I0610070

A JUDGE GONE WRONG

A SLIM CALHOUN, BULL MORRISON
WESTERN

JOHNNY GUNN

WOLFPACK
PUBLISHING
— EST 2013 —

A Judge Gone Wrong
A Slim Calhoun, Bull Morrison Western

Paperback Edition
© Copyright 2019 Johnny Gunn

Wolfpack Publishing
6032 Wheat Penny Avenue
Las Vegas, NV 89122

wolfpackpublishing.com

All rights reserved. No part of this book may be reproduced by any means without the prior written consent of the publisher, other than brief quotes for reviews.

Paperback ISBN 978-1-64119-567-6
eBook ISBN 978-1-64119-568-3

Library of Congress Control Number: 2019934215

A JUDGE GONE WRONG

CHAPTER 1

"AIR'S GOT A CHILL TO IT THIS MORNING, PURDY."

"Yup it do, Sam, it shorely duz got a bite to it. Strawberry comin' up and hot coffee while they change up the horses. Gonna be a long winter, I think."

The emigrant trail from Mormon Station in Nevada Territory to Placerville in California was long on miles and hard on endurance for horses, drivers and their shotgun toting protectors, and for those riding in the coaches. The Carson Road hosted thousands during the California gold rush and equally thousands during the rush to Washoe following the Comstock Lode discovery.

"Got me some rabbit skin gloves comin' in from San Francisco. No more cold fingers for me." Sammy Fredericks was riding shotgun on this westbound trip through the majestic Sierra Nevada. They'd be making stops every twelve to twenty miles either to rest or change horses. At some of the stops there would be hot food. Fredericks had a reputation of being a hard-nosed, shoot to kill stage coach messenger, and with the gold they were carrying, he was needed.

Virginia City was pumping out silver and gold ingots by the ton, it seemed and the mint in San Francisco was the final destination for much of it. There were only two roads, the Donner Road and the Carson Road; and stage coaches on both were often laden with gold and silver. Both roads ended in Sacramento, and those going toward San Francisco took the steam boats, as did the gold. There were gangs in those mountains waiting for their chance and many places to hide if they got lucky.

Businesses and banks wanted railroads in the worst way, passengers prayed for the day they could ride the rails, but the stage operators were quite happy with they had. Employees numbered in the hundreds and money flowed to the owners.

The driver was Purdy O'Neil, known for his love of horses, his foul mouth, and his hard knuckles. "We got a heavy load this time, Sammy. These horses are pulling hard today. Between too many passengers, their stuff and all, the mail sacks runnin' full, and that gold, it's gonna be a long haul."

The Sierra Nevada range was laid out north and south, with towering peaks of granite, great pine, fir, and cedar forests in the north and magnificent Giant Sequoia stands in the south, which were a wonder as fall made its approach. Those in the coach were given sights never seen anywhere else in the land, and the drivers never tired of the magnificence of the grand views.

It was winter everyone feared. Sierra Nevada; translated from the Spanish to English meant snow-covered mountains. And they are that; just ask those that survived the Donner expedition. Thirty, forty, even fifty-feet of snow over a winter was usual, and travel suffered.

It was a busy road and had been for years, first from

those thousands making their way to the great California gold strike, and lately from many of those same miners now heading east to the Comstock silver strike in Virginia City, Nevada Territory.

"Never have liked this run into Kyburz and Strawberry. The road is set up for outlaws, Purdy. Them rocks and turns and trees, all jammed together. Never have liked this part of the run."

The six-up were moving along smartly when three men on horses rode out from behind a large stand of fir trees, rifles pointed at the coach. "Pull 'em up or die," a big man in a heavy black-bear coat, black hat, and black mask hollered. His companions were dressed the same. Purdy pulled hard on the reins, slowing and stopping the chargers. Sammy Fredericks never had time to pull the double-barreled, sawed-off shotgun up.

"That's fine, boys. Just fine." This was the smallest of the three speaking and obviously the outlaw leader. The other one had a deep growly voice slightly muffled by the over-the-head mask. The leader seemed very young, his voice almost weak when he rode up alongside Fredericks. "Throw down that scatter piece and your side arms, nice and slow." He had his rifle aimed at Sammy's face. "Don't want you to miss sunset tonight, do we? Driver," he yelled. "climb down from that high seat of yours and come around to this side. Easy does it, now."

One outlaw jumped off his horse and began unhitching the wheel horses while his companion took hold of one of the leaders to drive them off. This was a well-organized group of men who had apparently done this many more times than once. "All right, driver. Get your passengers out here. It's inspection time. Guard, you make one more move and I'm gonna splatter your brains all over this mountain."

Fredericks had tried to reach a little revolver he kept hidden in his boot and the outlaw saw it. Sammy was steaming angry. Letting these men get to him with such ease was hard on his pride, and he was going to do everything he could to stop this insult. *Mangy bastards. That little one sounds like Gus Emerson. Gettin' mighty bold, that boy is.*

The passengers included federal judge, Lemuel S. Chastain and his wife Abigail, Carson Valley, Nevada rancher Fred Willoughby and his seventeen-year-old daughter Sharon, and Dangberg Lumber Company executive, Clarence Jacoby. Sharon caught her breath and hid her face in her father's chest when the outlaws appeared.

"Take it easy and keep calm, folks." Jacoby was tall and thin with a hard look to his face. He had large, gnarled hands that came from his work in the forest. "They will want our money but not our lives."

"You sound mighty sure of that," Judge Chastain said. "There's three of them. I say we should shoot 'em."

"I don't pack a gun and it looks like you're carrying a pea-shooter, at best. Maybe we could all jump out and throw rocks," Fred Willoughby snarled. "I agree with this gentleman. Just hand over the money and be through with it."

The judge slumped back in his seat, glared at the two men and took his wife's hand. "Stay calm, Abigail. Hopefully this will be over with soon. I'll notify the marshals when we reach Strawberry and see to it these ugly and dirty criminals are hanged."

Chastain was angry most of every day, had rarely found anyone he considered close to an equal, and despised criminals of every sort. Well, that is, except for those smart enough to not get caught, present company included. Chastain was working hard to get a railroad into his Monterey Bay community of Santa Cruz, where he presided as the federal judge. There was a lot of money being moved among several bank accounts, more than most belonging to the good judge.

His holdings in the redwood covered mountains surrounding that seaside community were worth millions, but the claims to the holdings were shady at best. He had bested a few interlopers but there was an investigation underway that bothered him. *Damn Spanish land grants being accepted by California need to be ended. Those trees, that river, and those lands should be mine without dispute.*

Sammy Fredericks always carried an extra weapon or two hidden away. He had tossed the shotgun and his big Navy Colt into the mud but had another tucked inside his heavy Mackinaw and was slowly letting his hand move toward it. Fredericks twisted in the seat and pushed off with his legs, tumbling to the ground on the other side of the coach. He rolled into the ditch alongside the road pulling his back-up weapon.

"Kill that sumbitch, Jackson," the gang leader yelled at the man unhitching the teams. Tom Jackson spun away from the horses reaching for his sidearm, but not in time. Fredericks shot him in the leg and fired a second round into Jackson's chest, killing the man.

The man on the horse, coming around after getting Purdy with the passengers, leveled his rifle and shot Fredericks through the chest, driving him back into the ditch. "Anyone else want to play hero? Hawknose, get them passengers lined up." The outlaw leader climbed down from his horse and watched the six-up rig run down the trail toward the Strawberry stage stop, five miles away.

Gus Emerson was still a teenager but had been terrorizing this line across the mighty Sierra for more than a year, had four or five men working for him, but only had Jackson and Mackenzie with him for this holdup. Emerson's father was a miner who came to California with the first wave of forty-niners, bringing his young wife and four-year old son, David, with him. He lost his wife on the journey to an Indian attack. Old man Emerson married a Spanish woman in California's capital, Monterey, and he re-named his son, Santiago Diego David Ortiz Emerson. The lawmen chasing Emerson called him Gus, his friends and gang members called him Chago, short for Santiago.

Despite his very young age, Chago Emerson was a born killer, born leader, and all of it without benefit of a soul, according to those who thought they knew him best. Emerson was a willow tree sapling of a man, five feet eight inches tall and one hundred thirty pounds light, and still didn't need to shave but once a week or so.

Hawknose Mackenzie came back around the coach and stepped off his horse but still cradled the rifle. "Time to empty the pockets and purses, please." He grabbed a flour sack from behind his saddle and opened it up. "Money, jewelry, and more money," he laughed stepping up to the first man in line. "My, aren't we dressed up all dandy like."

"You'll not get away with this," the gentleman said. "Do you have any idea who I am?" He puffed himself up to a full six feet or so and scowled at Mackenzie.

"I sure do know who you are. You're the man what's gonna give me all his money," he laughed.

"I happen to be Federal Judge, Lemuel S. Chastain," he said. "You'll hang for this."

"Well, well, well," Gus Emerson chuckled. "Ain't we got us a prize now. Well, Mr. Judge Chastain, just who's that pretty little lady standing next to you?"

"Mrs. Chastain. You'll hang for this outrage," the judge was beside himself. At fifty-three he was probably about fifty pounds overweight, jowly, and with thinning hair that needed trimming. Mrs. Chastain on the other hand was a slim, golden haired beauty of about thirty years. Her green eyes were on fire and her temper rose to the boiling point at the slightest test.

There was something in her eyes that caught Hawknose Mackenzie's attention. He had it in the back of his mind that he knew this lady and watched as she seemed not the least worried about being accosted by highwaymen. She was almost smiling when she looked into his eyes.

"Well, Mrs. Chastain, it's nice of you to join our little party. Would you be kind enough to put your jewelry in the sack, please?" Hawknose Mackenzie's eyes were giving the lovely lady full attention, from her cascading locks to her ankles. It was what was in between that he spent the most time with. "Wouldn't she warm up a cold night, eh Chago?"

"Keep your mind on your business, Hawknose," the outlaw leader said. "However, you most assuredly are right." Emerson's blood was warming at the thought and he was trying his best to stop it. He wasn't kind to the ladies and liked his activities more than rough. Many of the working girls up and down the gold camps of the Sierra Nevada wouldn't have anything to do with him.

It was when she smiled at Emerson's comment that Mackenzie remembered. It was along the waterfront in San Francisco, a little dive that had gambling tables and women, and the judge's wife was one of the women. "Yes, I am, Chago, very right, indeed."

"You keep your filthy mouths shut. My wife is a lady of the finest background. You are filthy pigs," the judge stormed. Hawknose Mackenzie whacked him across the side of the head with his rifle sending the heavyset gentleman face first in the mud.

"Temper, temper, Judge," Mackenzie said. "What do you suppose this lady of the finest background might be worth, Chago?" He gave Abigail Chastain a grand smile showing off yellowed teeth, one of which was made of California gold. "All right folks," he said, "let's fill the sack."

Chago Emerson was getting the heavy money box down from under the splash guard, the judge was coming to and stammering obscenities, and Hawknose had Mrs. Chastain hold the sack so the other passengers could put their valuables inside. Chago threw the box to the ground and climbed down giving the lady a full going over with his lust-filled eyes. "That's a heavy box this week. Lots of gold for us to have some fun with," he laughed.

"Well now, Hawkeye, you've just opened a whole new door to this world of ours. Taking the lovely young wife of a federal judge would surely bring dedicated U.S. Marshals down on us like cougars to fresh spring lamb. What a fine hostage the lady would make, though, with these nights getting cold and all."

"Her worth? Well, let's find out." Mackenzie swaggered to where Judge Chastain was still trying to get his feet under him. "What do you say to that, your muddy honor? Your wife worth fifteen or twenty thousand? Or maybe you're looking to drop her and go for another younger one?"

"Filthy bastards! Don't you lay a hand on that lady." He wiped a mixture of blood and mud from his face, ran a hand through his hair, and wiped more mud off.

"Or what, Judge?" Hawkeye reached over and slipped his arm around Abigail and drew her in. She tried to fight him off, dropped the sack of money and jewels and hit him with her little fists, bringing chuckles of delight from the outlaw. "She likes me, Chago," he laughed.

"Pick up that sack, woman. Let's get moving, Hawkeye."

He shoved the judge back into the mud, mounted his horse, brought Jackson's horse around for Abigail Chastain to ride, and Hawkeye tied off the sack of goodies and the big strong box on the back of his horse.

Sharon Willoughby had her arms wrapped tightly around her father, sobbing softly, terrified from the shooting and what had happened to the judge. "Take it easy, sweetheart," Willoughby whispered. "It'll be all over shortly." She peeked out in time to see Chastain thrown back in the mud, and Clarence Jacoby reach down to help the man to his feet. She felt like she was going to faint dead away and held onto her father even more tightly.

"Give our regards to those fine folks at Strawberry Station, will you?" Emerson was laughing as the three rode off. Judge Chastain was having trouble with his balance and was steadied by Purdy O'Neil and one of the passengers.

CHAPTER 2

"IT'S ABOUT FIVE MILES TO KYBURZ FLATS, FOLKS, SO WE better get started." O'Neil picked up Sammy Fredericks' shotgun and pistol and started moving toward the other side of the coach, now standing without horses attached. "Just follow the road. I want to tend to my partner's body."

"I'll help," Clarence Jacoby said. "What will happen now? I mean, is there a sheriff or something at this Strawberry place?" None of the passengers moved off down the road but followed Purdy and Clarence toward where Sammy fell.

"I'll tell you what will happen," Purdy O'Neil said. "Robbing the stage with a load of gold and killing the guard will bring the local lawmen, but Gus Emerson just made a fatal mistake. Abducting the wife of a federal judge will bring U.S. Marshals and that will be the end of the Gus Emerson gang."

"You know this Emerson?" Jacoby asked. "Seems rather strange."

"He's been on a spree for about year now, and even with his mask, that small stature and high voice marks him as

Gus Emerson. There's no doubt in my mind," Purdy said. "He's robbed his last stage, I'll wager."

Purdy O'Neil got down on his hands and knees next to the fallen Fredericks and was startled when the coach guard moaned. "He's alive," he yelped. "My God, he's alive." O'Neil rolled the wounded man over and saw blood oozing from a wound high on the man's chest.

One of the men tore open his shirt, despite the cold of the day, and handed it to Purdy. "See if this helps." Purdy opened Fredericks jacket and shirt and stuffed the torn rag inside and held it in place.

"Here, let me help," Sharon Willoughby said, kneeling down next to Sammy Fredericks. "I take care of most of our animals." She looked at Jacoby and smiled, taking the bloody rag from Purdy. "You men get a fire going and find some fresh water so I can wash the wound clean."

There was no doubt in any of the men's minds that Sharon was a child of the frontier, not the frightened little girl she had appeared to be when the outlaws first arrived. She had Sammy Frederick's shirt pulled away from the wound and was wiping blood away to get a good look. Jacoby bent down next to the girl and helped stem the blood.

"It looks like the bullet went in high on his chest. He's bled some but I think a doc could save him." Purdy was beside himself with hope. He and Sammy had been with the company since the first coach rolled over the Johnson Cutoff, had fought off some of the worst bad men in the Sierra Nevada, and fished and hunted together in off times. "Hang on, Sammy. We'll get you help."

"I can get him help," Clarence Jacoby said. "I can make those five miles fast. I'm a lumberman and run in these mountains every day. I'll bring a doctor and wagon back as quick as I can," he said, jumped to his feet and took off at a good lope down the muddy trail.

"Thank God," Purdy O'Neil said. Sharon whispered the same prayer and watched the tall man run down the road. She knew that living and working in the high country allowed a man to breathe deeply of the thin air. Jacoby's legs were pounding in the dirt and mud, churning his way to Strawberry.

"ABIGAIL," Chastain whimpered, over and over as the group stood in the middle of the Carson Trail on a cold fall day watching Jacoby take off running. Chastain still had visions of the outlaws riding off with all their possessions, gold meant for the San Francisco Mint, and his wife. "I'll see to it those men hang if it's the last thing I ever do," Chastain bellowed. "They'll feel the wrath of Lemuel S. Chastain and the fires of hell, so help me, God."

"Speaking of fires, let's get one built, folks. We're gonna be here for some time, I fear." Purdy was already tired of the judge and his sanctimonious ways. "We need to keep Sammy warm and alive, and we need to make ourselves as comfortable as possible. Judge, go find some water, and Willoughby, see if there are any blankets in the coach. I'll get the fire going."

With fall in the air, O'Neil knew that as soon as the sun dipped below the horizon the air would cool off quickly. They were almost seven thousand feet above sea level, and it would get cold quick in that rarified air. "We might have help by sunrise. Did anyone bring food along for their journey?"

CHAPTER 3

IT WAS CHAOS INSIDE THE RAMBLING STRAWBERRY STATION that evening. Most of the talk was the arrival of Clarence Jacoby and news of the stagecoach hold-up. A wagon was dispatched immediately, with a doctor, to bring the group in. The six-up team arrived without its coach and passengers well before Jacoby set off the alarms.

"My name's McCall, Judge, Tubbs McCall, the station operator. The telegraph lines between here and Placerville have been down for several days following that last storm. I've sent a rider to Placerville to alert the officials in San Francisco. The El Dorado County sheriff from Placerville will also be told of the holdup, of course."

Judge Chastain was a blustering maniac demanding this and that until McCall was able to calm him down with a bottle of vintage brandy and a large snifter. "I'm sure Sheriff Bellows will bring a posse and will have your wife returned safely."

"Bellows? Never heard of him. I want the marshals."

"The marshals will be notified, Judge. Alex Bellows is a fine lawman, has a strong sense of duty, and will be here sometime tomorrow, I'm sure." McCall was a heavy man, a good stage station operator, and proud of the food he offered every coach that came through. He dreaded the many hours ahead with a judge who seemed to think that what he said was law. In Santa Cruz, Chastain acted more like a Spanish Alcalde, lord of the land-claim.

Strawberry was a beautiful stop in magnificent country, built of local fir and pine, redwood from the coastal mountains, and had the feel of a European hunter's cottage built to a larger scale. There were fireplaces in every room, magnificently large and elegant lamps which provided light and a feeling of warmth, giving the effect of welcome and good cheer.

"We'll get supper served shortly, folks, good beds are waiting you, and you'll be off first thing in the morning." He had dispatched a team and driver, and a guard to retrieve the coach and was glad to tell the passengers that their baggage had not been rifled and everything seemed to be there.

Everything except for Mrs. Abigail Chastain, much personal worth, and some twenty-thousand-dollars in Comstock gold. Purdy O'Neil was up for forming a posse to chase the bandits but was quickly talked out of that, when Tubs McCall reminded him that there were only three men available to ride.

"How bad is it, Doctor?" Purdy O'Neil was just outside the door of the room where Sammy Fredericks had been taken. "Is he gonna make it?"

Silas Smith, nearing sixty years on this planet, had been a frontier doctor in more than one wagon train or mining camp, and was hoping for a nice quiet old age in the craggy mountains of California. He built a cabin close to the Strawberry Lodge and his services were seldom needed. "He's a tough old bird, Purdy, but that bullet did some serious damage. Missed his heart and lungs, somehow, but busted up some bone and tore up some muscle.

"Your shotgun guard won't be riding any stage coaches for some time, but I'm sure he'll live. Have a good supper and sleep well, Purdy. Sammy's gonna be fine."

AL BELLOWS WAS PACING around his office waiting for his posse to form up. His chief deputy brought seven men from around what had been called Dry Camp, was later called Hangtown after three men were strung up, and now carried the moniker of Placerville. "We're ready, Sheriff," deputy Clive Sorenson called through the door. "Counting you and me, there'll be nine of us."

"Should be enough. You get Beartooth Johnson to come?" Johnson, at least according to him, was one of the finest trackers on the west slopes of the Sierra Nevada, and Bellows wanted him with them. He was hard to get along with, and had a great love of self, but he really was a fine tracker. Johnson picked up the nickname because of a heavy necklace of bear's teeth he wore at all times. Regardless of his loud boasting, the man knew these mountains, from the headwaters of the Humboldt River in Nevada Territory to the delta of the Sacramento and San Joaquin Rivers.

Beartooth Johnson had many stories behind those teeth, most dealing with him shooting the big California Grizzly before it ate him, or him wrestling with the monster for half an hour before he could do him in with a pocketknife. Beartooth had a story about those teeth for every occasion, and for every audience.

"He'll be half an hour behind us, Sheriff. Something about new laces for his moccasins. You know how he is. the only thing he didn't do is ride with Lewis and Clarke, I think."

"I know how he is, but he is one of the best." Bellows said. He mounted up, looked over the posse of drinkers, miners, bums, and ne'er-do-wells, shook his head and said, "Let's ride." Getting a posse put together usually meant offering a dollar and drinks, and it was the drinks that got him the men. He led the group out of Placerville and onto the main cross-mountain roadway. "We'll probably meet that stage coming this way and maybe get more informa-tion." He motioned for Sorenson to ride up alongside.

"The description tells me it's Gus Emerson again. We gotta stop that fool, Clive. This is his third holdup in the last few months, and he took a hostage this time. I want him in irons, Clive, not dead, in irons. He's making me look like a fool and I want to parade him right through town, in irons." He had his cigar half eaten before they reached the town limit.

Clive Sorenson had to chuckle on the one hand and was also angry on the other because of Emerson. Sorenson was a young buck, almost twenty, stood at about average height but carried considerable weight that was almost entirely muscle. His family came west looking for gold and found sickness and death. He was raised by an old prospector who taught him the ways of the world. That is, be friendly but expect the worst.

THE SHORT, stocky man with a chaw pouched in his cheek stood at the bar glaring at the bartender, daring him to not pour his glass full. The long, bright red scar that started from above his left eye and ended slightly below his lower lip, quivered as he spoke. "I said a glass of whiskey, Sparrow, not a whimpering shot of whiskey. Fill it up."

"This would be your third one, Bull," Sparrow Johansen said, very quietly. "You know how you get sometimes." Bull Morrison was in Sloppy Joe's Chop House, just two blocks from the federal courthouse in San Francisco, waiting for his partner, Slim Calhoun.

"I ain't gonna tear the place up, Sparrow, but I might tear your face off if you don't fill up that glass. I'm waitin' for Slim. We got business to take care of. Now," he slammed his ham of a fist on the bar, sounding the alarm in most of the noon-time crowd. "Fill it up."

Johansen knew that it was only two weeks ago that Bull Morrison took on five men and wrecked the place doing it. It was just three months ago that Bull Morrison stood back-to-back with Slim Calhoun and took on the crew of the good ship Monterey and wrecked the place.

"Aren't there other places you like to drink, Bull?"

"Not really," Morrison said. He had a little boy's grin on his face, chuckling some, too. "This is one of the friendliest places in Frisco. I like coming in here, Sparrow." He took his full glass of whiskey to a table near the front windows to wait for Calhoun, nodding to several patrons who seemed to want to edge away from the heavy man.

"Morning, Marshal," Slim Calhoun said, sliding into a seat at the table. "Your note said it was urgent. What's up?"

"Glad you made it, Deputy. We got a long ride to make, a lovely damsel to save, and a judge's way of life to preserve."

"Hmmm," is all Calhoun mumbled. Bull Morrison was U.S. Marshal Morrison and Slim was Deputy U.S. Marshal Calhoun, and together on the job they had the kind of reputation the service was very proud of. Together, off the job, was another matter entirely. Many saloonkeepers in the western states didn't always welcome them with open arms.

Morrison and Calhoun spent the next half hour discussing the situation in the Sierra Nevada. "You ever had dealings with this Judge Chastain?" Morrison asked.

"I've heard some interesting stories. He's from the Santa Cruz district, has strong ties with the railroad people down there. He runs his district like the Spanish and Mexican land grantees, is what I've heard."

"This might be fun, then. We're meeting him in Sacramento tomorrow. Right now, we have to catch the steamer. I've got orders in for good horses and mules for our ride into the mountains. We'll pick them up after our talk with Chastain."

"There are two gangs operating on the routes through the mountains- Gus Emerson's and one led by a man called Duke Hornaday. Was there enough description to figure out which one we might be facing?"

"Don't matter none," Bull Morrison said. "Either one would be fine with me. I'll just kill those that are the slowest and beat the hell out of the others," he laughed, leading them out of the saloon. Slim Calhoun knew it wasn't a joke.

"They say he wasn't very big and seemed young. That describes Gus Emerson to me. Abducting the woman, though, puts an entirely different frame on the picture. Road agents don't kidnap." Calhoun could tell that Bull Morrison was allowing himself to get more and more angry as he thought about what happened.

"Even more reason we catch him and get him hung just as soon as possible."

CHAPTER 4

"WHAT IS IT YOU THINK YOU KNOW THAT I DON'T, HAWKNOSE? You seem kinda tight with that woman." Gus Emerson was sure those that rode with him were out to get him or steal from him or hide information from him. They had been riding through rough country for two days and Hawknose Mackenzie had become far more than friendly with their prisoner.

"About five years ago, Abigail Chastain carried a slightly different moniker, Chago." Mackenzie liked the idea of Emerson having to ask him this, liked being able to tell him something. "Called herself Irene the Heaven Sent and worked the area around Angel's Camp. Had five or six lovely doves in her employ, and a traveling circus of pleasure up and down the trail." He had a smug look on his face and a gleam that told Emerson he knew a little more than he was saying. It had the desired effect.

"You've already toyed with that woman, haven't you?" He got a chuckle back, a wry look spread across Hawknose's face, telling Emerson all he needed to know, making his blood hot. One thing Emerson needed on a regular basis was a woman on fire.

"We've been riding in the high mountains, Hawknose. When did all this happen?"

"Only talked about it, Chago. She wants to go back to the judge, but will be our willing guest until she's saved," Hawknose cackled. "That woman enjoys being treated well."

"Well ain't that gonna make things nicer around here. We need to get hid-out quick, then. Let's backtrack over the summit and down to Spooner. We got that cabin up in the hills by Marlette. If we stay away from the wood cutters no one will know we're even around."

"We ain't lookin' to keep this woman, Chago, are we?" The sneer was lost on the boy-bandit. "She would sure bring us a full sack of gold."

Emerson caught his breath, stomped around the fire and collected his thoughts. The idea of a hot woman in camp was almost more than he could think of, but what Hawknose said about a sack full of gold, was even better.

"We got to get hid first, then get word to the judge on how much we want. Gonna be tricky, Hawknose, you can bet on that. We'll light out at sunrise and make Spooner late in the day."

"More like the next day," Mackenzie said. "We got a ton of gold to carry, some food, and the woman. We won't be travelin' fast up to the summit."

"We'll move fast if I say so," Emerson snarled. Nobody told him what to do. Then the idea of that hot woman took over. "She's good in the blankets, eh? I'll let you know in the morning."

"THAT LAST STORM was a wet one, Al. We been clawin'

through mud all day. We're still at least an hour out from Strawberry and we ain't seen that coach yet."

Bellows had the posse moving steadily up the trail from Placerville, but Sorensen was right about the mud. "Next storm'll be a cold one, Clive. You can bet on that and then we'll be cussin' the ice and snow. They probably held the stage until we get a chance to talk to everyone."

Bellows turned in the saddle and noted that he was already two men short of what he started off with. *They're always all fired up and ready for a good chase until they find out it's actually called work. I wonder what it would be like to put together a real posse make up of dedicated lawmen?* That thought made the next hour a little more pleasant.

Time was always an important element in trying to save someone who'd been taken prisoner or abducted, and Bellows was pushing the posse as hard as he dared. After making the uphill journey from Placerville these same men and horses would have to go out on the hunt, and those horses would be tired.

"If it's Emerson's gang they'll head to Nevada Territory as quick as they can. We gonna follow his trail if he does?"

"Can't. Jeppson said he was going to send a wire to the U.S. Marshal in San Francisco. It would be their responsibility if Emerson crosses the state line. We'll just have to see what we find."

The group rode into the Kyburz Flats and Strawberry a little later than planned because of the mud and bad road and found a furious Judge Chastain waiting for them. "You should have come at a hard gallop, Sheriff. That's my wife those gangsters are holding. You find her or so help me I'll have you strung up."

"Back it up, Judge. We're here and we'll find your wife," Al Bellows snarled right back. *Fat pecker-head talks to me like that a couple more times and he'll find himself flat on his back. Damn, I hate people like him.* "Let's get the passengers and driver together. I have a few questions and we'll know more about who we'll be chasing."

"I know who you'll be chasing. You don't have time for talking, Sheriff," Chastain bellowed.

"Back off now, Chastain. You might get away with that in your courtroom but I'm the sheriff of this county and I'm running this investigation. Push me too far and I'll arrest you for impeding an investigation." Bellows glared at the fuming judge, shook his finger in the man's face, and growled. "No interference, sir." Bellows turned and walked over to the fire, then spun back around.

"You're upset and I know that, but there are at least three gangs roaming these granite mountains and I need to know which one abducted your wife. Now, calm yourself and let me do my job."

It took another fifteen minutes or so to get everyone in the large sitting room by the fireplace. Questions were asked, the judge stormed and cussed, and Bellows led his posse back out to their horses. "That man is a fool, Sorenson," Bellows said. "Sure glad he's not in our district. That little Willoughby girl is a looker, eh?"

"Couldn't keep my eyes off her, Sheriff. She is the reason Sammy Fredericks is alive, from what I gathered, talking to those people." The sheriff smiled, nodded at his young deputy and continued into the barn. Sorenson ducked his head, knowing he was blushing some, wishing he could stay at the inn and get to know that charming little gal.

"I wonder, listening to that judge, if Mrs. Chastain may not want to be rescued," Clive Sorensen snickered, stepping into the saddle. "Living with that fool must be a chore. I thought for sure you were gonna pop him."

Bellows had to laugh at the comment and almost had to
agree with what Sorensen said. "You seemed to enjoy asking
questions of that pretty little girl in there, Clive. It got to be
'Clive and Sharon' after just a bit."

"She's about the prettiest young lady I ever laid eyes on,
Sheriff. Her father's a tough old bird, too. I hope we run into
them again, soon. I'd let her doctor me any time I got all
busted up like Fredericks."

"We're gonna be on the trail for a while, Clive, so hunker
down and do your job. At least we know it's Gus Emerson
we're after." Sheriff Bellows led the group out onto the main
road. "The dead man was Tom Jackson and he's been riding
with Emerson for some time. The other one they were
talking about, the one with the smart mouth and bad attitude sounded a lot like Hawknose Mackenzie. Mackenzie
kills for pleasure, gentlemen, so keep that in mind. Don't
give these men the slightest edge or you'll be dead."

There wasn't much to see at the site of the holdup, but
Beartooth Johnson did pick up the trail Emerson left riding
off. "They didn't take the main road out, Sheriff. Left us a
good trail to follow. They're going cross-country, at least for
a while. That storm was our friend, Bellows. Look how those
three horses leave their trail."

They wound their way through great stands of pine, fir,
spruce, cedar and hardwood, climbing all the time. "They're
making for the summit and they'll drop down toward Lake
Tahoe and work their way into Nevada, sure as we're sitting
here, Clive," Bellows said. "Send one of the men back to
Strawberry to wait for the marshals. He can tell them where
we're going and where we think Emerson is going.

"You get in this country, you have to have a destination,
and it's gonna be somewhere around Spooner. Those boys
are hauling heavy packs of gold and a woman hostage. They

need to find a hole to crawl into." The sheriff knew the country but not as well as Beartooth. "If you say they're heading for Spooner, I'll go along with that."

"It's gonna be a cold one tonight, Sheriff, did you bring enough food for a two- or three-day ride? We're gonna hit tree line shortly and that wind will cut right through us like a hot knife in bear grease. We'll be riding in it all day tomorrow, too."

"I think so, Beartooth, but if you think we would be better off with fresh venison over the coals, well, you just high-tail it out there and shoot us one." He hadn't finished the sentence before Beartooth hit the saddle.

"READ that wire back to me again, Slim. The judge ain't coming? Damn." Bull Morrison and Slim Calhoun were in the federal building in Sacramento expecting to meet with Judge Chastain. "We could have left late yesterday after we docked. Damn these people that try to make our decisions. I'm gonna shoot that judge," Bull snarled.

"Apparently, El Dorado County Sheriff Al Bellows picked up the trail, believes it is the Emerson gang, and they appear to be heading for Nevada Territory. The judge is waiting for us at Strawberry and will join our hunt."

"Like hell he will," Morrison barked. "Bellows give any more information?"

"Yeah, there were two wires, Bull. One from the judge, another from one of Bellows' men. Bellows is sure Emerson is headed for a known hideout area near Spooner Summit, which would put him in Nevada Territory." Calhoun handed the wires to Morrison.

"If we ride hard, forget the pack animals, we can make Strawberry in two days, Slim. We'll have Buck Antonelli and

Warren Fitzgerald bring the pack animals. Did you hear what that banker said about the gold? More than twenty thousand was in that strong box."

"Those mines in Virginia City are gushing gold and silver like it's coming from a well house, Bull. Banks are buying it up, the government is buying it up, and the outlaws are doing what they can to get theirs too. The horses are saddled, old man. Let's ride." Their saddlebags held coffee, dried meat, and hard biscuits along with a jug of Kentucky's best.

"I hope we meet some ugly people on the way, Slim. I need to get in a fight with some mean, ugly people." Morrison wasn't laughing and spurred his horse into a strong lope up the Carson Trail. "Any mean people in Placerville that you can direct me to?"

"THIS IS TOO crowded for us to be hanging around here, Hawknose. We gotta find a better hideout. All these wood cutters are sure to give us up."

"They're cuttin' every tree in sight, Chago. Must be for those mines on the Comstock. Let's ride on down to the Carson Valley. Good hiding places in the mountains along near Mormon Station. Nobody'd pay any attention to us down there."

"That woman throw another fit like she did last night, and we won't be gettin' no ransom money from her. Look at my face, all scratched and bleeding. You said she was a willing part of all this."

"She don't like the rough stuff," Hawknose said. There was the slightest sneer in his voice. "Got to be gentle with her kind." He was gloating more than Emerson liked, and enjoyed seeing this kid bandit brought down by a woman he knew intimately. He wore a cockeyed grin on his face.

"I ain't gentle with nobody. Don't you get cocky with me, Hawknose. Bring her here. I want some more of her and then we'll leave. Did you get a mule?"

Hawknose nodded and went to bring Abigail. "Chago wants you," he said. She was washing blood from a shirt she was wearing the night before.

"That man hit me or hurt me again, and I'll kill him, Mackenzie. Look at this," and she held up the torn shirt spotted with Chago's blood. Hawknose wasn't going to let himself get in the middle of the two, so he shrugged and turned to leave the room. He didn't see that Abigail pulled her dress up and checked to make sure a dagger was tucked neatly to her ankle. "Little boy outlaw ain't gonna get nothing from me, ever," she muttered, letting her skirt fall back.

"Best not to press him too hard, Irene. He's a killer, even if he is a teenager. I've seen his nasty work, so you be careful. You're worth a lot of money to us, my lady."

"Little boy killer? He just better be careful, Hawknose. I've been known to whip my knife toward places men don't much like to see." Hawknose was chuckling as she walked off. *I just bet she has.*

"What do you want?" she said, walking into the bedroom. Chago was sitting on a rumpled bed, making sure his Navy was fully loaded. He had a sneer on his face when he looked up, and it turned sour as she approached.

"I want you, and you better be willing, woman." He reached out and grabbed her arm, pulling her down onto the bed. She raked her strong fingers across his face again, slicing new rows and opening those partially healed from the night before. "You bitch," he howled in pain.

Emerson jumped from the bed, grabbed the Navy and pumped three shots through Mrs. Abigail Chastain, late wife of federal judge Chastain. Hawknose came running into the room and stopped, staring at the still bleeding but very dead lady who should have brought them lots of money. "You fool," he said.

"Look what she did," Emerson screamed.

"You were warned, Chago. Get your kit put together, we gotta be on the trail now." There were wood cutter camps scattered all over the surrounding hills and three gunshots were sure to draw attention. "You need to learn that not everybody's afraid of you. Some women don't much care for that rough stuff. You just cost me a lot of money and probably they'll have big posters plastered from Canada to Mexico in the next week or so."

"You ain't got no call to talk down to me, Mackenzie. You want to split up that gold in the strong box and be on your way? Fine. Let's do that. You ain't good enough to ride with me, no how." He was still holding the smoking gun and brandished it in Mackenzie's face, daring him to make a move.

The two men, Emerson holding a weapon, stood over the body of Abigail Chastain, glaring at each other. Chastain was too young to fully understand what he had just done, too sure of himself to understand Hawknose Mackenzie's reaction. Having someone like Mackenzie riding with you should have given Emerson a strong feeling of security, but then again, Emerson just killed the wife of a federal judge. Thinking was not a large part of his makeup.

"Bring that box in and we'll split it up, all even." The youngster in him was talking, not the man he thought he was.

A mature man would know just how much trouble had

been started, first with the abduction and then the killing of the wife of a federal judge. Hawknose Mackenzie could almost feel the rope around his neck, but Chago Emerson was too young to grasp the situation. If they hadn't already taken the trail, Mackenzie knew that the U.S. Marshals would be riding hard with orders to kill on sight.

Hawknose had saddlebags filled with gold, coffee, and hard tack as he rode out of the canyon and onto the plains of the Carson Valley, working on a plan to get as far from where he was as possible. "I ain't never been to Texas," he muttered. "It's somewhere south of where I am, so that's where I'm heading." Hawknose Mackenzie was born in Oregon Territory in 1842 and had never been east of where he was at the moment. "I gotta get miles between me and that young fool."

"IT's about time you got here, Marshal. Where have you been? Do you think this is supposed to be some kind of pleasure ride? My wife is out there, somewhere, being held by killers. You find her, bring those killers to me."

"I'm U.S. Marshal Bull Morrison and you're U.S. Judge Lemuel Chastain. You know your job, I know mine." Bull Morrison stood face to face with the judge, his eyes blazing, that horrible scar across his face scarlet in his anger. "Where is that man Sheriff Bellows sent back. I want him now."

Thomas Burke stepped forward. "I'm with the posse, Marshal. I have a note here from the sheriff for you." Burke was a businessman in Placerville and Morrison knew Bellows sent him back to keep him alive. Some men are made for the mountain trail, some are made to stand behind counters.

"It's Emerson, all right," Bull said after reading the letter.

"Looks like he's headed for Spooner Summit, Slim. Probably already there."

The hard ride from Hangtown had been a cold one and Morrison wasn't going to waste any more time on what he considered frivolous nonsense from the judge or anyone else. They hadn't been at Strawberry Station fifteen minutes and he wanted away as quickly as possible.

"Listen, Burke, here's what I want you to do, and it's very important. I have two deputies coming, probably tomorrow, with full packs on good mules. You give Buck Antonelli this letter and tell him to get it on.

"Slim, fill your saddlebags and mine with whatever you can find in the kitchen and let's get out of here."

"I'm coming with you," Chastain said.

"No, you're not," Morrison snapped. "We're riding hard and fast following a cold trail. Ain't got time for teachin' you the ways of the trail. Let's move it, Calhoun."

Slim Calhoun had never been to Strawberry before and looked around for this kitchen he was supposed to go to when Sharon Willoughby motioned for him to follow.

"Yes, Ma'am," he smiled. "Thank you. I gotta be quick about this before Bull shoots that judge."

"Somebody needs to," she laughed.

Calhoun found himself looking into deep blue eyes attached to a most welcome and comely face. "Were you on that stage when it was robbed?"

"I'm afraid so," she whispered. "I've never been so frightened in all my life. That big man was the most scary but the young, skinny one was the most dangerous, I think."

"You're not far from wrong," he said as she led him into the kitchen. He had Tubs McCall make up a food pack for three days and headed out to the stables to join Morrison. Sharon walked him to the door.

"Will you catch those men?"

"We'll catch them, Miss Willoughby. You can take that to the bank." Under other circumstances, Slim thought, I would certainly want to spend a great deal of time getting to know that young lady. He found Morrison talking with the coach driver.

"You do got room for me, Marshal," Purdy O'Neil said. "I was the driver of that coach and know these mountains better than the goats that live here."

"Then quit talking and get saddled, damn it," Morrison bellowed. He had to almost shove the judge out of the way, heading for his fresh horse. The last words he heard were from the judge screaming for him to find his Abigail.

"Think they'll keep her alive?" Slim Calhoun knew some of Emerson's background, knew he was an impetuous teenager, not a seasoned outlaw. "He's got a potential ransom if he keeps her alive but he's probably not smart enough to realize that, Bull."

"No, he ain't smart about nothin', Slim, but he's riding with Hawknose Mackenzie, and Mackenzie might be smart enough to know what they have. That judge would pay a king's ransom for her return."

"If they hole up in the Spooner area, what are we looking at, Purdy? And if they should run down the hill into Nevada, where would they most likely head?" Morrison was more than a day away from his man and was already planning his attack. Morrison would tell anyone that fighting was the best thing in life and right next to it was planning for the fight. He could feel the itch of a good fight coming on.

CHAPTER 5

"Looks like you got in a fight with a nasty little kitten, son. What'll you have?" The bartender at the Silver Palace in Carson City had a sneer mixed into his comments and the smile wasn't a friendly one. The Silver Palace was in the heart of the territorial capitol city and was filled with miners, ranchers, and travelers. Gambling tables were filled, there was music of a sort coming from two men with banjos, and working girls were working.

"Whiskey," Chago Emerson snarled. "And a clean glass." Emerson had back tracked from the wood cutters and followed the well-worn emigrant trail, the Carson Road, out of the Sierra Nevada, through the Carson Valley and into Nevada Territory's capitol city of Carson. He had tried to clean up the deep cuts and scratches when he stopped along the Carson River but they still leaked blood, and at least some showed signs of infection.

The barman wasn't smiling when he filled the glass with whiskey and shoved it at Emerson. "One dollar," he said. Emerson had to look through a couple of pockets before finding a cartwheel for the barman. He snickered as he walked to a table far in the back of the smoky saloon, away from the gambling tables, and dipped his neckerchief into the whiskey. *I've got more than ten thousand dollars in gold bars in my saddlebags and can't spend a dime of it. Damn that woman.*

Some, sitting close to Emerson's table, heard him grunt when he tried to clean the cuts with the whiskey. He was almost crying in pain when he finished. He was in trouble and knew it but wasn't wise enough to know how to get out of the mess he created. His face stood out like a red flag, nobody would forget seeing him, and he needed both a friend and a doctor.

The friend part would be the hardest to come by with his natural bad attitude. He had to be the toughest, the meanest, no matter the situation. He could never lower himself to ask for help. That would be a sign of weakness, and he would prove to the world that he was not weak.

Nevada Territory was still in flux with thousands of men heading for the mines in Virginia City, men and families settling in the valleys and creating large ranches and farms, and not much in the way of organized law enforcement. Some settlements had a town marshal, each county that had actually organized, had a sheriff, and for the most part, only the really serious crimes were even noticed.

Saloons were filled with a mixture of miners, buckaroos, and businessmen, all being accosted by gamblers, whores, and confidence players. Stock market manipulation by high rollers was at the top of the fraud market with horse stealing and strong-armed robbery at the bottom. Maybe a very young man with multiple scratches and cuts on his face wouldn't be that much noticed, Emerson came to believe as he sat at the back of the Silver Palace Saloon and Dance Hall.

"Buy me a drink, mister?" She was almost as young as he was, and twice as good looking. She sat at the table and smiled into his torn-up face. "Don't know who you've been with but I'm a bunch nicer."

"Yeah, well, I ain't got time for game playin' lady. You know how to doctor some? That's what I need." He was looking into pale blue eyes set deep in a long thin face outlined by dark blond hair. Her nose was thin, and her lips were full and smiling. Most men would say she was too thin, almost gaunt, and used hard despite her young years. It was the sadness in the eyes that gave it away.

"My regular rate is two dollars silver and that gives you twenty minutes of bliss, mister. You want a doctor, he's down the street and to your left." The eyes were still pale blue, but it wasn't a warm and cozy blue, more like ice in February. He reached out and slapped her across the side of the head sending her sprawling onto the filthy floor.

The sound of the slap, the surprised yowl and thud from a falling body, and those around Chago's table were quiet, ready for whatever happened next. "You bastard," the girl screamed, getting back to her feet. She pulled her skirt up and grabbed a little piece of iron tucked into a garter. The shot echoed around the room, Chago felt the bullet nick his left shoulder as it tore through his heavy coat, and he was on his feet, Colt in hand.

Why he didn't shoot immediately, he would never be able to answer, but when a bruiser of a miner stepped up and smashed him in the face, he did fire point blank into the man's gut. The miner wheeled around, staggered, and fell face first to the floor. Chago, thrown back against the wall got his feet under him, waved the revolver at those standing around, edged around the table and carefully made his way to the swinging bat wings, keeping the crowd back with threats. His bleeding face, smoking gun, and high-pitched threats allowed him to escape. He left Carson Street in a cloud of dust.

The acrid smell of burnt gunpowder filled the now quiet saloon and people were hesitant to make any kind of move. It was a single shot, they remembered preceded by that almost muted scream from that pretty little girl. The new girl in town who hung out with Three-Fingered Jack.

"He's dead," the saloon girl said. Shirley Berkshire knelt down next to the gut shot miner. "Three Finger Jack is dead," she whimpered. "That bastard shot him dead," she whimpered. She cradled the man called Three Finger Jack and whispered, "Somebody get the sheriff." Three-Fingered Jack would never rob another stage coach on the road to Virginia City again.

AL BELLOWS KNEW he was wrong to follow the trail on down to Lake Tahoe and up to Spooner Summit, but Beartooth Johnson was sure the trail was hot. "They can't be even a day in front of us, Sheriff. If we can get them, it sure would make you look good." His eyes told the whole story. He wasn't thinking of making the sheriff look, good. More than likely, "it would sure make old Beartooth look good."

"We'll follow 'em on in," Bellows said. "The trail they're leaving is fresh. We're moving into an active timber cutting area, so we're sure to lose that trail. If we do, we'll scout around some while we're waiting for the marshals."

Heavy timber cutting was evident as they made their way through the granite sides of the Carson Range of the Sierra Nevada. The mountain sides were being laid bare by the incredible amount of timber being cut for the mines of the Comstock. Besides holding up the mines even more timber was needed to feed the voracious steam engines used to power everything.

As they neared Marlette, the trail became almost impossible to determine because of so much activity. Let's make up a good camp, boys. Gather fire wood, then we'll scout around some." Bellows called Beartooth over.

"You've been here before, Johnson?" The scout nodded. "Are there any permanent or semi-permanent cabins where these yahoos could hole up?"

"There's a couple just over that rise there. They were put up by some sheep men a couple of years ago. Don't run the sheep through here now, cuz of all the timber cutting."

Bellows called a deputy to join them. "Let's the three of us ride over and check out those cabins. Bring your rifles."

As they neared one of the cabins, Beartooth stepped off his horse to get a closer look at some tracks in the mud. "These are the horses we been a-followin', Sheriff."

"All right, then, nice and slow and spread out." He pointed to a deputy, "Go over to your left but keep me in sight. Beartooth, take the right side there, and I'll sneak up from the front. Stay as much out of sight as possible. There is one man dead and another bad hurt from these fools."

They were well above the six-thousand-foot level and the day was cold. A goodly wind was blowing, signaling another storm in the near future as the three men moved closer to the thrown together cabin. The front door was standing open and blowing in the wind, and there was no smoke coming from the rock chimney.

The deputy was able to sneak right up to the cabin since there were no windows on that side. He edged around the corner of the building and got as near to the front window as he dared. Al Bellows was behind some large granite boulders, just fifteen feet or so from the front door, and

Beartooth was behind a large sugar pine, rifle at his shoulder, ready to fire at anything that moved.

"See anything?" Bellows yelled. The deputy shook his head and Bellows made a run for the side of the cabin next to the open door. He kept his rifle in his left hand, pulled his big Navy, and stormed into the cabin yelling as loud as he could. Nothing moved. "Come on in," he said. "You, too, Beartooth, we got some work to do." He was looking at the crumpled body of Abigail Chastain.

Beartooth rode back to bring the posse up to the cabin while Bellows and his deputy buried Abigail. "They didn't leave together, Sheriff," Beartooth said before he rode off. He spent some time searching around the cabin while the grave was being dug.

"We'll make a camp here. The federal marshals won't be too far behind us, so we'll just wait for them. I'm so far out of my jurisdiction now, a day more won't matter none," he laughed.

"Did you see the lady's hands, Sheriff?" Deputy Oren McMillan climbed out of the grave he was digging. "Blood and skin all over those fingernails. She must have put up a pretty good fight before one of them shot her."

"We better remember to tell the marshal that," Bellows said. "Either Emerson or Hawknose Mackenzie, or maybe both," he chuckled, "might be scratched up some."

"ALL RIGHT, settle down, now, damn it. You can't all talk at the same time. You," Carson City Sheriff Jeremy Wilson said, pointing at the young girl. "What's your name?"

"Shirley, uh, Berkshire," she stammered. "He hit me and knocked me down."

"Yeah, I can see that," Wilson said. "What else?"

"Well, Three Finger Jack helped me to my feet and challenged the kid and the kid shot him dead." She was sobbing, her shoulders shaking, and her face hidden in her skirts. "It was horrible."

"Anybody disagree with that?" Everyone said the same thing.

"One thing, Sheriff," the bartender said. "The kid's face was all scratched up and bleeding. He was angry as all get out, too, when he came in. I don't think he was sixteen or seventeen years old but mean as any snake you've seen."

Wilson got five or six men to ride with him and after finding out which way Emerson went, lit out after him. He sent a man back to wire Douglas County to the south and to send the chief deputy to join them. They crossed the Clear Creek Canyon road and headed into the wide plains of the Carson Valley.

Chief Deputy Charles Baker joined the posse within half an hour. "That description mean anything to you?" Wilson asked.

"Sounds like Gus Emerson to me, Sheriff. Young, high voiced, and ugly mean. He's been working the stage route from Spooner to Strawberry for a year now."

"Something brought him out of the mountains. Well, we can't go any farther. We're in Matt Rogers' territory now. I'll send some wires out. From holding up a stagecoach to flat out murder in a saloon is a big step for an outlaw. Hope wherever he's ridin' to, keeps him away from here for a long time."

CHAPTER 6

"Nice to meet you, Sheriff. We'll take it from here," Bull Morrison said. "You did a good job tracking him here. Glad it's you has to tell the judge about his wife. I'd just as soon shoot the old fool."

"I'll be heading back in the morning. That lady did some serious damage to one of those boy's faces. The strong box is empty, so they have money to spend. Anything else I can help you with?"

"That box was filled with gold bars, not coins," Calhoun said. "They won't be able to spend any of it until they knock it down to spendable size." He was chuckling and his eyes were dancing thinking of the irony of a robbery netting cash that couldn't be spent.

"Yeah," Morrison said. "I've got a couple of deputies a day or so behind me with pack mules. Give 'em good directions on finding us. If he'll stay, I'd like to keep Beartooth Johnson. Likes himself some but he's a fine tracker." Bellows tried to hide his grin and chuckle and wished that would be the case. He agreed about Johnson's tracking ability but would be very happy not to have to spend another night around the campfire with him.

"I'll send him to you. Good luck," Al Bellows said. He walked over to where his posse was camped to find Johnson, and Morrison walked into the cabin to find Slim Calhoun. Bellows was hoping Beartooth would ride with the marshals. "Cantankerous old buzzard gets in my craw and enjoys it," he muttered.

"What's your take, Slim? We got some riding to do."

"From what that tracker said, these boys must have got in it and split up. Maybe that's why the woman is dead. They have to be in Nevada, and I'd go to Carson City first, but that's a big open territory. About ten billion places to hide."

"If hidin' is what you're lookin' to do," Morrison chuckled. "I want to whup on that Emerson kid, Slim. That bad little boy needs a good whuppin'. Bellows is leaving out in the morning and I think we should too. Ever been to Carson City?"

"Before I joined the service, I came through headin' for the gold country. That's when I met you, Bull. Would have been different if I'd have found gold," he laughed. He was jerked back two years to when Bull Morrison rode into that wild Angels Camp to arrest a bank robber. Calhoun remembered telling Morrison that he had never met a U.S. Marshal before and how Morrison just laughed at him.

"Why don't you join the service, then, youngster. You can meet even more of them." He was a smart alec, Calhoun remembered. *Hell, he is still a smart alec, but I surprised myself by joining the service. Damn me, but we've been together three years now.* Those early days with Bull Morrison were an education most men would not enjoy.

Slim Calhoun walked over to the strong box and kicked it, looked at where Abigail Chastain breathed her last, and scowled. "Yeah, both them critters need a good whuppin', Bull. Let's head to Carson City and see if there's a trail to follow."

"I think you'll find the two of 'em somewhere near Mormon Station," Beartooth Johnson said walking into the cabin. "They both rode back and took the Carson Road, which would take them there.

"Sheriff said you want me to do your trackin', you better listen to me, then," Beartooth had that swagger and cock to his head that usually got a man a broken jaw when it was used on Bull Morrison. Morrison would not suffer fools, accept self-pity or self-importance from anyone.

"Oh, my, Mr. Calhoun, did you hear that? We better listen to this old fool." Morrison had his dander up and cocked and Calhoun wasn't about to slow him down.

"Yeah, I heard that 'bout as loud as be. My goodness, Bull, we better listen then. After all, we're just lonely and lost federal marshals what don't know east from north."

Beartooth Johnson wasn't used to being mocked and Morrison and Calhoun watched him bristle and anger up some. "You want the best tracker, then I'm the man, but you will listen to me when I tell you somethin'." He had his fists on his hips, his face pushed forward, and his eyes shining when he said it.

"I already got the best," Morrison snarled. "He's standin' next to me right now. Old Slim here's been knowed to track a salmon in a waterfall, Beartooth. Guess we'll just have to do without your services." He shook his head in wonderment, hoping to high heaven the tracker would take a swing at him. "Would have been good pay, too."

"So long, Beartooth," Calhoun said. He walked over to the rock fireplace and stirred the coals some before throwing in a couple of split logs. "You just ride on back with Bellows, we'll just have to stumble our way to success."

Both men were chuckling as Johnson stormed out of the cabin, cussing. "Ain't enough daylight left to leave out tonight, Bull. You still good with Carson City?"

"Yup," is all he said, pulling his old bear skin coat off and standing near the fire. "Think you can find the way?"

"Probably get lost," he said. "How about we bring that stagecoach driver, Purdy O'Neil along with us? He knows this country well, driving that route several times a month. Bet he knows people in Carson City and Mormon Station."

"Good idea. He's been naggin' to come and he is a tough old buzzard. Go see what he says, I'll attend the fire."

HAWKNOSE MACKENZIE WAS STANDING at the Mike and Dan's House Saloon bar with a bottle in front of him when Emerson stormed in. Both stood rock still, staring at each other and the barman was sure he was about to witness a killing. The kid with the scratched-up face was shaking but not from fear while the ugly man at the bar was letting his hand get mighty close to the big iron at his side.

"Didn't 'spect this," Emerson said, slowly. He edged his way down the length of the bar and stopped a few feet short of Mackenzie.

"Nope. Just about to pour me one. Join me, Chago?" He left that right hand close to his weapon but had a slight smile on his face. "Looks like someone added to your facial treatment, Chago."

"Might be people coming."

"Not my problem," Hawknose said. He nodded to the barman to put another glass up. "Got time for one, do you?" When they were robbing coaches, Emerson was the boss, but since the Marlette dispute, Mackenzie figured he was on his own.

Emerson looked around the long and narrow saloon and saw a couple of tables in the far back corner, almost in the dark. "Yeah, back there," he said. Hawknose put a double eagle on the bar, grabbed the bottle and glasses and followed Emerson to the table. "Bring the change," he said.

"You been ridin' hard, Chago."

"Had to shoot a man in Carson City. Damn women, Hawknose. Damn 'em all. You got a place where I can hide? Hell, they're probably not far behind me." Hawknose saw fear in the young man's eyes for the first time and almost had to chuckle.

"This is a different county, old man, but I'm sure they'll be lookin' soon enough. You just don't know damn nothing about women, do you? You're bringing a damn posse down on us and you want me to hide you? If I just shoot you, I might get a reward, you know," he laughed in Emerson's beat up face, watched the kid tense up, then felt sorry for him.

"Yeah, I got a nice little hole up in the mountains, but don't you be bringing John Law down on me. I don't know why I should share my place. Tell me why, sonny."

"You mean us, Hawknose. You're in as deep as I am. You shot the messenger on the stagecoach and we robbed the stagecoach. It's us, Hawknose."

"I guess so," the ugly man said. He wasn't willing to give it up just yet. Mackenzie knew he wanted someone like Emerson to ride with. He had a fast gun, killed at will, but couldn't think very well. "I suppose you were in a place with a lot of people with that messed up face. And the barman here can't keep his eyes off you. Hell, this place will be swarming with law. Let's leave and take a couple of bottles with us. It's a good half hour or more to my hidey hole. You get anywhere near a woman and I'll shoot you dead."

Hawknose led them high into the mountains west of Mormon Station. The canyon they followed opened onto a small meadow where the cabin stood in a copse of pine and aspen. A small stream spilled out of some rocks on the far side of the meadow and heavy brush helped obscure the view. The granite peaks of the mighty Sierra Nevada towered over the bucolic scene.

"How'd you find this?" Emerson asked as they put up their horses in a small brush and log corral behind the cabin. He could see that it had been occupied for some time.

"Met the old prospector who lived here yesterday, and he brought me here. He's buried off behind those rocks over there. We can stay for now, but we'll have to move out in the morning. It looks like many in the valley know about the old codger and this cabin, so any posse coming in would come here.

"I've got his mule and riggin', so we can carry what we need. The old boy had a good store of food we can take. We can ride east to the Walker River and then go south, maybe to New Mexico Territory. I had the old man draw me a map on how to find that river, and then we just go south."

"These cuts really hurt, Hawknose. I need a doc bad. I can't ride off with these cuts festering like they are. I got shot, too, but it was just a little scrape. We gotta find a doc."

"Ain't gonna see one, Chago, unless you want to go to jail for the rest of your worthless life. Or hang."

"Don't talk to me like that," Emerson snarled.

"Don't be gettin' huffy on me, boy. You're ridin' for me, now. You do as you're told or get the hell out." Hawknose Mackenzie had his hand resting on his sidearm, just daring Emerson to say or do something stupid. "Wash those wounds and put some bear grease on 'em." He glared at the young outlaw, smiled a wicked grin, and told him to be ready to ride at sunrise.

"I ain't gonna play nursemaid with you. I'm leavin' out at sunrise, with or without you. Killin' a man in Carson City and runnin' to me for help was just another stupid thing to do."

The hate came quick and Emerson couldn't control it, didn't want to control it. From the time he could remember, the idea of someone telling him what to do grated bad. He killed his first man because he was told to watch his language. His second kill came from that woman screaming insults in his face while gouging great scabs of skin. Now, he's killed his third, and that one came with some ease.

He stepped forward, his hand swiping that big Navy out and up, but not quick enough. Hawknose saw it coming well before Emerson made his decision and slapped the youngster's hand away knocking the heavy revolver loose. He followed through with a massive fist that knocked Emerson clear across the cabin and bouncing him off the log wall. Every cut and scab on his face opened up from the force of the blow.

Mackenzie jumped on the weakened Emerson and had his arms around the man's head, his fingers reaching for his throat. Emerson grabbed at Mackenzie's hair trying to yank the man off him. "Let go my hair," Mackenzie yelled.

"Let go my throat," Emerson grunted.

"What's more important, my hair or your throat?" Mackenzie said and felt Emerson slowly let go the hair.

Hawknose picked the gun up and walked over to the crumpled boy outlaw. "Get up, Chago. You ride with me, you do as I say. You pull a gun on me again and you're one dead youngster. You'll get this back in the morning," he said, stuffing the revolver into his waistband.

Sleep was out of the question as hate battled with pain hour after hour. Emerson got up three or four times, wanted to kill Hawknose, wanted to ease the pain from his now badly infected face wounds. He saw Abigail's angry face, saw the Carson City saloon girl, Shirley Berkshire's face laughing at him, and wanted to see Hawknose's body spread across the rough boards of the cabin's floor.

It was a long and slow sunrise coming that morning. Hawknose Mackenzie gave him no quarter, forced him to clean his own wounds, pour his own coffee, saddle his own horse, and the hatred grew with each chore.

"You're in no position to talk to me like that, Judge," Sheriff Bellows growled. "The U.S. Marshals have that job of goin' over state lines, not a county sheriff. I'm very sorry you lost your wife, but I'm also very sure Marshal Morrison will capture or kill those two men."

Chastain had been in a rage since Bellows told him about Abigail and that Emerson and Mackenzie had escaped to Nevada Territory. "I should have been allowed to ride with the marshals. They'll hear about that. They work for the judiciary. They should have taken me with them."

"If I were you, Judge, I'd thank your stars that you're not riding with Morrison and Calhoun." Bellows was almost chuckling, thinking about what a confrontation that would be.

"You want to find those killers, Judge?" Beartooth Johnson walked up to the two men. "I'll lead you right to them. I told the marshal where they'd be, but he just shrugged me off." Johnson had a glass of whiskey in his hand and nodded to the sheriff. "That Bull Morrison is a bastard." Bellows just shook his head and walked away.

"If you know where they are, I'll be ready to ride first thing in the morning." The judge glared at Sheriff Bellows and turned his attention to the tracker. "You get what you need for the trek from Tubs McCall here at the station. Tell him it's to be on my account, and we'll go."

"We'll just take one mule and be in the Carson Valley in two days, Judge. I'll bet all these fine bear's teeth those two men are at or near Mormon Station. They took the Carson Road and it leads right there. We'll leave at sunrise," he said and walked off toward the kitchen to find McCall.

"BIG DIFFERENCE, AIN'T IT?" Morrison said as they drifted into the vast Carson Valley. "An hour ago, we were in the wilds of the Sierra Nevada, and just like that we're riding through tall grass. This'll be a state one day soon, Slim, a rich little state."

"Driving the stage down off these mountains can be a chore," Purdy O'Neil said. He gestured back toward the steep road behind them. The Eastern flanks of the Sierra Nevada are almost perpendicular in places and roads and trails up down use cut-backs to make the descent. The Carson Valley was one of the lushest valleys in Nevada Territory, originally settled by Mormons. The church called the settlers back to Salt Lake and Western Utah Territory became Nevada Territory.

"Looks like four riders comin' up, Bull. We better spread out some." Slim Calhoun had led them off the mountain and into the valley. They were riding on almost flat ground now, toward Mormon Station when the riders were spotted coming toward them. Calhoun and O'Neil moved as far to the left on the trail as they could get, and Bull moved well to the right. All had their hands near their weapons.

Calhoun spotted the tin star on the lead rider first and held up his hand to tell Bull. "Looks like lawmen, Bull. Better open our coats so we don't get shot." He had to chuckle knowing what Bull looked like to most lawmen. That scar, the way he dressed all in black, and his welded-on scowl were open invitations to a fight. Bull grumbled but opened his bearskin coat so that big badge could be seen. Calhoun did the same.

"Mornin'," Calhoun said when the riders pulled up in a cloud of dust. "Looks like you're in a hurry."

The man with the badge gave the three men a good looking over before speaking. "U.S. Marshals, eh? I'm Sheriff Matt Rogers. We're looking for two men who have killed a couple of people."

"Yup," Calhoun said. "Us too. This is U.S. Marshal Bull Morrison, I'm Deputy Marshal Slim Calhoun. Tell us about these men you're after and we'll tell you about those we're after."

They moved off the trail and tied their horses to some nearby trees. A fire was lit, and the coffee pots broken out. Rogers got right to the point. "There was a killing at a saloon in Carson City by a young man who rode off toward Mormon Station. He was described as having bad scratches and cuts all over his face.

"We trailed him to a cabin in the hills behind the town and found the body of the prospector who lived there and signs that two men had been there."

"Looks like our boys," Morrison said. "So, Sheriff, why are you riding this way?"

"Seems like the logical thing to do. They probably want to hide out in the Sierras. Most outlaws seem to want to."

"Not these two," Calhoun said. "They're runnin' away from a stage holdup and killing. The one with the torn-up face is Gus Emerson and the other is Hawknose Mackenzie. Name's mean anything to you?"

"I've seen posters on both. Don't remember anything about torn up face."

"Those wounds are still bleeding, for Pete's sake, Sheriff," Morrison snarled. "Damn. Where you figure they're headin' Slim? Won't go north if Emerson killed somebody in Carson. Didn't come this way."

"Best bet would be to follow the Walker River into Mono country. Easy to get lost in that open country. Plenty of game and water. That's where I'd go."

"Yeah," Purdy said. "There's a good road too. Been over that route many times."

"Then that's where we'll go," Morrison said.

"I won't be able to help you, Marshal. You'd run out of my jurisdiction right away."

"Just as well. You take care of your little county, we'll take care of the country." Morrison stood up, threw coffee grounds in the fire and walked to his horse. "If you should run into them, remember they ain't got a friendly bone in their bodies."

"Glad I'm not riding with that bastard," Sheriff Rogers muttered. "He might be a marshal but he ain't got much else goin' for him. All right, men, let's head back. First drink's on me."

Morrison, O'Neil, and Calhoun rode off cross-country, through tall grass and sparse brush. They worked their way through herds of fat cattle, Morrison wondering if one would be missed, thinking fat steaks over an open fire. They forded the Carson River and rode toward the Pine Nut Range, which they would have to cross to come to the

Walker River. It was steep hills filled with rocks, canyons, and more rocks. Great stands of piñon pine covered the hillsides.

"Figure to pick up a trail, Bull?"

"Figure you will. Heard someone say you were the best tracker in the country," Morrison laughed, putting the spurs to his horse.

They were high in the Pine Nut Range for the first night and hadn't picked up any kind of trail. "Probably still a bit north of us," Calhoun said. "We'll hit the Walker River tomorrow and should pick up their tracks. A wise man would follow it south."

"That would leave Gus Emerson out of the picture," Morrison chuckled. "But not Hawknose Mackenzie."

"We'll follow that old river and come home with a couple of bad old outlaws," O'Neil said.

"You said there's a good road along the river," Morrison said. "Is that the one that leads into Body and the Mono Lake area?" O'Neil nodded. "I've been there, but it was some time ago. Lots of places to hide in that big canyon."

"Yeah, and a few angry Indians, too. Good deer country and they don't much care for us ugly old white men shootin' them." He spat a wad tobacco juice onto some rocks. "More than one coach has been stopped by those Injuns. They're mean as hell and simply hate white men."

CHAPTER 7

"IF YOU'RE GONNA WANT TO STOP AND REST EVERY TWO OR three miles, we ain't gonna catch no outlaws, Judge." Beartooth Johnson and Judge Chastain weren't five hours out of Strawberry and not very many miles either. Chastain hadn't been on the back of a horse for years, went everywhere in carriages, well sprung and padded. He would never be willing to admit that, but he knew deep down that demanding he be included in this chase was a mistake.

Maybe he could get this bruiser of a man to take on the chase. Maybe if he thought hard on the matter, he could convince the man to do it at his own expense. Play on his ego, the judge snickered. That generally works with these low fellows.

Chastain knew he should not be on this chase before the horses were saddled when Beartooth wanted him to help pack the mule and handed him something that had to weigh close to fifty pounds. Judge Chastain hadn't lifted anything heavier than a brandy snifter in ten years or more. Johnson wanted him to saddle his own horse as well, all the time telling the judge what a fine tracker he was. "I'll have those men in chains for you before you even realize we're chasing 'em," he said.

The skies were that beautiful high-altitude shade of deep blue that seems to sparkle and dance, and despite the bitter wind, the day was more than tolerable. "We've got a storm comin' our way, Judge, I can taste it in this wind. We've simply got to keep moving." Beartooth had no patience on a good day and was ready to ride off and leave the codger.

"I'll give you one thousand dollars in gold if you capture or kill those two men, Beartooth," Chastain sputtered, stepping down from the saddle for the third time that morning.

"You make that fifteen hundred and I'll go it alone, Judge," Beartooth said. His heart picked up a beat or two and he stepped down to talk a little more business.

The morning had been cold at the start but a bright sun warmed things up nicely on this fall morning, despite the wind. Standing behind massive granite boulders and out of the wind, it was a nice day. Aspen trees were showing off their bright yellow leaves, the hardwoods were glowing in many hues of orange and red, and the few clouds scattered about were white balls of southern cotton. Chastain saw nothing of this, only the faded memories of Abigail. He knew that Beartooth Johnson thought he had him over the barrel and seemed to reluctantly agree to the fifteen hundred.

"I'll want proof, Johnson. Absolute proof that those men are dead or in irons because of you. I'll not accept anything less."

They shook hands and Beartooth saw to it that Chastain was back on his horse and headed for Kyburz Flat and Strawberry Station. "Stage will be along in an hour or so, Judge. You can flag 'em down and ride on in, trailing the horse. I'll have Gus Emerson's head mounted for you, if you want," he laughed, mounting his horse and getting ready to ride off down the main highway over the mighty Sierra Nevada.

The judge wasn't ready for him to ride off just yet. He needed a hook, something he could use down the road to protect that fifteen hundred dollars. "Don't do anything illegal, Beartooth, while you're chasing those men, or when you're arresting them."

Beartooth Johnson quit chuckling and allowed himself to get very serious. "I'll need something from you, Judge, to let others know I'm working for you. Something to show the marshals or any local lawmen I might run into. They don't much care for people showing them up."

"I could write out a quick note, if that's what you mean." Chastain could feel it coming, could almost feel the man's ego ready to accept just about anything.

"No, I was thinking more along the lines of something I could pin to my coat or shirt." He had ridden with Sheriff Bellows many times, but the sheriff would never deputize him, never let him wear a badge. It was a simple point but a sore one for the simple but egotistical tracker. He had always wanted to wear a badge.

So many times, he had led Ballard to his man and was unable to flash a badge and tell the man he was under arrest. He longed to introduce himself as Deputy Johnson, and Ballard never deputized him.

Chastain reached into his satchel tied behind the saddle and brought out a shiny badge. "My court guards wear these. I suppose it would work. It doesn't really have any law enforcement value, though."

"This will do just fine," Johnson said. He pinned it on, saluted, and rode off.

"Ungrateful, uneducated, unwilling to be gentlemen," Chastain muttered, smiled some, and walked his horse slowly down the road. "These vulgar men who live their lives in the mountains wouldn't last a minute in the city where society's best live. But now, Mr. Johnson, you work for me," and he had to give just a hint of a smile.

"I'll be so glad to get out of these mountains." He let his thoughts wander to Abigail and how her death would affect the rest of his life. He had to admit he would have a little more gold rattling around with her gone. "That woman can spend money just looking through a store's window. She was always a bit rough around the edges, but she was the most wonderful bed partner a man could ask for. A bauble for her neck or ears and I would be in heaven for a week."

The stage was right on time and they allowed the judge to ride on into Kyburz Flats and the Strawberry Station. "Well, that was a mighty short trip, Judge," Tubbs McCall said helping the gentleman off the stage. "Was there a problem between you and Beartooth? He can be difficult at times."

"Book me on the next stage to Mormon Station in Nevada Territory, Mr. McCall. I'll ride as a gentleman, not some kind of animal, thank you. Are the telegraph wires back up?" McCall shook his head. "I wanted to let the authorities know I was coming and to prepare a proper posse to chase those filthy men down."

"Man has a serious attitude problem, I do believe," Tubbs McCall walked away shaking his head in wonder and muttering. "World revolves around him," he chuckled heading into the kitchen. "There's half a train load of people out there searching for those murderers. Two sets of marshals and now Beartooth Johnson, soon to be followed by the good judge. God help Nevada Territory."

. . .

"Too many bones, Slim. Damn trout would be fine without these bones. Gimme a grouse or fat rabbit any day instead." Camp was set up along the banks of the Walker River along the west side of a long canyon. They had scouted the river for several miles before Slim spotted the tracks of two horses and a mule, and they followed them into a meadow. The grass was good still and the cottonwood trees along the canyon hadn't lost all their leaves yet.

"I figured they'd be travelling a little faster than this, Slim. Wonder if we should just ride on after dark?" Bull Sorenson was aching for a fight. Slim Calhoun had to talk fast to keep him from slugging or shooting Sheriff Matt Rogers when he refused to put a posse together and join the chase. It was Purdy O'Neil who took the time to fashion some willow stems into a fishing rod and catch some trout for their supper.

"That sheriff's still in your craw, eh?"

"Damn right he is. He had a posse and was on the trail when we met up with him, but wouldn't join us? Man's a coward, Slim, not fit to wear a badge. Let's just ride on."

"Sure, Bull. Right into their camp? No, they're hours in front of us and neither we, nor they, know this country. It's about to get desolate and there won't be a lot of places to hide. We'll catch 'em."

"I've been on this road many times, Slim," Purdy said. "If they get deep into the Walker River Canyon, they won't have anywhere else to go but follow the river. Those prints they're a-leavin' are easy to follow, though. The canyon is deep and narrow in many places, so we'll catch up with them soon."

"In San Francisco we can eat fish without having to work

around five thousand bones. I want you to shoot something we can eat without digging around bones. Tomorrow, Slim."

"Anything you say, Bull," he laughed. He looked around the meadow and the entrance to that canyon and thought that Bull might just get his wish. The country was lush with feed, there was obviously plenty of water, and winter was still weeks away. "I'll conjure up an antelope or something, Bull. Just for you," he laughed.

"I'M GONNA DIE, ain't I?" Chago Emerson was sitting on a rock near a hot fire, wiping blood and puss from open wounds on his face. Some of them were two inches or more in length and deep into moldering flesh. "It really hurts, Hawknose."

"I don't know about kicking off from those wounds, but I do know I'll leave you to die if you keep up this cryin' stuff. Big old outlaw? Big old crybaby if you ask me. You got rough with a woman like Abigail and she taught you a lesson, sonny." He walked down to the river and filled a pan with water. "Maybe you'd be happy if I make up a sugar titty for you?" Hawknose Mackenzie was ready to ride off, leave the boy bandit, but he didn't and what's worse he wouldn't be able to tell you why he didn't.

He liked riding with Emerson when they were robbing stage coaches, rode with another outlaw called Jameson, down near Columbia City, robbing banks, but with Emerson, stopping the coaches was best. But now? He's still just a young boy and Hawknose Mackenzie was a much older man.

"I'll heat this water and clean those scratches, but this will be the last time. You get your head screwed on, Chago. We're runnin for our lives here and we can't stop every time your ugly face hurts. I killed a stage guard, you killed two people. We kidnapped a judge's wife, even if she was a whore, and I ain't slowing down cuz your face hurts."

The anger boiled and Emerson knew he couldn't do a thing about it. The infection was taking its toll. He was weak, couldn't hardly keep even a biscuit softened in coffee down, and wanted to kill Hawknose Mackenzie in the worst way. He let Mackenzie clean the wounds with the hot water, almost screaming from the pain.

There were two empty bottles of whiskey back at that cabin they had brought from the saloon. "Damn shame we don't have some whiskey to clean out these wounds," Hawknose said. "These are gonna get worse before they get better, if you live long enough."

Emerson wrapped himself in heavy wool blankets and stretched out near the fire. Half an hour later he flung the blankets off, waking in a sweat. Then the chills came back, and he shivered, pulling the blankets back up. This went on all night. Sweating hot and freezing cold. He was almost helpless when the sun came up. The wind was blowing, and Emerson couldn't get close enough to the fire.

"There ain't nothin' else I can do for you, Chago. I ain't gonna sit around and wait for whatever law is following us. You either get on your horse or stay here. I'm riding out when I'm packed." Hawknose wasn't going to let himself get caught and hung just because Emerson was about to die. He had the same conversation with himself over and over as the night wore on. Self-preservation far outweighed any short-time friendship. The thought of shooting Emerson was always in the front of his mind. It would make things so much easier, he thought.

"You ain't got the brains of dead flea, boy. You beat on a woman and she whupped you good, then you damn fool, you shot a man when you were already on the run. They be people following us, Chago. Maybe they'll fix you up before they hang you."

"Don't leave me," Emerson cried out. "My God, man, you can't leave me to die alone. We been partners, Hawknose."

Emerson watched Hawknose load the mule and saw that both sacks of gold were on the mule. "You taking my gold?" He hollered out, reaching under the blankets for his gun. Hawknose turned, gun in hand, and watched Emerson fumble through the blankets.

"I am, and you ain't gonna do nothing about it." The big ugly outlaw slipped his weapon back in leather and tightened the ropes on the pack, walked around to mount his horse and saw Emerson aim his big Navy at him.

Hawknose spun away, drawing his gun and firing. Both men fired almost simultaneously, and both hit their targets. Emerson felt his shoulder explode with pain as the big lead slug tore through where the arm and shoulder came together. He was flung back into his blankets, the Navy hanging loose from a helpless hand.

Hawknose was thrown off balance and toppled to the ground, grabbing for his left foot. The bullet tore through his boot, his foot, and the boot's sole, breaking several bones on the way. He got up, hobbled to his horse and jumped into the saddle, grabbing the mule's lead rope, and loped off, southbound, along the banks of the Walker River.

"Don't leave me," Emerson cried out, softly, before he passed out. Hawknose Mackenzie didn't look around, just rode on. Was it survival or was it all the gold? Regardless, Hawknose felt no stab of remorse, only the pleasure of being alone.

.   .   .

BEARTOOTH JOHNSON RODE into Mormon Station the next day and found Sheriff Rogers talking with the barman. "Trailing a couple of outlaws for federal judge Chastain," he said. "Name's Court Deputy Johnson."

"Court Deputy? What the hell does that mean?" Sheriff Matt Rogers laughed. asking the question. Rogers saw a man of about forty years, dressed almost as a mountain man and with a cunning look to his eyes. "Explain yourself."

"Men I'm after robbed a stage, killed two people, and are known to be coming this way. Federal District Judge Chastain has retained my services to bring them in." Johnson was doing his best to remember how lawmen had talked when they discussed such things about him.

"You might be a bit late, Court Deputy," Rogers chuckled. "A couple of U.S. Marshals are on the chase a couple of days ahead of you. Ain't never heard of a court deputy and you ain't got no jurisdiction around here. You try to play lawman and I'll lock you up tight.

"You want to follow the marshals, that ain't no crime. They headed across the Pine Nut Range toward the Walker River. Between here and them mountains, Mister Court Deputy, you're in my territory and don't forget it."

"Why ain't you chasin' 'em, too?" Johnson asked.

"Don't you get smart with me," Rogers snapped. *That was the same question that marshal asked. Just who do these people think they are, suggesting how I should run my office. I'm the sheriff here and I do things my way.* His way had always been the easy way. Don't make work for yourself, don't try to be something you ain't. He was a man who took life the easiest way possible. "You better be on your way before I lock you up. Impertinent old fool."

Johnson tipped his hat, growled a "thankee" and turned on his heel. He was cussing long but quietly as he mounted and rode out of Mormon Station leading his old mule. "Uppity old bastard," he growled. He was about ten miles out when he noticed a lone rider coming up behind at a lope and turned his horse into a stand of laurel trees. He let the man ride past and stepped his horse out behind.

"Whoa up there, mister. You following me for a reason?" Johnson had his Henry rifle out of the scabbard and held at the ready.

"I am," the rider said. "Heard what you said to Sheriff Rogers and figured you might need a little help."

"Why would you be concerned?" Johnson kept his rifle at the ready. He saw a long scrawny man in his early twenties at the most, with long stringy blond hair, light eyes, and a scrubby beard.

"The man you're after shot Three Finger Jack, my friend, in Carson City and beat on a woman I like. That Sheriff Rogers should have ridden with the marshals just like you said but wouldn't. I'll help you catch those two."

"What do you get out of it?" Johnson had never done anything for anyone without some personable gain. "You ain't getting' none of my bounty." He wondered if he should have said that but then took another look at the kid. *No, I don't have to worry about this fool trying to hog in on my bounty. He ain't strong enough to lift my rifle.*

"I'm lookin' to kill my first man," the kid said. "Killin' an outlaw ain't a crime, I figger and ridin' with you might just give me that chance."

"You got a handle to go with that bad-man attitude?" Beartooth Johnson laughed.

"Don't be laughin' at me just cuz you're holding a rifle. I'm pretty quick and a damn fine shot," the kid snarled. His eyes were narrowed some and Johnson saw this youngster in a different light.

"Name's Duff. Duff Dorman and you need a second gun goin' up against those men. I saw the one with the torn-up face shoot my friend, and he's pretty good."

"You're ridin' light, boy. You expect me to feed you too?" The kid was right, Johnson thought. He knew a second gun would come in handy, if the kid was as good as he said he was. "You get us some good camp meat and we might make a deal, but you can forget about getting' part of my bounty."

Dorman gave Johnson the slightest nod and rode off in the direction they were heading at a steady lope. Johnson walked his horse and mule on behind wondering just how this would play out. Dorman figured he would play along until he could kill the man with the torn-up face and in the meantime find out more about this bounty that might be available.

"Bounty hunter, eh? I've heard the phrase but sure never thought I'd be riding with one. How much bounty?" he muttered. "If it's enough to get his attention, it sure has got mine."

Following the tracks of Bull Morrison and Slim Calhoun was easy since they weren't trying to hide anything. Beartooth could read track better than most and had been through this country before. "I don't think Gus Emerson or Hawknose Mackenzie have been through these canyons, Dorman, but I have. We'll go through a long canyon and head south. We'll have those boys in two days if I'm pickin' right."

CHAPTER 8

These tracks are fresh as a ripe peach, Bull. We can't be half a day behind Emerson now. Wonder why they're ridin' so slow?"

"Cuz they're outlaw stupid, Slim. As much as I know about chasing stupid outlaws, if I turned outlaw, you'd never catch me, Slim," Bull Morrison chuckled.

"Hell, Bull, I'd have you roped, tied, and beggin' for mercy inside two days. I bet one of these men is wounded. Sheriff didn't say nothin' about gunshots or knives, did he?"

"Nope. Just the cuts on his face. Maybe they ain't just scratches. Maybe he's been hurt bad and they're all infected. Damn, that's always so ugly to deal with. Usually smells bad, too."

"You just got a tender streak about somebody hurtin' bad," Slim Calhoun laughed. "Let's ride into dusk before making camp, Bull. We might be close enough to see their fire when it gets dark."

"Might be close enough for them to see ours you mean. You're lookin' for this fight, ain't you?"

"Just learnin' from you, Bull." He nudged his horse into a

trot but knew that Bull Morrison, U.S. Marshal was right. He was looking for a good fight from this Gus Emerson character. The Marshal Service was created by President George Washington and dedicated to serving and protecting the federal judiciary. Emerson kidnapped the wife of a federal judge and that was one big thorn in Slim Calhoun's foot.

Calhoun looked over at Morrison and saw an angry man riding next to him. "You, too, eh?"

"Man kidnapped the wife of a federal judge, Slim. My duty to kill him."

"Well, supposed to be our duty to apprehend him, Bull, if you want to get technical."

"I don't believe in technical," Morrison chuckled. "Yup, my duty to kill the man while apprehending him. There's your technical."

They made camp in a stand of cottonwood trees as the sun drifted behind the rocky hillsides to their west. Calhoun was still chuckling as he tried his best to shield their fire but that wasn't going to work. "Can't shield this fire if you continue to add broken cottonwood branches to it. I thought we would look for their fire, not make ours so visible."

"It's cold, Slim, and I don't like the cold. Did you shoot something today or are we still on smoked elk rations?"

"Smoked elk coming up along with hot coffee and hard tack. Tubbs McCall said he packed beans for us, but I sure can't find 'em. Still got some whiskey, though. Bought a bottle while you were jawin' with that sheriff."

"Good boy, Slim. That's why you're my deputy." He poured a generous cup full and settled back against a rock. "Speaking of that sheriff. How do men like that get elected? He ain't no more a lawman than Emerson. I'm gonna bring these two yahoos back to that little town and dump their bodies in the middle of the street and invite the town-folk to demand the sheriff do something about it."

'You're gonna get a fight going no matter what, Bull. That's why I ride with you."

"Where's Purdy? He's gonna miss a fine supper of dried up elk."

"He went north for a bit. Spotted some antelope. We'll probably have antelope steaks for breakfast, Bull. Probably so."

"I woke up twice last night lookin' for some firelight off in the distance but there weren't none. Looks like we got us a storm comin' in, though. Wind picked up just before sunrise. You gonna get up or what?" Slim Calhoun loved the morning, saw most sunrises, made good strong coffee, and couldn't understand Morrison's reluctance to get moving early in the day.

Purdy had an antelope half butchered, steaks hanging over the fire. "Sun's been up for some time now. Can't you smell that fresh meat, Marshal?"

"Day's gonna be here no matter what time I get started, Slim. Um," he whispered, taking his first swallow of camp coffee. "Shoot something, did you? I like elk but damn, man, everyday? That does smell good, Mr. O'Neil. Anybody grow cows out here?"

Calhoun was laughing, spilling his coffee, watching Bull Morrison fight his way out from under a heavy buffalo blanket, and almost jumped straight up at the sound of gunfire off in the distance. Calhoun had his sidearm out and cocked, Morrison was trying to find his in the quiet that followed.

"Get an angle on that?" Morrison asked. "Sounded like almost in direction of where we were riding."

"Yup," Calhoun said. "Long way off, though. Maybe they killed each other, and we can go home. Let's pack up."

The ride into the long and deep Walker River Canyon was easy on riders and horses, the road in good condition. This time of year there was little traffic, mostly because of the threat of storms. The canyon's funnel actions created winds of hurricane strength along with massive amounts of snow.

"We might call this fall," Bull said as they forded the river for the third time that morning, "but my bones are telling me it's winter." The wind was swirling, seeming to come from all four points of the compass, and was icy cold. "Hope both those boys are dead," Morrison grumbled.

"You're the sheriff in this county and I'm telling you there are criminals runnin' loose out there." Federal Judge Lemuel S. Chastain was on a rampage moments after the stagecoach slid to a stop at Mormon Station. He jumped from the coach and stomped across the muddy street into the sheriff's little office. "It's your duty to chase them down, and I'm ridin' with you to see to it that it's done right."

"You ain't in no position to tell me what my duty is, judge." Sheriff Matt Rogers snarled right back at the man. "These men you're talking about killed somebody in California and somebody else in Carson City, neither place happens to be in my jurisdiction." He couldn't help but wonder why all these people from out of the area were telling him what his duty was. "I know what my duty is. It's to the people of this county, not to you, from California, not to the Carson City sheriff."

Rogers neglected to remember the dead prospector who was killed in his county. Rogers was not a fearful man, he simply wasn't cut out to be a lawman. He was a fine politician, understood what a round of drinks was worth at the local saloon, knew how a few key words about protection were far more productive at the polls than actually chasing an outlaw.

"Now if you want to hike on out of here and chase 'em down, don't let me get in your way, but I ain't goin'." Rogers walked out of his office and across the muddy street to Mike and Dan's House saloon. Chastain was right on his trail, yapping like a cur dog smelling fresh meat.

"Now you listen here, Sheriff, I want those men hanged and it is your responsibility to catch 'em. They killed my wife," he howled, almost sobbing in frustration. He was still berating the sheriff as the two walked up to the oaken plank.

Sheriff Rogers spun around, his Colt Navy out and cocked. He shoved the barrel into Chastain's face so the man could see the bullets in the cylinder. "One more word about my responsibilities and you're going behind bars. Judge or not, nobody talks to me that way.

"Now, you listen to me and listen hard cuz I ain't gonna repeat myself. There are two groups of U.S. Marshals following the outlaw's trail. You have some kind of court deputy out following the outlaw's trail. It's the marshals' responsibility to trail and capture those men. By now those two bad men are probably out of my county anyway."

Listening to the judge's jabbering made him think about his own deputy, Cliff Martin, and his constant yowling about duty this and duty that. *Martin's gonna run against me at the next election and what's going on right now will be a big part of his campaign, but I'm not gonna get involved in this mess.* He let his mind turn to how to counter that, maybe with a little organized set of parties, some special appointments, but not chasing after these outlaws.

Chastain stood at the bar glaring at the sheriff, understanding that the man probably would arrest him if he said anything else. The working end of that revolver was enough to put a cork in the good judge's mouth and he turned and stormed out of the saloon. "That man has no sense of responsibility and no respect for the law. I'll see to it that he's removed from office," he growled all the way to the stables.

He was almost at a trot coming into the livery and blacksmith barns and was breathing heavy. "I'm federal judge Chastain," he almost panted to the smithy. "I want to rent a carriage and trotter and need directions to get to the Walker River from here."

The smithy was choking back some serious laughter and finally said, "We don't get much call for carriages and trotters around these parts, old timer. I can fetch up a nice little spring wagon and working team. You're talking about some rough country between here and the Walker. Roads are primitive at best and used by heavy teams and wagons. You up to that kind of drivin'?"

"Just put it together for me while I get some gear," Chastain said.

The smithy nodded, muttering, "Be two dollars a day for the wagon and five for the team. In advance."

"I'll be back in half an hour," Chastain said. He handed some bills to the smithy and headed for the general store.

"YOU BEEN IN THIS COUNTRY BEFORE?" Beartooth Johnson was looking at the trail left by the marshals. "This river is about to join up with another coming from our south." The kid smiled.

"This is the Walker and we'll join another branch of it in just a mile or so. I'm sure the marshals and outlaws are following that. We'll ride south into some prime game country in a long canyon." Duff Dorman surprised the old Sierra tracker with his knowledge of the area.

"My call on this," Beartooth said, "is that we're half a day behind the marshals and at least a full day or more behind the outlaws. Let's pick it up some. I want to be the one to take those men into custody, not the marshals."

Dorman nodded and the two put their horses into a solid trot turning south when they joined the Walker. "Got a storm comin' our way, I think. Winds kickin' up some." Dorman knew this long craggy canyon well having made more than one trip to the Mono country and up to Bodie. There weren't any places where they would be able to get around the marshals without being seen. He decided he would ride along and live with whatever happened as long as it wasn't too illegal. The thought of bounty kept bouncing joyfully around his young head.

That was just nonsense about killin' somebody. What I want is a pocket full of that bounty money. This Beartooth is a wily old devil, but I am too, the youngster was chuckling some as they rode on.

BEARTOOTH WASN'T aware that the tracks he was following were of the marshals following Calhoun and Morrison, the ones bringing mules and supplies. They were at least ten hours or more in front of the old tracker and not moving fast at all. Deputy Buck Antonelli and Deputy Warren Fitzgerald were seasoned lawmen backing up Morrison. "Old Bull is leaving us a clear trail to follow, Warren. I wonder how long it'll be before he and Calhoun trap those two bad men?"

"That dumb ass sheriff said they had blood in their eyes talking about the death of the judge's wife. They'll ride 'em down hard, Buck, and God help 'em if those two bad boys fight back," he laughed. "Think we should pick up the pace? Morrison might need some help."

"Naw, there's only two outlaws," Warren Fitzgerald chuckled. "If there were six or more, maybe, but not for just two. Old Bull would feel hurt if we tried to move into his play."

The trail was well used, the river was down this late in the fall, and travel through the deep canyon was pleasant. "See a buck, let's put him in our stores, Warren. I think the only thing Tubbs McCall had on hand was smoked elk. I could use some fresh meat. Let me have your mule's lead rope and you ride out and see what you can find."

Fitzgerald had a camp set up, a fine young buck hanging from a tree, all cleaned and skinned when Buck Antonelli led the mules in. "Now we're talking my language, Mr. Fitzgerald, sir. Venison back strap cooked over an open fire, a cup of Kentucky's finest, and no rain or snow.

"These tracks we've been following are fresh," Fitzgerald said. "If we step it up tomorrow, we should catch up. But about that rain and snow, I think it's comin' our way and soon."

"Good. Let's leave out at first light and push some. Mules might not like it, but we will. Sure would like to be on hand when Bull takes those two into custody."

"Or just shoots 'em," Fitzgerald chuckled. "I rode with him on one job against four mean bank robbers. The Peterson mob, it was. Chased 'em down the Stanislaw River for three days before cornering them. Bull hollered out, got shot in the leg for his efforts, and was so mad he walked right through their gunfire and killed all four. Never seen anything like that in my life. He took two more bullets going in and simply didn't care."

"Hush up for a minute," Antonelli said, twisting his head around. "Listen."

The two men dropped down behind some brush and heard animals walking slowly up to the camp. "They're about a hundred yards out, Buck. Sounds like two men horseback, and maybe a pack mule." Fitzgerald motioned for Antonelli to move out of camp to his left and he snuck through the brush the other way.

Beartooth Johnson and Duff Dorman spotted the camp when they were out about thirty yards and pulled up. Johnson motioned Dorman to walk slowly into the camp, but the young man shook his head. "Good way to get me shot, old man. No. Holler out that we're coming in."

"You holler out and ride in slow. I'm gonna skirt around and keep going. Those killers have to be right in front of us, only a few hours away."

Dorman could almost see his part of this thing called bounty slip away. "Don't you ride off on me," he said. "Don't you cut me out of this," he snarled but nudged his horse forward, and hollered out. "Hello the camp. Coming in slow." He watched Johnson disappear into the brush and trees along the trail.

"Well, come on in, then. You keep those hands where I can see them," Antonelli said. He stood up, a lot closer to Dorman than the young man thought he would be and walked into the camp area. "Step down slow. I'm Deputy U.S. Marshal Buck Antonelli, who are you? Why have you been following me?" He knew there were two riders and hoped that Fitzgerald had a handle on the second one.

"Name's Dorman, Duff Dorman," he said, not saying anything else. He walked to the fire, saw the hanging deer carcass, and warmed his hands. "Nice fire. You been hunting?"

"You might say that." Antonelli started to say something else but was held up by a ruckus taking place in the brush several yards off to the side of the trail. Several grunts, dust flying, and some serious cussing and Buck pulled his weapon, aiming it at Dorman's head. "Stand quiet, boy. Seems like you didn't tell me about a friend along with you."

Dorman froze, didn't even give a nervous shake. He had never seen a weapon drawn, cocked, and aimed that fast. He looked down that long barrel right into the cylinder filled with lead. Then the shakes started, and he couldn't control them. "You take it easy, boy. I only shoot people when they get dumb."

Fitzgerald came through a stand of sagebrush pushing Beartooth Johnson in front of him. "Caught this one trying to sneak up on us," he said and pushed Johnson face first into the dirt. "Don't care to be snuck up on," he growled.

Antonelli relieved Dorman of his weapons while Fitzgerald took Johnson's. "Just about time for you boys to introduce yourselves. You know who we are, and we are not nice friendly people. You first, great mountain man. Speak up."

"I'm working for Federal Judge Lemuel Chastain. I'm Beartooth Johnson, court deputy," Johnson said, trying to pull his coat aside to show that shiny badge of his.

"There's a new one, Buck," Fitzgerald laughed right out. He walked over and poured a cup of coffee. "And you're the court deputy's deputy?" He snarled it out at Duff Dorman, turned and whacked Johnson across the side of the head, spilling some coffee. "Fun is over, boys," he said. He finished the coffee and put the cup down. He pulled his weapon, checked for load, cocked it, and aimed it at Johnson's left eye.

"Why are you here? No more games." Dorman fell to the ground almost crying, while Johnson set his jaw and glared at Fitzgerald. After all, he too was wearing a badge, one that came from a federal judge.

"We thought you were the marshals chasing two murderers," Dorman whimpered. "We were gonna catch 'em first for the bounty."

"Shut up!" Johnson screamed at the boy, trying desperately to get to his feet. Fitzgerald hammered him again across the side of his head, this time with his pistol.

"Go on, boy. What's this about a bounty?" Buck Antonelli sat down on a stump with a cup of coffee. "Guess we haven't heard about that."

"Some judge is gonna pay Beartooth some money to kill the men that killed his wife is all I know," Dorman whimpered. "I rode along hoping that if I helped, I'd get part of that bounty." He was no longer the tough young man he thought he was. Watching Beartooth get knocked around, having a big chunk of iron pointed in his face changed all of that.

"Is that a fact?" Fitzgerald chuckled. He used his revolver's barrel to poke Beartooth in the ribs. "Well, Mr. Beartooth, is it? You just a bounty hunter pretending to be a lawman?" He used his boot toe to prod the man again. "You better start talking, Mr. big shot, or I'm gonna break every bone in your ugly face."

Beartooth sat up in the dirt, glared first at Duff Dorman then at Fitzgerald, and tried to get to his feet. "Judge Chastain offered to pay me to catch Emerson and Hawknose. They killed his wife. He swore me in as his court deputy. I ain't no bounty hunter." He was wobbly as he made his way to a log to sit down. "That boy don't know nothing."

"You being paid to hunt down a man makes you a bounty hunter, Mr., and makes the judge a criminal. Damn, Buck," Fitzgerald laughed. "I ain't never had to arrest a man I was hired to protect."

Buck Antonelli got Dorman on his feet and sat him next to Beartooth. "Put your hands behind your backs, gentlemen."

"Whatcha think you're doin'?" Beartooth started to jump up and Buck flattened him with a heavy fist, sending the man face first into the dirt again.

"Have to put you boys in irons. Can't have you running around threatening U.S. Marshals in their peaceful camp, now, can we? Get up, bounty hunter, and put those great paws behind your back."

With the two trussed up, Buck and Fitz prepared some nicely cooked venison and beans, offering beans and coffee to their prisoners.

"We got to be movin' early, Buck if we're gonna catch up with Bull and Slim. I'll take first watch, you get some sleep."

"LET'S MOVE, Bull. It's light enough." Slim Calhoun gave Morrison a gentle boot toe in the back, stepping back quickly. He's seen the man explode from his blankets more the once. "Fire's hot and coffee's fair. Side meat and biscuits are almost ready. Move it, big man."

Fall in western Nevada was coming on hard, with a cold wind blowing, heavy gray clouds gathering, and trees showing empty branches. The rocks took on a different color in the bleak conditions, and even the river looked black.

"It's still pitch dark, dammit. Go away. Shoot somebody." Bull Morrison, U.S. Marshal slowly fought his way out of his blankets, found his crumpled hat, strapped on his big Navy Colt, and stumbled toward the fire. "Ain't decent getting up before the sun. I'm a dignified member of the Marshal Service, and don't you forget it. Where's the coffee? You put any Kentucky in it?"

Calhoun was laughing at every comment and move Morrison made, poured a healthy shot of whiskey in both coffee cups, and handed one to the marshal. "You are one dignified U.S. Marshal early in the morning, Bull. Grab a biscuit and fill it with some fresh antelope meat. We got to get moving. Somebody out in front of us got shot, remember?"

Purdy O'Neil was already packing the mule and had to nudge the marshal out of the way to grab his bedroll. "Hot meat'll make you feel better, Marshal. Those gunshots weren't more than a mile or so in front of us."

"I wonder where Antonelli and Fitzgerald are? They can't be too far behind us. We need to keep leaving good trail for them. Hope they're carrying some fresh food for us." He wolfed two biscuits loaded with fried side meat, slurped two cups of boiling coffee and yelled at Calhoun to get a move on.

"We got criminals to kill, boy. Let's ride."

Calhoun was still chuckling as they moved onto the trail left by Emerson and Hawknose the day before. "We want to move as quietly as possible, Bull. Remember that somebody shot at somebody right where we're riding." He had a heavy wool jacket on and saw that Bull was wearing his buffalo robe coat, too.

"These late fall mornings are a little more than crisp, Slim. There was ice on my blankets, I swear there was. We need to make it a rule that we can only chase people in the spring. It's just not right."

"You saying it ain't dignified?" Calhoun laughed. They rode through the early morning, Bull grumbling, Slim trying to keep him quiet. It was a long two hours later when Morrison finally sat straight up in the saddle.

"Something moving up ahead, Slim." He pulled his horse up and stepped off, grabbing his rifle on the way. They tied off their mounts and spread out in the brush and trees, moving slowly to where Morrison was pointing.

The Walker River was low at this time of the year, and the willows that grew along its banks were back some from the water. "You take the river, Slim, I'll stay on the trail. Keep those eyes of yours wide open. Purdy, hang back some and back our play. Don't let anyone get behind us or too far to the side."

The two marshals had worked together on so many chases, kills, and captures that each knew what the other was going to do, but Morrison knew that Purdy wasn't trained in chases like this.

Slim nodded and moved along through the dirt and rocks of the river-bed, staying as low as he could, his eyes sweeping back and forth, trying to pick up some kind of movement. It was sound instead of sight that made him stop. He caught Bull's attention and pointed off toward a stand of cottonwood trees.

CHAPTER 9

"CLIFF, COME OVER HERE FOR A MINUTE." SHERIFF MATT Rogers was sitting at a table inside the Carson Valley Café. Cliff Martin, his chief deputy was flirting with Daisy Crawford at the counter. "I got a problem."

Martin, about twenty-three or so, long and thin but strong and fast agreed, but silently. *Yeah, Sheriff, you do have a problem and you'll find out just how much of one at the next election.* Cliff Martin nodded to the girl and turned his attention to the sheriff.

The single girls in the Carson Valley, those few that existed, all had their eyes on him, and he took great pleasure in letting them. "You worried about all that activity around the killers? Me, too, as you well know. What's on your mind?" He sat down and watched Daisy sashay over with a big pot of coffee.

Cliff Martin had his eyes on the sheriff's job as well as on the local girls. He told everyone in sight, more than once, that when that posse from Carson City turned back, Rogers should have taken up the chase. When the old prospector's body was found, he was adamant about taking up the chase. In Martin's mind, the situation was now out of control.

"There's a whole circus going on out there, Cliff, and the main attraction ain't the killers, it's that fool judge. He took a spring wagon with two-up to cross the Pine Nut Range and get on the Walker River Road. He's gonna die out there and sure as old Abe is an honest man, I'll be blamed."

"You know my feelings on that. You're way late. You plannin' on bringing the judge back? Or joining him?" He didn't hold back his contempt for the sheriff. Matt Rogers hated having to make decisions. It was too easy to hold off, or just say no. He also didn't like being scorned by his own deputy while at the same time he knew what did get done around the sheriff's office got done because of Cliff Martin.

"I'm thinkin' we will join him, Slim. You may have been right, but right now you're still my deputy, working for me." Rogers was just slow to get his horses all in a line, but he did hear Martin's contempt. "Go make up a three-day pack and we'll leave right out. The only real lawmen out there will be us and those bloodthirsty marshals. The rest of 'em are all fools on a fool's mission."

Martin had to hold back a guffaw at the comment about real lawmen. *Real lawman?* he thought. *The only real lawman at this table is me, you fool. Now, at last, a chase will begin.*

Martin had been waiting too long for this and jumped at the chance to join the chase. They were on the trail within the hour and following such a broad path made by so many people within the last few days wasn't the least bit hard. "They're making a new highway across the Carson Valley, Sheriff. That judge ain't much of a wagon master. He's trying to keep those horses on the same path as the riders, knocking down sagebrush and everything else in his path."

"He left out about three hours ahead of us, Slim. We'll

catch him before sunset. Hope we can talk that cantankerous old fool into turning back. Stubborn as my first wife," Rogers laughed.

"Well, it was his wife who was murdered by that Emerson feller. I think I'd be pretty hard to get along with, too. The broadsheets on Emerson describe him as being just a teenager but a known killer. Think the marshals will bring him in alive?"

"Highly doubtful, Slim, highly doubtful. I'm worried about that fool that calls himself Beartooth. There's a problem in the making. Court deputy? Should have just arrested him for pretending to be a lawman and got it over with."

"Hell, Sheriff, the judge called him that, too," Cliff Martin chuckled. "Maybe there is such a thing over there in California. Just look at these tracks," Martin said, pointing at the wagon tracks taking off to the south, and twisting and turning through the sage and scrub brush.

"That ain't the judge's doing. Those horses spooked, Cliff. Let's go. That judge is in trouble right now."

Chastain drove single pacers inside towns and cities, horses that heard loud, even boisterous sounds constantly, worked where people walked in front of them, where papers blew in the wind, where bells clanged, and whistles blew. He was driving a team of farm horses cross country, making them walk or trot right through the brush, and at the slightest unexpected event, they panicked.

More than likely, so did the judge. He was probably screaming obscenities, whipping them too, and they were trying to flee. He had no idea how to stop a run-away, and his panic level probably equaled that of the horses.

Rogers and Martin had their horses in full flight following the erratic trail laid out across the open plain of

the Carson Valley. Those wagon horses knew all the preda-
tors of history were on their tail and ran as fast and hard as
they could, not trying to evade anything in their path. They
bolted into deep gullies, bounced the wagon off large rocks,
tried to take out scrub pine and cedar bushes. It took but
half an hour of hard riding to find the crumpled remains of
the spring wagon. Four horses, lathered and panting, still in
harness, stood quietly nearby, chomping on green grass.

Federal District Judge Lemuel S. Chastain was crumpled
as well, in the remains of the wagon. "He's alive, Sheriff, but
hurt. Can you make that wagon useable? He needs to see a
doc right away."

Rogers helped Martin get the judge untangled from the
mess and laid out in the dirt. "Keep care of him while I get
the wagon put up right. Damn fool has no business being
out here in the first place."

Martin watched the sheriff start work on the wagon and
had some bad thoughts about the situation. *You should have
been with him, damn it. If we had made up a posse in the first
place, we wouldn't even be here right now. Rogers is too willing to
say no when all the facts point to him saying yes. If this judge
dies, Rogers is responsible and I'm gonna make sure everyone in
this county knows it.*

Martin got the judge covered in a blanket, got a fire lit on
a cold late afternoon, and built a pot of coffee. "You need a
hand?"

"I think it'll hold together. Hit that big cedar bush with a
wheel and flipped it right over. It looks a bunch worse than
it really is. Wheels are still on and all the fittings are sound.
How's that judge doing?"

"He's got busted up ribs on both sides, at least one arm is
broken, and his head is beat up pretty bad. Probably bruised
up inside, too." He helped put all the stuff the judge brought

along back in the wagon. "What's your plan now, Sheriff?" He wanted to say something like, are you gonna suggest we call this off to take the judge back to town? He wasn't going to call it off. Somebody from this county needed to be in on capturing those killers.

"We got to get this old codger back into town, Cliff. He's hurt real bad and sure can't drive himself."

"Well, I think you can handle that all by yourself," Martin said with about a ton of sarcasm in his voice. "I'm gonna ride on and see if those marshals might need some help. Emerson and Mackenzie committed murder in our jurisdiction, so I feel justified."

"Up to you but it ain't necessary. Help me get these horses all hooked up and I'll be on my way. Hope he lives long enough to get to town."

The sheriff watched Martin ride off and got the team started. He was thinking that Martin was just grand standing when he heard moans coming from the back of 5he wagon and pulled the team up. Judge Chastain was trying to sit up and couldn't.

"Take it easy, Judge. I'll have you back at the doc's in a couple of hours." He stepped into the back of the wagon and handed the judge a canteen. "You took a pretty good tumble back there."

"A sip of brandy would help some, Sheriff," he whimpered. Rogers handed him his flask and got back up in the seat, unwound the reins from the brake lever and got the teams back on the trail for Mormon Station.

"THERE, Bull, under that tree. See him?" Slim Calhoun worked his way out of the dried river-bank and spotted Gus Emerson, wrapped in a blanket, propped up next to a cottonwood. "He ain't moving. What is it you thought you saw?"

"Got me. Just some dust. I'll come around from behind him and you ease up from the side. He's not moving but that don't mean he's dead." Bull stayed in the bushes and slowly crept around until he knew that Emerson couldn't possibly see him and moved a bit faster.

The move forward was a little more difficult for Calhoun, coming almost straight on. "He's either dead or asleep," he murmured, creeping through the thin brush. He was twenty feet or so from Emerson when Bull stepped up and confronted the young outlaw, gun in hand.

"One little move and you're a dead man," Bull said. Emerson didn't move but Morrison wasn't gonna take that kind of chance on him playing dead. Coming up from the side gave him the advantage since Emerson was flat on his back. He reached down and ripped the blanket away, exposing the horrible wound to Emerson's shoulder. The stench from the open wounds on the man's face drove him back a step or two.

"He ain't dead but it won't be long. Come on in, Slim." Slim was already on his feet, striding in to back Bull's play.

"Stay with him until I can sort out this camp," Slim said. He made two big circles around the campsite, stopping often to take close looks at the ground. "Looks like his good old partner shot him and left. We heard what we thought was one shot last night, Bull, but I think there were two, almost together. Hawknose Mackenzie was also shot, but he left out. Going south, following the river. I got a blood trail that ends where horse prints start."

"You get on him, Slim. I'll stay with Emerson until Antonelli and Fitzgerald catch up. They gotta be close. Take as much of the supplies as you want, and I'll light out after you as soon as those yahoos catch up."

Ten minutes later, Slim had his saddlebags filled with food and extra ammunition. His bedroll was tied off and he was on the trail. "I'll have him in irons when you catch up," he said, watching Bull light a fire.

"He's already gonna feel caged, Slim, and if he's shot it's gonna make him meaner. You be careful."

CHAPTER 10

"I NEVER SHOULD HAVE TIED UP WITH THAT FOOL," HAWKNOSE Mackenzie muttered, nudging his horse into a gentle lope. He was following the Walker River through the deep canyon, the trail was well used but even so, he noticed his prints stood out some. "Ain't nobody been down this way for a spell. I'm gonna be easy to follow, damn it."

He thought again that he probably should have brought the mule. He did bring some food but didn't account for all the extra weight his horse was packing, in particular some twenty thousand dollars' worth of gold. How far should he follow this river before leaving it for safer country? Are there hostile Indians in this country? Hawknose had been working the western slopes of the Sierra Nevada for years and had never met a hostile Indian.

The Walker River boiled out of the Sierra Nevada and over the eons carved a deep trench in the eastern slope of those mountains, eventually cascading into Nevada's high mountain desert. The slopes of the canyon were steep, filled with timber and brush with great towers of granite reaching for the stars. Incredibly beautiful country to ride through if you weren't afraid of those who might be following.

Some of those towers had fallen, crashing into great fields of boulders while parts of the mountains eroded leaving overhangs of granite in which foxes, bobcats, bears, and lions made their homes. It was a country wild with energy, dangerous for the unwary, and beautiful to behold if one wasn't running from the law.

Hawknose had to ford the river often, had to make long detours around fallen rocks the size of goodly cabins, and figured that outlaws and maybe the Indians in the area considered lone riders fair game. Wagons coming from or to the Mono country often had several well-armed outriders. The Walker River was full of fish and that, of course, meant the possibility of bears, particularly this time of the year.

"I can't climb out of this canyon, it's just too steep and the country up high ain't the least friendly, I sure ain't turning back, and I'm weighed down with all the gold a man could spend in a life time," he muttered. He could see so many ways that nature could keep him from escaping, could make him fail. The pain from his foot wound was awful and he feared gangrene or other infection. He was starting to panic and knew that would kill him for sure. "I will get out of this alive," he said right out loud, giving his horse a good kick in the ribs.

The night was cold, a wind following the river, coming down from the majestic peaks of the Sierra Nevada bit right through his heavy coat. "I should have just finished that fool off and taken the time to grab all the food. I gotta stop, though, and soon." Emerson's shot had gone right through Mackenzie's foot, coming in from the side, breaking bones on its way through, and splashing out the other. The pain was throbbing as he rode south. He could feel his boot half full of blood and felt the weakness from its loss.

He put off stopping for another hour and finally pulled his horse off the trail and into a grove of aspen trees, fifty yards or so up the hillside. Hobbled as he was, he pulled the saddle and gear from his horse and tied him off in good grass before putting together a small fire near an outcropping of rock. He had to fight to stay conscious when he jerked his boot off. Blood poured from the two open wounds on his foot, and he could see mangled bone.

"Oh, what a mess you've gotten into this time, Mackenzie," he muttered. His saddlebags held only enough coffee for three pots, maybe two scant meals of hard tack and sidemeat, and almost twenty thousand dollars in gold. "That old horse can't take much more of that weight. I gotta hide that gold, get this foot fixed, and get the hell out of this territory." He fought off the rising panic, tried to walk and fell back. He found a broken limb and used it as a cane.

He hobbled down to the river and filled a pot with water. "Damn," he said, looking back toward where he had his camp. "Fire stands out like a beacon. If anyone's chasing me, they gotta be at least twelve hours or more behind." He got the water boiling and cried out in pain, cleaning the wounds. "I won't be wearin' that boot for a long time," he muttered, wrapping the remains of a shirt around the foot. "Oh, Mackenzie, you've done it this time."

He fought off panic, tried to stay busy, and didn't allow himself to think about how this might end. His foot hurt like the blazes, he was suffering from shock, knew he had a fever, and finally knew he had to sleep in order to have any strength for tomorrow's long hard ride through the canyon and into the safety of open spaces.

He built up the fire, wrapped in his blanket, and tried to

sleep, but it wasn't gonna happen. "What about the gold? I got to get it hidden before leaving out. That horse can't carry it. I ain't worried about food, but I'm trapped in this canyon, and I'm the richest sumbitch in the territory." Just a touch of black humor as he fought off the pain and finally fell asleep, tossing fitfully for no more than three hours. It was slowly coming daylight in that deep canyon when he awakened.

The wind had a knife's edge, the clouds weren't a warm white, they were as black as Mackenzie's mood and the outlaw knew he would be riding in a cold storm that day. He had enough water left to make a single pot of coffee, boiled some hard jerky in it, and tried to plan his day.

"Fire, coffee, clean the wound, and go," he said, trying to get to his feet. He searched his saddlebags twice before cussing up a tornado of anger. "I left the damn whiskey with Chago. Stupid!" With the remains of that shirt as a pad tied under his foot, and the broken limb, he could barely hobble about but knew he would be able to ride.

It was a cold morning with wind whipping through the canyon. Clouds could be seen building over high peaks of the Sierra Nevada. Summer thunderstorms were normal, but these clouds were filled with the first hints of winter snow that often built to twenty and thirty feet in those high towers of granite.

"I gotta get that gold hid," he said, draining the last of his one-cup of coffee. He found another rock outcrop, up the hill and behind three tall pine trees. He hobbled up the steep incline, used his hands only and got a good hole dug out underneath it. Getting the gold up the hill took almost all his effort. Canvas sack after canvas sack was carried up the side of that hill. He was covered in sweat from the effort despite the icy wind that was blowing. The rags tied around his foot were dripping with blood and the pain was relentless.

He realized after the third trip that he was also running a high fever. He was sweating and cold, then hot, then cold. The foot was bleeding heavily when he finished burying those sacks of gold and it was more than painful. "I'd give half that gold for a bottle of whiskey right now."

He spent a full ten minutes taking in where he was, exactly. He etched that scene in his mind, where the rocks were, where those three trees were, where his camp was in relation to the river and those trees. "I'll be back," he hollered up the mountainside to the gold as he mounted his horse for what he hoped was a good escape. "But I know there are people following and I gotta get moving." The wind was nearing gale force, blowing leaves, twigs, even limbs, and it had the full measure of winter in its force. He was bent low in the saddle, fending off the wind, and was fighting the effects of infection in those wounds.

Over the eons the Walker River had cut a canyon deep into the flanks of the Sierra, and now, winds of hurricane force are funneled through those rocks doing their part to make the canyon even more difficult to navigate. Hawknose Mackenzie was well aware that death was his companion on this ride.

"How many times have Bull and I been on the trail of outlaws only to have one of us pulled off because of something as dumb as this," he chuckled, following the obvious trail left by Hawknose Mackenzie. "Old Gus Emerson, boy outlaw, shot and dying, and Bull has to stay behind. Isn't the first time I've had to go it alone. Feels like winter is about to ride along with us," he said, as much to himself as to his horse.

Towering slabs of granite filled the sides of the deep canyon, the river was at fall's lowest level, and there was nowhere else Hawknose Mackenzie could have ridden. Following his trail was as simple as staying on the main road. "Bull said this road leads to Mono country and that means we're gonna be climbing into some high mountains before long, old man," he muttered.

He was about three hours into the ride when he saw relatively fresh prints leading off the trail. "Well, now, looky here. Can't be anyone else but Hawknose." He followed slowly and after a short time got off his horse and tied it off, following the track on foot. "Has to be Hawknose," he muttered. "Nobody else on this trail last night or this morning. The trail led up toward a rock outcrop and Calhoun figured he was walking right into a rifle's sights.

"Just in the last three hours I've seen at least three million spots where an ambush could have been set up. Half the Sioux Nation could be hidden back in these rocks. He pulled his rifle and gave the sides of the canyon another quick look-see. "Of course, this ain't Sioux country," he chuckled. "Whoever they are they probably don't much care for me being here, though."

He stayed low, moved well off to his right, and slowly advanced on what became obvious as a campsite. An empty campsite. Calhoun tested the fire and found it still warm and looked around for other signs. Bloody rags meant that Mackenzie had been shot for sure, but other signs told him the outlaw made several trips up the hillside from the camp.

"Those bad boys still had the gold from the stage robbery," Calhoun chuckled, digging out some fresh dirt from under the outcrop. "This is what the prospectors look for," he laughed, holding a heavy canvas sack. "A decent outcrop of quartz that will lead to a gold vein, and looky here, will you? I've struck gold."

A lesser man might have given thought to filling his saddlebags with that heavy metal, but it never entered Calhoun's mind. "I need to make this location known to Morrison."

He pulled several heavy sacks from the hole, almost laughing as he did so. "Now, I've got myself a little problem here. The same one that Hawknose had. What to do with all this gold? That is a bunch of weight that my horse can't carry for long." He did what Mackenzie did, re-buried the gold and made sure he could remember where that rock outcrop was.

"Always wanted to discover a big gold strike and now I have. Shame I can't just stake a claim," he chuckled. "Well, horse, let's get on with it. Mr. Mackenzie can't be too far in front of us and he's hurt. Let's catch up and make him hurt some more."

"About time you boys caught up," Bull Morrison called out as Buck Antonelli rode into camp. Buck brought a full menagerie with him, with Duff Dorman and Beartooth Johnson in restraints, and Warren Fitzgerald leading their ponies. "Who are these people?"

"Had some visitors last night, Bull. You'll enjoy this story. Where's Calhoun?"

"Well, old Emerson and Mackenzie got into it, shot each other up, but Mackenzie was able to ride out. Emerson's over there tryin' to die. Purdy's doing some doctoring on him. Boy's gonna die from infection, though. Slim'll get

Hawknose but I do need to follow, to keep him on his toes, you know," he laughed.

Antonelli told him the story of Beartooth and the boy, how the judge swore in Johnson as a court deputy, and how he was also guaranteed a bounty from the judge. "That old badger is so full of himself it's a wonder he don't fly off somewhere 'cuz of all that hot air."

"You talking about Beartooth or the Judge?"

Buck Antonelli had to laugh and said, "Both, I guess."

"I've about had my fill of these people, Buck. You'll need to build a travois to haul Emerson out. I got an idea," Morrison said. "I want you to take Johnson on the ride back. Now listen, I don't want you to say anything about bounty or anything. When he puffs himself up and confronts the judge is when you tell him who it was caught this little boy bandit." He had a good laugh, Antonelli could almost see that scene, and had to chuckle along with Bull.

"Get that great Sierra Nevada tracker over here, Buck, and don't be nice about it." Bull Morrison had a nasty look on his face. His confrontation at the scene of the murder of Mrs. Chastain was still like bile in his throat. *The greatest tracker in the world he said. He's lucky he can find what he needs to relieve himself.*

Antonelli was laughing all the way across the campsite. "On your feet, Johnson. Marshal Morrison wants to talk to you. You might get out of this with your pants on yet," he snarled, jerking the manacled man to his feet. He pushed him along as they moved to where Bull was sitting.

"So, Judge Chastain gave you some kind of badge and then offered you a bounty on this here feller, eh? By golly, ain't that something? Well, then, Deputy Marshal Antonelli, why don't you take those irons off this upstanding tracker-man and have a chat with him."

Beartooth Johnson was in a rage, anger spilling from every pore in his body. "You take great pleasure in humiliating people, don't you, Marshal. I plan to give the judge an earful of this. You'll have to account for your actions."

"I plan to, Johnson," Morrison growled, those eyes boring into the man. The scar across Bull's face was crimson and his distaste for Johnson was as plain as the day was stormy. "Before you go off half-cocked, I have a proposal for you. I want you and Deputy Marshal Antonelli here to escort this prisoner back to Mormon Station. See to it he gets medical attention so we can hang him and contact the judge."

Beartooth Johnson stood quiet for a minute letting his anger cool and realized what just happened. "So, you accept the fact the judge named me a deputy? About damn time. The judge ain't gonna like what I plan to tell him."

"I don't doubt that for a minute," Morrison said, holding back his chuckle. Bull turned to Antonelli, gave him a quick little grin. "What are we gonna do with this other boy, Buck?"

"His name's Duff Dorman and he's just a young kid drifting around. He hasn't committed a crime or anything but was sneaking up on our camp. He might be a help to me and old Beartooth here on the ride back. Sure wish we had a wagon to haul Emerson in, though. He sure can't sit in a saddle."

"Haul him out on a travois," Beartooth said. "Good enough for injuns it should be good enough for a killer."

"See, Mr. Antonelli? Mr. Tracker-man is gonna be a help to you, for sure. Why, my heavens, that's a wonderful thought. Go build one," he snarled. "Would you have ever thought of something like that, Buck? Maybe that's why you're known as the great tracker-man. Get him out of here, Buck, and tell Fitzgerald to find me."

"You gonna keep Purdy along with you?"

"You bet. I wish I could keep you, too, but you're gonna have more trouble than us, I think. Old tracker-man there is gonna fill your days with fun and excitement, I'm afraid." He wandered off to the fire and filled his cup with a little coffee and a lot of whiskey.

"PUT TOGETHER a good pack for us, Fitz. We'll leave out of here right away. Sure as hell Calhoun is gonna need help. We could use another gun or two, but it'll just be you, me, and Purdy O'Neil on this run. Hawknose is wounded, and that might make him even more dangerous."

"Like a trapped wildcat. We'll split the rest of that venison between Antonelli and us, and the same with the coffee. Won't have to worry about water, though." He walked off to where the mule was to make up a pack.

"We'll carry our stores," Bull hollered after him. "Let them have the mule. And we ain't eating fish with bones."

They were ready to hit the trail about half an hour later when a rider approached the camp. "Now what?" Bull snarled. "What is this cross-roads on the main emigrant trail? Who are you?"

"Name's Martin, Deputy Cliff Martin. I work for Sheriff Matt Rogers."

"Oh, yeah, the guy that doesn't want to get involved," Morrison said.

"That's the man."

"Why are you here?" Morrison asked, and Martin spent the next ten minutes telling how the judge hired a wagon to follow on, got injured, and how he came along alone.

"I might just have room for you on our next move, Martin. Find some coffee and I'll tell you what me and old Fitz here are gonna do." He gave a moment's thought and hollered at Fitz. "I guess we'll need that mule after all, Fitz. Hell, we got us a whole troop about to ride out, now."

CHAPTER 11

"WHERE'S THE SHERIFF?" BUCK ANTONELLI BARGED INTO THE sheriff's office in Mormon Station followed by Duff Dorman. "We got a badly wounded prisoner for you."

"Holding down table three at the saloon, Marshal." The deputy didn't stand up, didn't offer help, simply turned back to his wonderful paperwork spread out on the desk.

"Help me get this man inside and send for the best doc you got around," Buck barked. "I'm Deputy U.S. Marshal Buck Antonelli, and I need help. Get off your lazy butt and help me or so help me God I'll shoot you where you sit." He had his hand resting on the butt of his revolver and took great delight in watching the deputy jump to his feet.

Buck, Dorman, and Beartooth Johnson had been on the trail three days, threading their way through sagebrush, cedar brush, rabbit brush, and just brush with the wounded Emerson riding in a travois. It was dodge this and that, lift it over this and that, for three full days and nights. They had kept him alive, somehow, and Antonelli was ready to kill anything that moved. Dorman gave Antonelli the impression that he was slow witted, and Johnson refused to help in any way.

He spent more time trying to keep that travois moving than he did trying to get Beartooth to do any work and thought how many ways he would be able to get even with Bull Morrison for sending him on this fool's mission. Anger and frustration were boiling over. All that and a man who should have died the first day out, but simply refused to.

"Dorman, go get the sheriff. Deputy, help me get this man laid out on a bed and then you find that doctor and I mean now," he snarled. Antonelli couldn't understand how Emerson could still be alive but he was. Not conscious, not eating, but able to swallow water when it was poured slowly into his mouth. "What's your name?"

"Owens. Hal Owens," the deputy said, almost running from the cell where they laid Emerson out on a straw mattress.

Beartooth found some blankets and brought them into the cell. "Thanks for your help, there, Tracker. You just along for the ride or just waiting for your bounty? Three days pulling this man on a travois and you haven't turned a hand. No fresh meat, no cut wood for the fire. Just me and that youngster, Dorman. Why don't you see if you know how to make a pot of coffee?"

Johnson didn't say a word, just turned and sauntered toward the front of the jail. "That man's a piece, just like Morrison said. He won't like it when the judge gets here," Antonelli muttered.

It took ten minutes for Dorman to return with Sheriff Matt Rogers. "So, you caught the gunman, eh? Good. Where's my deputy?" Rogers didn't bother to shake hands or say hello, either.

"Getting the doc. Emerson's been shot but he's still alive.

He ain't gonna die from the gun shot, but from those cuts on his face. Nice to see you, too," Buck snarled. "Your other deputy, Cliff Martin is riding with Marshal Morrison, chasing the other killer. You run a strange department, Sheriff."

Rogers didn't say anything, just walked over and took a look at Emerson. "Had to shoot him, eh?"

"Nope, his partner did. Where's Judge Chastain, and where's the telegraph office?"

"Telegraph office is in a building behind the saloon. Chastain is at the doc's house. It doubles as our hospital. Nearest real one is in Carson City. He got busted up some in that wagon wreck," Rogers said. "Guess we'll have to move Emerson over there, too."

This wasn't what Buck Antonelli wanted to hear. Now he was stuck with Dorman and Johnson in Mormon Station and the judge laid up. *I'll cut Dorman loose, but I've got to keep an eye on this fool Beartooth Johnson. That damn judge is liable to pay him that bounty if he gets to him first.*

Beartooth was on his way into the jail-cell area with a pot of coffee and heard the sheriff's comment. He turned and put the pot back on the stove, walked out of the office and mounted his horse. He was off to find that judge, collect his reward, and head back to Placerville with a pocketful of money. Antonelli gritted his teeth when he heard a horse gallop off.

THE DAY's ride through the Walker River Canyon was taking its toll on Hawknose. His foot was infected despite a hot water bath that morning, and he was fighting a fever that clouded his thinking. He couldn't climb out of the canyon and it seemed to go on forever. He had wandered up one side-canyon only to come to a solid granite wall at the end and was rapidly running out of energy.

"I gotta quit thinking about getting out of this canyon and think about finding a place to hole up until I can fix that foot," he murmured. "If there is someone following me, I need to hide out soon. This canyon might go on for days and I'm not going to."

There were little canyons that emptied into the big one, but none seemed to offer any safety. He needed an overhang or cave where he could see someone approaching, where he could have an unseen fire, and where water was close by. The canyon narrowed down considerably, and he had to ride into the Walker River itself to get through the narrows. He found a broad meadow spread out more than half a mile before the canyon narrowed down again. The sides of the steep canyon were stepped with shallow shelves. Many of those flattened areas held stands of aspen, pine, and cottonwood.

There were great cascades of rock littering the mountain sides that had tumbled from the steps and cliffs. It would take a strong horse to climb up to one of the plateaus and Hawknose hoped he was riding one.

A large grove of aspen trees was prominent on a flat area above the steep hillside to the east where a spring fed stream poured down to the river and Hawknose smiled for the first time in days. He rode about a mile through a tumble of rocks up the steep climb, cutting back and forth across the sidehill, and into the trees. The grass was thick and there was plenty of downed wood for fire.

He long lined his horse between two aspens and built a fire ring, hobbling around gathering rocks and wood. He filled a pot with water and waited for it to boil. "Coffee can wait," he muttered, tearing more rags from one of his shirts.

"Gotta get that infection cleaned out. One bottle of whiskey would do it, damn it."

He almost passed out twice cleaning the wounds, one on one side of his foot, the other where the bullet came out. The rotten flesh peeled away along with other putrid parts of his foot, including bone. He gagged as he wrapped the foot and laid back on his bedroll, crying in pain. He was asleep or just unconscious in moments.

"THAT BOY'S not making good time, horse," Slim Calhoun said, looking at the prints left in the sand along the river. He had followed at a fast walk through the day, up one long side canyon that dead-ended as a box canyon, and into a couple of others. "He's trying to find a way out of the main canyon, and he won't. I'm gonna find a man dead from infection or one that's gone mad from the pain.

"The mad one would be very dangerous, horse. He'll have to hole up here, pretty soon, I think." He rode on keeping his eyes moving back and forth between the hoof prints and the country on both sides of the canyon. "Wouldn't be hard living in this long wide canyon. Fish, venison, quail. Man could live well here. Wonder if that's what Hawknose is thinking? Wonder if he's now looking for a long-time hole to climb into?"

It was getting late in the day when Calhoun noticed the canyon coming narrow. He had to ride into the river to get through the narrows and thought what a perfect place to set up an ambush. "If Hawknose Mackenzie is in the rocks on the other side of these narrows, he could pick me off as soon as I came out."

Calhoun stepped off his horse and wrapped the lead rope around a rock. "You stay put for a minute, old man," he muttered, splashing along the vertical side of the narrows. He crouched down and slowly emerged into a broad meadow in bright sunlight. He took long minutes to view the area and spotted smoke high up on the eastern side of the wide canyon.

"Found your hidey-hole, did you?" Calhoun had a smile on his face walking his horse out of the narrows and mounting up. "Well, Mr. Mackenzie, you're about to become a prisoner of the United States Marshal Service, that is, if you're still alive, which I hope you are. That's quite a climb up there horse. I think I'll leave you down here and snake my way up to that fool."

Calhoun found a tumble of big rocks at the base of the narrows where he could tie his horse off safely out of sight and started the long climb to the aspen grove. "Looks like this old mountain-side levels off where those trees are. Mackenzie has probably found good grass and maybe even water up there.

"Well, he's about to find Deputy Marshal Calhoun as well." He chuckled about that for some time, working through rocks and brush on the climb. "Got to stay behind as many of these rocks as I can. He's got the advantage, looking down at me."

He didn't go straight up the mountain but rather zig-zagged and tried to stay behind the large rocks that had fallen over the years. He could see wisps of smoke from time to time but never any movement. "That boy's got himself nested in pretty good, I think," he muttered. The climb was getting more difficult, there were areas of loose shale that threatened to give way under his weight, and rocks that turned when he stepped on them.

Calhoun was about fifty yards from the aspen grove, well off to the north along a rock wall when his feet went out from under him on a steep climb. He tumbled about ten yards, knocking rocks about, before catching his balance. The noise brought Hawknose out of his sleep instantly.

Mackenzie came out of his bedroll, grabbed his rifle, and crawled to a rock overhang where he could look out over the entire meadow. He spotted the dust that rose from where Calhoun slipped. "Company, girls. Company coming," he growled, scanning the rocks below. He saw Calhoun get to his feet and scramble back up the slide area, brought his rifle up and fired one quick shot just as Calhoun slipped again.

The bullet whistled past Slim's head as he crashed to the rocks. "Damn," he sputtered, again finding his feet, and rushed behind some rocks, pulling his rifle up. He worked his way through the tumbled rocks and brush, keeping as low as he could. "Well, at least I know I'll be bringing a live prisoner back," he said.

He took a couple of minutes to see what damage had been done. Many bruises, cuts, and scratches, but no broken bones or serious cuts. "Good rip in my britches and wounded the hell out of my pride, but I'll live. Which is more than I can say for that yahoo up there." He continued his climb staying low and behind anything he could get behind.

Evening shadows come fast in high mountain country and along with the darkness comes the cold. Wind, iced down by altitude, whistled through the peaks, trees, and boulders as Slim Calhoun edged up the incline to a level spot behind a high outcrop. "Won't have a fire tonight," he muttered, crouching low and moving again. He could see the flames of Hawknose's fire.

Hawknose built up the fire but wasn't fool enough to stay by its warmth. He moved well away from the light and crouched behind some rocks, straining to get a look at who might be following. "Can't be Emerson," he snickered. "I gut-shot that puppy. He killed that woman then shot some fool in Carson City and I'm runnin' for my life. Damn that boy." He neglected to remember that he killed the coach messenger, or that he robbed the stage, or that he helped abduct the judge's wife. He completely forgot the old prospector whose cabin he used.

Night came quickly and with it more icy wind now filled with large, wet snowflakes. Calhoun moved slowly back down the side of the mountain and pulled his bedroll off his horse. He figured since Hawknose took a shot at him when he was on the north side, he'd work his way up toward that fire from the south side.

"This ain't gonna be easy with all this snow and wind, but it might keep me from being heard. If I don't fall on my butt again." He wrapped the blanket from the bedroll around and moved slowly across the face of the mountainside until he could no longer see the outlaw's fire then turned uphill. The rocks were covered now in a thin coating of snow and ice and Calhoun had to take his time, making one slow step after another.

He remembered making a climb like this in the mountains near Monterey, chasing some Mexican bandits. There were three of them and they had hidden themselves in a stand of live oak trees on the side of a mountain that stretched right down to pounding surf. One slip and he'd find himself in the Pacific Ocean.

It was a hanging root from a cypress tree that saved him. He caught it to boost himself up just as his feet went out from under him and he became wedged in next to the tree. "Old Bull was laughing so hard he almost couldn't get me pulled free of that damned tree," he chuckled.

It took almost two hours for Calhoun to sneak close to Mackenzie's camp. He had a good sight line but the wind and blowing snow hampered his vision. "He ain't all cuddled up to that fire and I can see his bedroll is empty. I'll just wait him out," Calhoun said, wrapping up in his wool blanket.

"You're one quiet man, Marshal Morrison," Cliff Martin said as the three worked their way up the long Walker River. "You worried about your deputy?"

"Nope. I'm just wondering why you're here and not the sheriff. Those two men killed a man in your jurisdiction and you're riding to join the fight, two day's late and without the sheriff or a posse. We're chasing a man who helped rob a stage, steal twenty thousand dollars, kill a man, and kidnap a judge's wife. That man then shot another man in your jurisdiction.

"Where I come from that would give a man with a badge a pretty good kick in the butt to catch that outlaw. Where's your sheriff?"

"Can't answer for the man, Marshal but I plan to replace him at the next election." The snicker told Morrison that Martin was also a bit devious. "The man with the torn-up face shot a man in Carson City and ran into our jurisdiction and that fool Rogers did nothing then, either. This Hawknose Mackenzie we're following has a lot of paper out."

"He shot my coach guard, Deputy," Purdy O'Neil said. "Don't know to this minute if old Sammy's gonna live. You people ain't much for keepin' the law."

Morrison nodded at what O'Neil said and commented on Martin's paper speech. "We'll wrap him in that paper when we bring him in," Morrison chuckled. "Those prints on the left are Calhoun's and the others belong to Mackenzie. There ain't any others that would be fresh, so keep an eye on them."

"Looks like Slim is riding considerably faster that Mackenzie," Fitzgerald said. "He's got that horse in a solid trot."

"Well, then, why don't we do the same thing," Morrison said.

The ride was fast since they had nothing else to do but make up a lot of time and distance. Two hours or so later Fitzgerald pointed out where Calhoun and Mackenzie left the trail. "They went up the side of this hill and came back down. Let's go see what they did up there."

Morrison stepped off his horse at the campsite and walked around seeing where Mackenzie had his bedroll and where Calhoun left a canvas sack. "See this? It's from the stagecoach money box, and see the arrow?" He pointed up the hill toward a stand of pine trees. "We're gonna have us a little problem, boys. There's twenty thousand dollars in gold under those trees if I'm not mistaken."

"Yeah, that's a lot of weight but we're gonna have five horses and a mule to carry it back," Fitzgerald laughed. "How far ahead of us are they, Bull?"

"We're runnin' out of daylight and they're a long ride in front. We'll camp here tonight and find 'em tomorrow."

"You know we're in Indian country, Marshal," Martin said. "More than one express wagon and more than one rider has been attacked in this canyon. More than likely we're in California right now and the Washoe Indians claim this country."

"Then why don't you do us a favor and stand first watch, Deputy Martin."

CHAPTER 12

THE LONG AND DEEP CANYON ACTED LIKE A FUNNEL, DRIVING the windblown snow at hurricane force as Slim Calhoun moved closer to Mackenzie's campsite. Fall turned to winter that fast, the temperature dropped well below the freezing mark, and the snow began to stick to everything it touched. This was high country where snow levels were measured in tens of feet in mid-winter and winds topping the seventy mile an hour mark were not unusual.

"Is catching this fool really worth all this?" His murmuring couldn't be heard above the fury of Mother Nature. "You never think about chases like this when you're accepted into the service. Oh, hell no. The glamor of strutting down the street with that beautiful badge pinned prominently on your chest is what you think about." He grumbled on, knowing he was getting closer, knowing that the man at the end of this chase was a killer, a sadistic killer. The scowl eased into a boyish grin when he muttered, "You're mine, Hawknose Mackenzie."

Icy wind in his face and icy footfalls meant danger with every step he took as he made the slow climb to the outlaws' camp. Fallen branches were hidden in the snow, rocks tipped when they were stepped on, and Calhoun had no idea whether the killer already had him in his rifle's sights. A frozen biscuit washed down with cold water was what followed a long night without a fire, and Slim Calhoun wanted this capture or killing over with soon.

"Just another few feet and I should be able to see Mr. Mackenzie well enough to shoot the fool," Calhoun muttered. Sliding on his belly through snow covered rocks, he raised up a bit and could see the fire pit was out, not even any smoke coming from embers, and Mackenzie's horse was standing between two aspen trees, kicking snow off the grass. Was the killer still alive? Calhoun knew the man was wounded, but how badly? He had no idea.

Tracking down this killer had more meaning to it than most. This killer was responsible for the death of Judge Chastain's wife. Kidnapping, abusing, and murdering a woman was incentive enough for any lawman, but when the woman was the wife of a federal judge, that incentive level increased dramatically for a deputy U.S. Marshal. Calhoun brushed off the cold, did not concern himself with typhoon winds, nor did he worry about how this would end. He knew how it would end.

"That judge is a foul-mouthed tyrant with questionable judicial ethics, but he is a federal judge and his wife was killed by the man I'm about to have in my sights. No one but me would know if I should just shoot him on sight," he muttered. "And there it is. I would know. Bull would take one look into my eyes and he would know. You're one lucky man, Hawknose Mackenzie. You're gonna live through this."

The deputy marshal tucked himself behind a large aspen tree and stood up using the trunk for protection. He was stiff as the frozen tree limbs he had been crawling through. His legs ached from the cold, his shoulders wouldn't move, and his fingers were numb. "I really hope you're already dead, Mr. Mackenzie."

He couldn't see the man anywhere until the slightest movement up the hill and to his right caught his attention. He watched as Mackenzie slowly emerged from his snow-covered blankets. Calhoun could clearly see the bloody rags tied around one foot.

Something must have caught Mackenzie's eye, too. He was fast despite his wounds and rolled out of the blankets with his revolver in hand. The outlaw fired a quick shot in Calhoun's direction. Before Slim could pull his heavy Colt, Hawknose dashed behind some rocks. Calhoun ducked down and slipped away from the tree, moving behind another large rock formation.

Visibility for both was hindered by blowing snow, both men were cold to the bone, but only one was wounded and suffering from a bad infection and high fever. Calhoun had the upper hand and knew it. "I've played the game so many times," he muttered. "That man is desperate and I'm not. He's wounded and I'm not. Make your move, Mackenzie, cuz I'm waiting for you, and I can wait longer than you can." He muttered with anger but had just a hint of a smile on his weathered face

Hawknose had the blanket wrapped around him but his injured foot was naked in the snow, double its normal size, and putrid from infection. On top of that, Mackenzie knew it would become frostbitten in no time. He moved slowly around the backside of the rocks hoping to get a better view of where Calhoun might be and stepped on a pine cone buried in the snow with his wounded foot.

Screaming in pain, he fell to the ground, the sun dried and brittle cone with its sharply pointed seeds stuck in his foot. Both wounds opened with the movements and blood flowed onto the snow. He never heard Calhoun race up behind him and smash his rifle across the back of his head.

"The waiting game is always the winning game when we have to play with stupid outlaws," he chuckled. "That didn't come out right. All outlaws are stupid."

Slim dragged Mackenzie's body over to the fire pit and started working to get the fire built back up. "Got yourself a nasty wound there, Hawknose," he muttered, stirring the ashes back to life. He threw some downed wood on, found Mackenzie's old tin pot and ground some beans for fresh coffee. "Probably gonna lose that foot, old man." Mackenzie was still out from the blow to the head, but Calhoun just kept up a regular discussion, one sided, but regular.

Calhoun trussed the gentleman up with his own rope, slipped and slid his way down to get his horse, and nursed it back up that steep hill to camp. Hawknose was conscious when he arrived. "Have a nice nap, did you? We got us a bit of trouble, now, Hawknose Mackenzie, and if you want to live through this, you will have to do exactly as I say. Got it?"

"Who the hell are you?" Mackenzie growled, but the pain from his foot was obvious in his dull, almost lifeless eyes.

"Oh, well, I guess introductions are in order, eh? I'm Deputy U.S. Marshal Slim Calhoun, sir. It's my pleasure to have you as my prisoner. Oh, by the way, you are under arrest for a whole mess of crimes, which I will be more than happy to explain for you. There are multiple murders, kidnapping, and grand theft, among others. If you live through the next couple of days, the judge will explain it all before you hang. You see, killing the wife of a federal judge makes other judges really upset."

The coffee was boiling, and Calhoun poured two cups,

handing one to Mackenzie. "You ain't much of a talker, eh? Well, enjoy that coffee and I'll get some side meat cookin' shortly. Then we're gonna have to do something about that foot. Best if we just cut it off, but I ain't much good at that. Last time I tried, the guy died on me."

Hawknose winced at the comment but didn't say anything. Calhoun had the man's hands tied off in front so he could have his coffee and be able to eat after a while. Hawknose was working his hands back and forth, trying to get the knots loosened. Calhoun chuckled watching him and allowing him to get just to the point where they might come loose and he doubled up his fist and hit him smack in the middle of his nose, busting half a dozen little blood vessels open.

"Now, aren't you a sight," Slim laughed. "Bleeding all over everything from your head to your feet." He retied the ropes as tight as he dared. "One more dumb move and I tie them behind your back, and you get nothing to eat or drink. Just another stupid outlaw. Ain't no such thing as a smart outlaw, I guess. If you were smart, you wouldn't have to be an outlaw." He kept up the chatter all through breakfast and saw that it was having its desired effect on Mackenzie.

"Pretty soon, old man, you'll come to really hate me, and maybe even try to get away. It's a lot easier to transport a dead criminal than one that's wounded. I'd just flop you over the saddle and tie you down. This way, I gotta keep you awake enough to not fall off your horse, got to stop and get you some water, got to make food for you and clean your wounds.

"You're a serious pain in the butt, alive. So, go ahead, get angry, try something dumb, and I'll shoot you and get it over with." Calhoun had to chuckle when Hawknose started cussing, kicking at the snow, and then howling in pain. "Good boy," he said.

BULL MORRISON HAD his group together around the fire, ready to make the day's ride up the canyon. Deputy Marshal Warren Fitzgerald, Purdy O'Neil, and Sheriff's Deputy Cliff Martin were fighting off the bitter cold wind blowing down the canyon. "It's gonna be a nasty ride today, boys. This wind has a kick to it. Snow'll be deep within the hour, I think." He walked over to where Fitzgerald was retying some leather on his saddle. "You got the feeling we're being watched?"

"Ever since we woke up, Bull. This is Indian country. I 'bout wore out my eyes lookin' up and down these hills. Wind's blowing stuff everywhere, but I swear I've seen more than twigs and leaves moving."

"We're in Washoe and Paiute country," Bull said. "I don't want to ride off and leave that gold, but I know we have to. Calhoun is one on one with Hawknose Mackenzie, and we need to be with him."

"One on one? Don't seem right giving Slim that much of an advantage, but you're right, if we're being watched by Indians, they probably seen us stash that gold. Yeah, they'd pick it up right away."

"We got four horses and a mule so we could carry it out, but if we had to run for it, those horses would tire out real quick. Damn," Morrison said. He stomped around the fire pit trying to stay warm. "Fighting the snow and wind will be hard enough on them." He called Cliff Martin over and told him about their feelings of being watched.

"I haven't seen any but I'm sure I've seen movement in the trees and rocks above us," Martin said. He started to point in the direction of a stand of trees and Morrison cut him off.

"No! Let's not let them know that we know they're around. Let's stay close to the fire and brew up another pot of coffee and keep our eyes wide open. We need to protect the gold, save Calhoun from capturing that killer all by himself, and keep our scalps."

"Odds are good," Fitz said without the slightest chuckle. "Four of us against a hostile tribe of Indians? I'm gonna get my rifle from my saddle and join you at the fire."

"Good idea. When he gets back, I'll saunter over and get mine," Bull said, "and, Cliff, you better do the same. Purdy, you, too. Make it casual. Wherever those boys are, we don't need to get 'em too riled yet."

The second pot of coffee was boiling hard, the men standing as close as they dared, absorbing the warmth when Fitzgerald told Bull to look up high and to his left. "At least three moving down the hill, using every tree and bush up there to hide behind."

"There's bound to be more. Let's find some cover, gentlemen," Morrison grumbled. They moved behind some large rocks scattered about, a downed tree or two was used, and they checked their weapons one more time. They concentrated their sights on the mountainside with its scattered trees, brush, and boulders. The warriors were several hundred yards up the hill but moving down quickly.

"Looks like half a dozen or more, Fitz. You and Purdy cover the left side, I've got the right, and Martin, you shoot anything we don't kill." Morrison's eyes were blazing, that mean scar across his face was bright red, and anyone looking at the man would understand the meaning of the word anger. That look would terrorize the meanest man. "Martin, from time to time look behind us and make sure we ain't gonna be jumped from behind. I've been on this trail for more than a week now and haven't got in one single fight. These bastards are gonna die hard, Fitz."

Bull was still chuckling when Fitzgerald took the first shot at an Indian more than a hundred yards up the canyon wall. "Missed him," Bull shouted. "Shootin' uphill, Fitz. Make the correction." He watched Fitzgerald take a long slow aim at something and squeeze off a round.

"Didn't miss that time," the deputy said. Return fire came quickly and from at least eight weapons. "Got their attention," Fitz laughed.

"Pick your targets, don't just be shooting," Bull growled. He watched as the Indians moved slowly down the steep side of the canyon. "They're being almost military, Fitz. One group moving, then another. They seem to think they might win this little skirmish." Morrison watched one group move tree to tree, picked his target and put a bullet deep in the man's chest.

"Reminds me of our fight with the Mojave's a couple of years ago," Morrison hollered.

"That was in the desert, it was a hunnert degrees, and we didn't have any water, Bull," Fitzgerald yelled back.

"Yeah, but we was fighting Indians and we was winning," he laughed.

"There's three moving to our far right, Marshal. I'll move on them. They want to come from off to the side." Cliff Martin moved from behind his rock and took up a position about ten yards or so to their right. The hostiles saw him move and fired several shots at him without scoring, but Purdy O'Neil was backing Martin's play and shot one right through his head.

"Got me one, anyways. Come on down, boys, my rifle's ready for you."

Morrison liked the way the man saw the danger and made a move on it. He wondered how it was that Matt Rogers was sheriff and not Martin. "That man might even make it as a deputy marshal someday," he muttered.

"You talking about Martin or Purdy?" Fitz was chuckling watching Purdy shake his rifle at warriors on the hill.

The foremost group of Indians made a dash for the campsite and Fitz and Morrison opened fire on them, taking two to the ground. "Odds are getting better, Fitz."

Fitzgerald saw a third man tuck in behind a large pine tree and waited for him to make a move. Out of the corner of his eye he saw one of the wounded warriors crawl toward a rock, his rifle still in his hand. One quick shot ended that threat. The man behind the tree sunk to his knees and took a look around the base of the trunk and Fitz put a bullet through the middle of his head.

"Damn, Fitz, there's four of us here. Let us get a shot, will you?" Morrison yelled.

Martin howled out, "Three coming right at me," and fired his rifle once, grabbed his sidearm and fanned off three quick shots. Two other shots rang out and Martin fell to the ground. Morrison spun and fired his pistol twice, killing one man running toward Martin's body. Purdy brought his rifle up. Morrison watched Martin crawl behind a rock and saw blood on the man's jacket, high on his chest. Purdy fired one shot as an Indian made a dive for Martin, all but blowing the man's head right off his shoulders.

"I gotcha covered, Martin. Can you get back over here?" Morrison had his revolver cocked and ready and his rifle sat right next to him. He had his eyes glued to the Indians on the ground and didn't see any movement. "We've still got some bad hombres up in those trees."

Cliff Martin crawled quickly over behind the large rock

formation, almost gasping for breath, holding one hand to his chest. "Hurts, Marshal. Hurts really bad." Morrison pulled his jacket open to see where the bullet hit and saw blood high up on the shoulder.

"If it didn't hit a vein or something, you'll be fine," he said. He ripped part of Martin's shirt and stuffed it into the wound. "Hold that in place until the bleeding stops. Good work on those boys," he said. Martin couldn't tell if there was a smile with the words.

"What's the scene, Fitz?" Bull was sure that all the Indians were accounted for, but knew Fitz had a better handle on it. "I count seven down."

"Yeah, me too, Bull. I'm sure there were at least eight coming down that hillside, though. Better stay covered and I'll poke around a bit. Purdy, keep me covered."

"Okay, but don't get yourself all killed. We need you, Pard. Watch those trees up to your left. We didn't see any action from there, and somebody might just be waiting for their shot."

Fitzgerald had his rifle to his shoulder as he got to his feet and moved slowly around the big rock. Morrison had his rifle up and trained in the general direction of the trees to the left, as did O'Neil. "Sure as all get-out, Fitz, there he is," Morrison growled, fired his rifle and chambered a second round. "Got him good, I did."

Fitzgerald slowly moved through the rocks and brush making sure all the Indians were dead. Nothing worse than walking up to a dead Indian and getting shot.

"I don't see nothing moving," Purdy said, lowering his rifle, not his eyes.

CHAPTER 13

"TIME TO MOVE, MACKENZIE. REMEMBER, I WANT YOU TO BE stupid. Try something so I can shoot you dead. It makes my job so much easier." The storm gathered its forces and was blasting the canyon with everything it had; wind, cold, snow, and an icy mountain slope to negotiate. Calhoun had the killer's hands tied behind his back and his feet tied together under the horse's belly.

"You got me trussed up like a hog goin' to market, Marshal. I couldn't do anything no matter how much I want to. That bastard Emerson shot me in the foot."

"Well, you might want to know you shot him too. You'll probably lose that foot, Hawknose, but Emerson will probably be dead when we get back."

"That's the only good news I've heard," Mackenzie said.

"When we get to the river and through that narrow passage, I might retie your hands in front, but not right now." He had Mackenzie's wounded foot wrapped in a blanket but was sure it would have to be amputated as soon as they returned to civilization. "I don't want to hear no crybaby crap either. You brought all this on to your own stupid self." All he heard back was some foul cussing.

"You got yourself a bad attitude, Hawknose. Hell, man, I just saved your stinkin' life." He chuckled as Mackenzie lit off a trail of words that would have made the meanest mule-skinner proud.

The ride down the mile or so to the river at the bottom of the canyon was long and slow, both horses stumbling over icy rocks often, sliding in the snow-covered grassy areas, and generally being nervous and flighty. They rode in the river through the narrows and came up onto the main road on the north side.

The wind howling through the narrows had the horses ready to bolt and Calhoun took an extra wrap around the horn on his saddle on the lead line to Mackenzie's horse. "You nudge that horse one more time and I'm gonna shoot you dead, Hawknose. That horse gets to buckin', you better remember you're tied to him."

"How could I forget. You got these ropes so tight my blood ain't flowing. We got to stop and get a fire goin'. I'm freezin' to death."

"Good. The sooner you die the easier my trip's gonna be," Calhoun snickered.

The ride on the main road was much easier and Calhoun was able to relax just a little bit. "We'll probably camp where you've got that gold all hid-out. Maybe I'll dig it out and let you see it again. Would you like that, Hawknose? Sure you would," he snickered. He was about to say something else when he felt his horse tighten up, raise his head, and point those antenna-like ears toward the mountainside to the west.

"Indians," he said, driving his heals into the horses side and turning them toward a stand of pine trees growing in a rock-strewn meadow just yards away. He bailed off grabbing his knife at the same time, cutting Mackenzie's feet loose and jerking the outlaw from his horse.

"Now see what you've got me into? Damn me but I hate outlaws." He had the man face down in the dirt and snow and saw half a dozen Indians moving down the side of the hill toward the stand of pines. "You die before the Indians if you make one wrong move, mister."

He had his and Hawknose's weapons, which gave him two rifles and two hand guns, plenty of ammunition, but only him to pull the triggers. "Scrunch up against that tree and if you know how to pray now would be a good time to do it."

THE RIDE to the doctor's house would have taken Beartooth about five minutes at the most except for the fact he didn't know where Doc Trask lived. He rode hard for a couple of minutes, enough time to get away from the sheriff's office. He yelled at a man picking apples asking where the doctor lived.

"Red house on the left, mister, but he ain't there, today. This is Wednesday, mister. You'll find him down at the hot springs."

Beartooth didn't say anything, just spurred the horse on, and rode hard into the yard at the red house. He ran up onto the porch and pounded on the heavy wooden door. When no one answered, Beartooth tried the door, found it open and walked into the large old farm house finding three beds laid out to the right of a massive rock fireplace, and what might pass for an examination table and two beds to the left.

"Judge Chastain," he yelled, rushing to the man sitting

up in his bed, reading. "I found him and he's in jail. Gus Emerson is badly wounded, but I have him in jail."

"Well, I'm glad to hear that, Beartooth. You did your job. What about the other man? There were two of them, I recall. Did you kill Hawknose Mackenzie?"

"No, the marshals are chasing him now. I did what you wanted, Judge and I'm here to claim my reward, my bounty, as you promised."

Judge Chastain closed the book he was reading and put it on the table alongside the bed, took a long time finding a cigar on the table, and even a longer time getting it lit. "Well, let's see, now, Beartooth, I do believe I named you one of my court deputies, isn't that correct?"

"Yes, sir, you surely did and I'm wearing that badge with pride right now. I served you well, even told Emerson that he was under arrest on your orders."

"That's fine, Beartooth, but that brings up a little problem as far as you getting a reward for capturing the killer. The bounty was for a citizen, not an employee of the court. You demanded to be a court deputy and as such, you were simply doing your duty as a deputy of the court.

"No, Beartooth, a member of the court can't collect a reward for doing his duty. I can give you a letter of gratitude for a job well done, but certainly can't pay you a reward." Judge Chastain had a slight smile on his otherwise benign face and settled back into his pillows.

Beartooth stood silent for a moment, the words slowly etching their way into his very soul, and when they were settled, he exploded. "You're cheatin' me! You planned this, didn't you? You never had no idea of payin' me. You miserly cheat!" He grabbed the judge by his housecoat lapels and jerked him out of the bed, slammed the already injured man against the rocks of the fireplace and raced toward the door of Doc Trask's farmhouse.

Judge Chastain had suffered many bruises in the wagon wreck and the crash into the fireplace rocks added to his pain. He was unconscious when Beartooth let him fall to the floor.

DUFF DORMAN SAW Beartooth race from the office and ride off, knew something was wrong and found his horse to trail the old tracker. "He's running for the judge and that bounty money," the young man snorted, sinking his spurs into his horse. "You ain't gonna cut me out, Beartooth."

He rode up to Doc Trask's house in time to find Beartooth coming out the front door. "Hold up there, Beartooth. Did you get the bounty? I want my share, old man."

"There ain't no bounty," Johnson snarled. He ran to his horse, but Dorman cut him off.

"You're lying. You got the bounty and you're trying to keep it all. We had a deal, Beartooth. I want my share, and I mean right now." Dorman took hold of Johnson's heavy coat and tried to wrestle the big man down, but the old tracker was far bigger and stronger and shook the youngster off.

"Get away from me," he howled and slapped Dorman away like he would a pesky fly. Dorman jumped up from the snow and mud, angry, hurt, and ready to kill, pulled his skinning knife and lunged at Beartooth.

Beartooth Johnson told stories about fighting off bears with his bare hands, about wrestling bouts he had with the mighty California Griz, and almost laughed as Dorman circled him, waving that razor-sharp blade in his face. "Come on, boy," he whispered, using his finger to beckon Dorman on. "Come to Beartooth, little boy, and die. I was cheated by that judge and I ain't gonna take no crap from the likes of a boy."

"You're lying, Johnson and I'm gonna kill you and take my share. I might take it all," he said and lunged again, slicing a piece of skin from Johnson's cheek. "You're bleeding, old man. My next jab and you die."

Johnson jumped back, pulled the heavy Navy revolver and fired twice, hitting Dorman in the chest with the first shot, and putting the second one into the Doc's house, breaking some china on a table. He watched the young man stumble back from the shock of the bullet and slowly let the knife fall from his hands. Dorman had both his hands grasping at his chest and fell to the ground, bleeding out.

Johnson walked to his horse, mounted up, and rode out at a fast trot, heading for Placerville. He wanted to kill the judge but knew he had to get out of Mormon Station as fast as he could. "You're responsible for this, Judge," he howled, shaking his fist back at the old farm house.

The gunshots brought several people out from nearby homes and two men spotted Dorman's body and ran to it. "Better get the sheriff," one said. "This man's dead."

CHAPTER 14

"I GOT A LIVE ONE, BULL. DAMN," FITZGERALD YELLED OUT. Morrison rushed up the hill to find Fitz and an Indian wrapped in each other's arms, Fitz with his handgun and the Indian with a knife. Blood flowed from a large cut across Fitzgerald's face and a stab in his leg. The Indian was bleeding from a bullet to his middle section.

Morrison smashed his rifle butt into the side of the Indian's head, knocking the man five feet away from Fitz. Bull then aimed and fired the weapon, killing the man. "How bad you hurt, Fitz?"

"You good at sewing?" He tried to chuckle, but it wouldn't come out right with his cheek skin flopping about. There was more than a leg wound involved. "Got me good, Bull. I walked right up on him like I was a damn city boy and he whipped that knife out. I know sorry don't work, but I am." The wound to Fitz's face was more than serious and Bull was doing his best to keep the skin together and stop the bleeding.

"Happens to all of us," Morrison said but his mind was on something else. Now they had two wounded men on top of needing to get to Calhoun as fast as possible and the need to bring all that gold back. He also knew if there was one bunch of Indians out wandering the canyon there surely would be others. This was prime hunting and fishing country.

"Let's get you doctored up and get on the road. Calhoun is not gonna get all the credit for taking Hawknose Macken-zie," he chuckled, getting Fitzgerald to his feet.

"The way these boys are dressed and the weapons they're carrying makes me believe they are from the Washoe tribe, Marshal." Deputy Cliff Martin was knelt down next to a dead one. "They have been pretty angry about losing tradi-tional country. They seem to think they own the Sierra Nevada. All of it," he snickered. "From south of Lake Tahoe north to Susanville. They've been raising dust around Honey Lake for more than a year now."

The pain in his shoulder was forcing him to speak slowly and he had trouble getting back to his feet. The bleeding had been heavy, and Martin felt the weakness.

"Probably did own all of it before we showed up," Morrison said. He gave the deputy a hand, helping him up. "Probably more of them moving about, too. Pack things up, Martin, you and Purdy, while I fix old Fitzgerald up. Don't be paying no mind to his screaming cuz I ain't much good at sewing skin back together." Fitzgerald moaned, rolled his eyes and wanted desperately to pass out.

"You did bring a bottle, didn't you, Bull?" He tried to smile and that didn't work either with flapping cheek skin getting in the way. Bull handed him a flask.

CALHOUN WAS SPREAD out on his belly behind a tall and stately pine tree, watching through some downed limbs as the Indians slowly worked their way toward him. They were a full two hundred yards up the mountainside. "Too far, boys," he muttered. When the man furthest away came within about a hundred and fifty yards, Calhoun put a bullet through the middle of his head, whipped the rifle onto the next one down the hill and dropped him. Within a mere second or two, the others all but vanished.

"Now I've done it," Calhoun whispered. "They've scattered and I'm alone. Could come at me from just about anywhere." He looked around the area close by, saw a rock outcrop that had a good overhang and judged the distance. "With that boy's leg messed up so bad I don't know if he could make it. I do believe I can, though."

He saw a warrior crouched and moving quickly toward a stand of trees off to his right, pulled that rifle up and fired. He heard the howl of pain but couldn't tell if the man was down and out. "Hawknose, we're moving to that outcrop. Follow me the best you can, and I'll try to keep you alive," Calhoun said, jumped to his feet, all the weapons in hand, and raced to the rock, diving and rolling under the overhang. He scrambled to get into a firing position and watched Mackenzie, in a panic, crawl on his belly through the brush and rocks, almost like he was swimming.

Two shots rang out, one kicking dirt and gravel in Mackenzie's face, the other ripping through the man's outstretched right arm. Calhoun spotted some white smoke just twenty yards or so from Mackenzie and fired two quick shots from his pistol. With Mackenzie squalling loudly, Calhoun couldn't tell whether he hit anything with his rounds.

"Come on, man, you're almost here," Slim yelled. Mackenzie screamed and pointed behind Calhoun as a buckskin clad warrior jumped on Calhoun's back, swinging a stone headed ax. The ax missed, but the momentum of the attack took the two men out of the little cave where they rolled through rocks and brush.

Calhoun didn't lose his grip on his revolver and smashed the heavy weapon into the warrior's head and face, over and over, until the man was unconscious. He pushed him off and scampered back to the overhang, bullets kicking up dust and rocks all about him.

He rolled into the cave and came face to face with the wrong end of a rifle pointed between his eyes. There was no hesitation as Calhoun brought his pistol up slamming Hawknose Mackenzie back against the rocks. "That sure ain't how they taught me to keep a prisoner safe," he muttered. "Damn, how many savages are still out there?" he said pulling another pistol into service. He took the one he had been using and without taking his eyes off the surrounding territory, reloaded.

Mackenzie moaned and Calhoun spun on him. "Thought I kilt you, Hawknose. Damn you are getting to be a pest. All right, then, if you want to live don't never pull a gun on me again. I ain't got a lot of time, here, Mackenzie, so hold still." He saw that he had hit the man across his head, ripping skin and hair, and probably cracking that hard skull. He ripped more of Mackenzie's shirt, wadded it up and handed the mess to the outlaw.

"Hold those in place and you might not bleed out. Don't make no matter to me which way it goes. I got enough trouble with some angry red devils out there looking for scalps."

The quiet is what gets to a man when those out to kill him slowly advance on his position. Where are they? Which direction will they come from? How many are left? Minutes went by and he couldn't see movement anywhere, couldn't hear anything but the murmuring of the river off in the distance. Even the wind had ceased its fury.

"Sounds like the Merced River," he said. He and Bull Morrison fought off a Mexican bandit gang along the lower Merced near where it joins the San Joaquin. "That was a fight. Bull got so angry when those banditos tried to rush us, he just stood up and started firing with a pistol in each hand. He walked straight at those boys, shootin' and cussin'. It worked and he didn't even know that he'd been shot twice." Calhoun was chuckling at the memory.

It was then he noticed that the wind had quit, too. Snow, great huge flakes of snow, were falling straight down, and that muffled what sound might be being made by those out to kill him. The two rifles and two pistols were fully loaded, and his knife was close to hand when he heard a whimper coming from some brush just yards to his left. He couldn't see anything move, couldn't discern a body, and wondered if he was being led into a trap.

"Want me to come help you?" He snickered. "Sure I will, with my knife." He hunkered down as low into the dirt and rocks under that overhang as he could get and watched the hillside until his eyes hurt. The whimpering continued for some time and then it ended, too. Just the sounds of the river, the beautiful scene of falling snow, and the effects of bitter cold remained on this late afternoon.

"What a damn spot to be in. Alone, surrounded by dead, wounded, and probably some alive Indians who want my scalp really bad. I could use a couple of Bull Morrisons right now." He thought about that for a minute and had to laugh. "I sure woud'nt tell him that, though."

After an hour, Calhoun knew he had to make a move. The little cave was a perfect spot in which to stay the long night ahead, but only if there weren't any Indians about, looking to count coup. Calhoun slowly crawled out from under the big rock, his pistol cocked and ready, and stood up, stretching his legs and body, looking for the slightest movement.

Something rustled in the brush, the same brush where the whimpering noises had been, and Calhoun darted, first left, then right, and crashed through the brush ready to kill whatever was moving. He found a seriously wounded man, writhing in pain, holding his hands tight to his middle section. Calhoun could see matted blood and fresh blood on the man's hands and buckskins.

The warrior looked up at the deputy marshal with pure hatred in his eyes and tried to reach for his battle ax. Calhoun kicked it aside and slowly knelt down next to the young man. "I doubt you're even sixteen years old," he murmured, moving the boy's hands aside to look at the wound,

"You ain't gonna see another year, I'm afraid." The bullet went into the boy's midsection, probably through all the things that are in there, and must have hit the spine, too. The warrior was unable to move his legs when Calhoun dragged him to the little cave. "I'll build us a fire, boy, but you'll probably be gone by morning. I ain't gonna try to fix anything cuz I simply don't know how, so just accept it."

He knew the boy didn't understand anything he said, but he had to keep talking. It was hard enough to kill a man, but killing a young boy was pretty tough, no matter how tough Calhoun thought he might be. "Don't much care for killin', son. It's part of my job, killin' people that do stupid things, but I still don't much care for it."

He brought his bedroll and saddlebags to the cave, had the horses hobbled in good grass if they kicked the snow out of the way, and got a nice fire burning. "If your friends come calling, I'm gonna kill you first, boy." He had the young warrior wrapped in one of Hawknose's blankets, boiled up a pot of coffee and had some smoked meat warming in a cup of the good stuff. "Gonna be a long night, I'm afraid and I ain't gonna get a minute's sleep, either." He had to snicker when he looked around the little cave. He was spending the night with a seriously wounded outlaw who already tried to kill him once, and a badly wounded Indian who also tried to kill him. Both appeared to be sound asleep enjoying the warmth of the fire.

"Yup, gonna be a long night."

He moved his bedroll out some from the fire, had Hawknose and the young warrior laid out next to the fire. "If them murdering bastards come down on us tonight, they'll work on those two before me and I might get out of this yet." He was wrapped in a blanket, sitting with his back to a rock, maybe fifteen feet from the fire, a cold cup of coffee by his side.

"You plannin' on riding into the night, Marshal?" Cliff Martin moaned, holding tight to a lead rope. He was in pain and leading the pack mule. Fitzgerald was slumped in the saddle on a horse being led by Bull Morrison, and Purdy was riding slightly in front of the group, ready to defend if Indians should attack. The night was quickly coming on as they made their way up river in that deep canyon.

"Matter of fact I am. We just fought off some Indians, Martin. You don't suppose there might be others dancing about do you?" He snarled his anger at what he considered a really stupid question.

"I've got one of the best deputies I've ever worked with trying to catch a desperate outlaw out in front of us somewhere. You damn right I'm planning on riding into the night." Bull Morrison was sure that an hour before he had heard gunshots way off in the distance. None of the others seemed to, though.

He found it interesting that this young deputy sheriff who not long ago told him he planned to run for the office at the next election didn't quite measure up to what he considered a real lawman. *Knowing a lawman is in front of you, chasing a known killer, and you're coming along for backup and protection would be foremost in a real lawman's mind. This kid sees the lack of professionalism in his current boss but not in himself. Even if he's elected, he'll never really be a lawman.* Bull rode quietly in the gloom hoping they would run into trouble. He needed to get in another good fight.

The wind had calmed down and maybe that's what made him think he heard something. It made riding the trail easier, but the snowfall was heavy, and vision was difficult. "We'll ride until it becomes dangerous. Get your mind on your business, Deputy. We ain't out of this yet. We're bound to ride into a whole damn tribe of hostiles before this night is over."

The brush along the sides of the roadway were covered in snow and most of the hillsides on both sides of the river were too. They were another hour into the night and Bull knew they couldn't safely go much longer. They came around a large pile of rocks that had tumbled from the canyon side and Morrison pulled up short. "Better get into those rocks and make up camp," he said.

"You take care of the horses, Purdy, and I'll get a fire going and try to make our walking wounded comfortable. Drop the saddle bags and bedrolls before you hobble the horses." He eased Fitz out of the saddle and helped him to a fallen log where he could sit with his back braced and cleared an area for a fire. Martin managed to get over and slumped down next to Fitz. "Keep your eyes open, Martin. We ain't safe here."

"If I sleep through the night, I'll be good tomorrow, Bull," Fitz said through a sliced cheek that had been roughly sewed back together. It was swollen, bloody, and had to be more than painful. "I ain't gonna die on you, Bull. Just need some sleep."

He was talking to hide the pain, Morrison knew, and would not sleep well that night. He thought about giving him the rest of the jug he had but didn't. Might need that for other wounds along the way. And to make his coffee taste better.

"We'll get our bellies full and take turns standing watch, Purdy. Fitz and Martin need their rest and we'll need them tomorrow. What have we got left of that venison?"

"Plenty for tonight and tomorrow, but then it will be time for looking for fresh meat."

"As long as it ain't fish with bones," Morrison snarled. "Snow's fallin' hard but that wind finally quit. Too quiet for my blood. I'm gonna take a little walk around. Keep that fire going good. Any Indians around already know we're here. No sense hidin' it."

Morrison made his way out of the jumble of downed rocks and into a stand of sage. He couldn't see twenty feet in front of him because of the heavy snow falling straight down. When he turned, even their own fire couldn't be seen. "That's a good thing, anyway," he muttered.

He was in a difficult spot but not one that worried him much. There were four of them, and, yes, two were wounded but still able to fire a weapon. They needed to find Calhoun who may or may not have a captured outlaw in tow, and all of them may be attacked at any time by hostiles.

"To hell with the bunch of 'em," Morrison growled. "I'm gonna eat and sleep and fight tomorrow." Back in camp he fixed a plate of venison, wrapped himself in a bedroll and told Purdy, again, to take first watch. "Wake me in four hours and keep close watch."

Cliff Martin was glad to be riding with the marshals. He had never been around men such as these, knew they were good at what they did, and hoped to learn as much as possible. He was terrified of Bull Morrison while admiring him at the same time. That horrible scar across his face made him fearsome even when he smiled, and his gruff manner and quickness with a weapon added to the fear.

"I'm gonna be sheriff after this election and I'm gonna be a good one," he murmured, pressing his hand onto the wounded shoulder, feeling the wet blood on the rag. The wound ached more than the searing pain he felt earlier and wondered if maybe the bullet did some bone damage as well.

The first few hours of the night passed quietly. The snow piled up and measured more than a foot by the time Purdy shook Morrison awake. "It's after midnight, Bull. All quiet around here, so far. Fire's hot and there's fresh coffee. Looks like the storm might be letting up some."

Morrison was awake and, on his feet, immediately, poured coffee, and gave a mighty stretch before walking off behind a rock to take care of business. As the night wore on, he was able to see more and more stars, and with the clearing skies the temperature fell dramatically. He kept the fire up, ripping complete sage bushes out of the ground and burning them.

"That Purdy's a good fighter. I guess being a stage coach driver, he'd have to be. I hope we don't run into a whole damn tribe of angry Indians before we find Calhoun. Purdy and Fitz will fight hard. I hope Martin will, too." He found himself pacing and forced himself to slow down, concentrate on keeping close watch on the surrounding area.

There was just a hint of light in the east when he got the others awake. "How's that leg, Fitz. I know your cheek hurts, but it's your legs that will keep you alive today."

Fitzgerald pulled the bedroll blanket aside and flexed his wounded leg some. "I'll be limpin' and cussin', Bull, but I'll be with you." He brushed his hand lightly across his wounded face, gritting his teeth from the pain. "Yeah, you could say it hurts, just a mite, though."

"You're gonna have a scar almost as ugly as mine, old man," Morrison laughed, piling more brush on the fire. "Let's drink coffee, eat something, and get on the road as fast as we can. We gotta find Calhoun today." He walked out of the rocks and into the brush to rip some more sage out and stopped dead in his tracks.

"Purdy, Martin, come here. Quick," he hollered. "Fitz, grab your rifle and hide in the rocks."

Martin came at a run, slipping through the icy rocks. He had his revolver in hand, but Morrison just pointed up the trail about a mile or so. "Is that a fire I see?"

Cliff Martin had a hunter's eye and looked in the direction Morrison was pointing. "It sure looks like one to me, Bull. Up the side of the hill from the roadway and in a stand of trees. Too far away to see any movement."

"Let's get packed and on the road. If it's Indians we're in for a fight, if it ain't we'll have coffee with Calhoun," he laughed. "Either way, we win"

"COLD SUMBITCH THIS MORNING," Calhoun said, piling some sage on the fire. "At least it quit snowing." Two things men learned coming west, cottonwood grows everywhere and burns good, and dried sage will burn hotter than hades and light quicker than coal oil. Many lives were saved knowing these things.

The fire was burning good and the coffee was boiling before he checked on the wounded warrior. He was cold and dead. "I hope you went in your sleep son," Calhoun whispered. He unwrapped the body and dragged it out of the cave.

"And you, old man outlaw that you are, are you still with us?" He knelt down next to Hawknose and pulled the blanket back a bit. He could see Mackenzie breathing and pulled the blanket back up. "Ain't gonna get no doctoring until I've got a pot of hot coffee in me, outlaw." He checked the other end of the blanket and saw that the wounded foot was almost black from frostbite and the other probably safe inside a boot.

A couple of chunks of dried meat softening in his coffee, a cold, hard biscuit to be washed down, and Calhoun started packing for the long trip ahead. It took more time to get Hawknose Mackenzie tied on his horse than it did to pack the mule. The outlaw wasn't able to help at all. He had a high fever, was weak from loss of blood, and only about half conscious. Calhoun was running out of material for bandages.

"Should make it back to where the gold is hidden before the sun goes down," he thought as he mounted his horse and took the lead lines for the horse and mule.

He was making his way down the mountainside when he spotted riders coming down the roadway. "Damn. Better get hid, old man," he growled turning the pack train back into the deep sage. He found a ridge that he could hide behind and tied off the animals. With the two rifles and two revolvers, he ducked behind some shale and watched the riders come up toward where his cave was.

They were a hundred yards away before Calhoun recognized Bull riding in the lead. He stood up and waved his rifle in a long arc, hollering a hello at the same time. "I was hoping that was your fire we saw," Morrison said. "Looks like Hawknose wasn't too willing to come back with you, eh?"

"We were attacked by Indians and he tried to gun me, Bull. Ain't nothing more stupid than an outlaw. Got jumped by half a dozen or so and after four of 'em died the others ran off. What's wrong with Fitz?"

"We got jumped, too. Fitz got in a knife fight with one of 'em. He'll be fine. Let's ride," Morrison said, urging his pony back onto the trail. Calhoun gathered up the lead ropes and jumped in the saddle. "You did a good job hiding the gold, Slim. Let's see if we can make it all the way back to that camp today."

He turned in the saddle and motioned Purdy to ride up. "Think you might be able to find us some fresh meat? We're gonna have a lot of mouths to feed for the next few days. Don't ride into a passel of Indians doin' it, though."

"It's the right time of the year to find a big old buck more interested in his love life than his own life," Purdy laughed, jogging off down the trail. "I'll meet you all back at gold camp."

"That's a good name for it," Fitz said. "I like my venison nice and tender, Mr. O'Neil. Don't be shootin' an old hobbled up buck just cuz he's got lots of horns."

"When we hit that camp, Slim, we got some serious plannin' to do. We're a long way from nowhere and more injured than not injured." The look on Bull Morrison's face told Calhoun just how serious things were.

CHAPTER 15

"THAT WAS BEARTOOTH RIDING OFF, SHERIFF. PROBABLY going to see the judge." Buck Antonelli wasn't going to get his chance to watch Beartooth lose his reward. "Dammit Sheriff, get you department in order."

Rogers cussed some under his breath, turned, and walked out the door. "My people are doing what they've been told to do, Marshal." Antonelli had to think about that for a minute or two and watched Rogers cross the street.

"Doing what they've been told to do," he mused. "That's coming mighty close to criminal behavior. Impeding the marshals in their duties might get your skinny butt thrown out of office," he muttered. Damn that Beartooth Johnson getting away before I got to watch him get shot down by the judge."

SHERIFF ROGERS WAS at his regular table at the back of the Mike and Don's House saloon, sipping on a cold beer as if he hadn't a care in the world. As usual, he had bought a round for the everyday crowd, which is exactly how he won election to the job of sheriff and was telling ribald stories.

He was about to describe how it was he was able to kill a deer a week or so ago when a man came rushing in. "Sheriff come quick. Man's been shot and the judge's been beat up."

Rogers started to say something but was interrupted when Buck Antonelli stormed in. "Need some help at the jail, Sheriff. Why is it so damn hard for you to be a sheriff? Do your job, man," Antonelli said, turned, and walked out of the saloon. "Good thing Bull is out busting sage cuz if he was here, he'd have you locked up or in the hospital. What was the ruckus when I came in?"

"Something about someone being shot and the judge. I didn't get it all just as you came in."

"Damn," Antonelli exploded. "Let's go," and he pushed the sheriff toward horses at the hitching rail in front of the jail. "We just got back with Emerson and that fool Beartooth thinks he has some kind of bounty coming. So does that idiot Dorman, and right now one of them is either dead or wounded." He was talking fast as they rode at a full gallop toward Doc Trask's farmhouse.

They jumped off their horses in a cloud of dust and ran toward a group of people standing around a body splayed out in the mud. Buck Antonelli moved a couple of men aside and shouted at the sheriff. "This is Dorman. Get in that house and check on the judge. Hurry."

He saw that Dorman's knife was close by and had some blood on the blade. "Anybody see what happened?" He looked around the crowd.

One man shook his head but said, "I saw a big man ride off fast after I heard the two shots. He had long hair and was really a big man."

"Two shots?" Buck asked and the man nodded. "Only hit

old Dorman with one of 'em. Beartooth's losing it." He ran to the house to see if the judge survived and found Sheriff Rogers helping the old man back into bed.

"Beartooth killed Dorman. How's the judge?"

"Got roughed up a bit. He'll be fine. What are you going to do?" The sheriff seemed puzzled by what had happened.

"What am I going to do? My God, what kind of a lawman are you? We are going to form a posse and chase down one Beartooth Johnson, that's what we are going to do. Let's go, and I mean, now." He turned and strode from the farmhouse, found his horse and was mounted before the sheriff hit the front door.

At the jail he brought Doc Trask up to date and called Deputy Owens to meet him out front. Owens brought another deputy out with him as the sheriff rode up and joined them. "Glad you could make it, Sheriff. Are these your only deputies?"

"Right now, yes. Martin is out riding with your marshal."

"Only one with any sense," Buck snorted. "All right, then, this will have to do. Put together enough food for a couple of days and we'll be leaving in fifteen minutes."

"Oh, no we're not," Sheriff Rogers said. "That man will be in California within the hour, way out of my jurisdiction. If you want to chase him down, that's what marshals are for, but I'm not sending any of my men with you."

"A man was just murdered less than two blocks from where we're standing and you're not chasing the killer? Oh, hell no," Antonelli said. "That would be something a real lawman might do." The sarcasm was getting too heavy for Rogers and he simply walked away.

Buck knew that Bull Morrison would have whipped that man into a bloody mess but also knew that time was what mattered right now. Beartooth Johnson was probably fleeing back to Placerville and that the faster he was on the trail, the better. "What's your name?"

"Henry, Joshua Henry, sir," the tall young deputy standing with Owens said.

"I'm Deputy U.S. Marshal Buck Antonelli, Mister Henry, and, if you approve, you're now working for me. Got a problem with that?"

"No, sir," he said, a bit of excitement in his reply. "I'd be honored to work for you, sir."

"You may come to regret that statement, son, but I'm glad to hear it. Best not be calling me sir, either." He looked over at Owens. "How about you?"

"No, sir. I work for Sheriff Rogers. You're wrong in doing this, Josh. Even if you catch that Beartooth fella Rogers won't let you come back to work here."

"Might be the best thing that ever happened to me," Josh Henry said.

"All right, then. Owens, you just nestle right up with that coward you work for and Josh Henry and I will do our duty. Henry, get a two-day supply of what we'll need, and we ride in ten minutes, and we'll ride hard." Buck Antonelli walked across the street to the general store to fill his saddle bags with some necessaries.

CHAPTER 16

"IT'S GONNA TAKE EVERY BIT OF EFFORT EACH ONE OF US HAS to live through this," Bull Morrison said. They had been riding for most of the day, breaking trail in the new fallen snow and keeping a close eye on the sides of the canyon. "I think we've all seen the movements in the sidehills as we've ridden today and I'm sure there are a lot more of them than there are of us. We're less than fifteen minutes from the old gold camp. Fitz are you in good enough shape to take care of the horses when we get there?"

"You bet, Bull, and I'm ready to fight, too." Fitzgerald had been in worse shape than this, he thought, remembering some of the fights he'd had with outlaws and Indians over the years. "You boys jump down with your rifles and saddle-bags and I'll tend the horses and join you."

"Slim, you and Purdy take point, and O'Neil, whatever Slim says is law. I want you two to be the eyes and guns of this fight. Me, Martin, and Fitz will back every play. Can we trust Hawknose not to try to run away?"

"Not for a minute," Calhoun laughed. "You'll need to tie him tight, and if he dies, that's just one less to be hung." He looked around as they neared the old camp site, spotted some movement well up the side of the canyon to the west.

"You feeling good enough for this fight, Martin?" Morrison didn't have much confidence in the deputy from Mormon Station.

"I am, Marshal, and angry enough if I wasn't."

Morrison gave a signal to stop and everyone jumped from their saddles, rifles in hand. Cliff Martin yanked Hawknose down and the bunch moved quickly to the rocks near the fire pit. Fitzgerald led the horses into a stand of brush and tied them off, grabbing his rifle and bags before running back.

Slim and Purdy O'Neil were down behind a shale outcrop about twenty feet in front of the fire pit. Morrison was ten feet or so to the right side, while Fitzgerald was set up well to the left. Cliff Martin took a position between and well behind Calhoun and O'Neil. "Let's not be shootin' at shadows, gentlemen," Morrison said. "When things get messy, we don't want to be shootin' each other, either. Let 'em get close and pick your targets."

How many times had he had to say that over the years? When a fight starts and the blood runs hot, young men let all their aggressions come to the surface, and just start shooting. "Hell, I've even seen it when hunting big game," he chuckled. "One old buzzard I remember emptied his rifle without even aiming at anything."

"I've watched men reload their muzzle loaders over and over without ever pulling the trigger," Calhoun laughed. "Out hunting, they call it buck fever." Calhoun felt his nerves tighten, felt the blood rushing and knew he had to calm down. *Always get these jitters just before a big fight. Gotta clam now, boy, and pay attention.*

It was late in the day and with the sun dipping behind

the tall peaks, the air turned frigid. "Gonna be dark soon, Calhoun," Purdy said. "Indians don't much care to fight at night."

"You're right but they do like to sneak about and slit throats. Wind's picking up again and if it brings snow that will be to our favor. I'll watch to the left, you to the right, and we'll just let 'em come to us." His mind was on the coming battle now and without even realizing it, he was calm as a horse in spring grass.

The wind was whistling down the canyon, blowing snow about, and making vision more than difficult. They would be crouched or sitting in the bitter temperatures for the night, Calhoun knew, and would be in bad shape for fighting come morning. He eased back to where Morrison was.

"I don't think we'll be hit until morning, Bull. They're gonna move around some and get in good position for an attack and it would be best if we got a fire going and set up watches. That way we'll be ready for a fight come morning."

"Let's do that. You and Purdy take first watch, Me and Fitz will take second. Go on back out there with Purdy while we get a fire going. Red devils might try to sneak in and slit some throats during the night, so keep those eyes of yours wide open, Slim."

Slim had to chuckle half an hour later as he and Purdy looked up the side of the hill and saw several small fires burning. "Looks like those bad boys are just as cold as we are, Mr. O'Neil. That wind's snakin' right through this big coat of mine. You holding up okay?"

"I'm fine, Marshal. I've driven a coach through worse than this. Sure wish old Sammy was with us. I swear he was the best man with a gun that I ever worked with. He proved that when we was robbed. He jumped off that old wagon, pulled his gun while he was still in the air, and killed that outlaw with one shot."

"When we rode out from Strawberry, the doctor said your messenger was going to be fine, Purdy. You'll be riding together one day soon." Calhoun saw just a hint of movement off to his left as he spoke and turned in time to brace himself as a single warrior leaped at him with a stone war club.

He and the Indian were a tangled mess of arms and legs rolling in the snow. The attack ended almost as soon as it started when Purdy O'Neil smashed his rifle butt into the warrior's head, once, twice, and three times. "Sure glad you saw him in time, Calhoun. That club was comin' for your head, true as an arrow."

"I'll never know how they are able to sneak up so close and not be seen or heard."

"We was talkin', Marshal. Stead of watchin'. Getcha in trouble every time."

"I think you're right," Slim chuckled. "Hope he didn't bring a friend." Calhoun sat back and thought about what that stage coach driver said. *Here we were talking about Sammy Fredericks instead of minding business. Take your mind off what it is you're supposed to be doing and bad things happen. We've already got two wounded and a prisoner about to die, I need to concentrate on nothin' but business.*

"You boys all right?" Bull Morrison hollered out from near the fire pit. "What was that ruckus?"

"We're fine, Bull. Just a friendly visit from one of our warrior neighbors. Purdy sent him to hell's fires. Go on back to sleep, we'll wake you in a couple of hours." He grinned at O'Neil and shivered as a gust of north wind howled through the area. "Gonna be more snow before sunrise, Purdy."

"Gonna be more Indians before sunrise, I think," O'Neil

said. "They're building up their fires now." He pointed up the hill where several of the fires were burning bright. "They'll eat, get good and warm. and attack, my friend. I've seen it before. They won't care a dime's worth if it's snowin' and blowin'."

"We better do the same, then," Calhoun said. He and Purdy moved back to the fire pit, getting the rest of the crew up and throwing wood on the fire. "Get warm, boys, cuz it's gonna get plenty hot soon."

"You figure out how many?" Morrison hefted some sage onto the already roaring fire. "Minus one, of course."

"No, but there's three fires up there, so I'm gonna guess there were twelve to fifteen braves. It's gonna be a fight."

"HE RODE OFF THAT WAY, MARSHAL," a man in a buffalo coat said, pointing off to the south. "I didn't recognize him. He was big, I know that."

He would gladly have shot the sheriff who offered no help, would have snarled a time or two at Bull Morrison for sending him on this fool's errand, and wanted to shoot that judge and Gus Emerson. "I've got a young deputy and a deadbeat sheriff to contend with, and Bull and Slim are riding through some gorgeous country without a care in the world."

They were in the saddle riding south and into the meadow where Antonelli figured Beartooth would be and found the old prospector's cabin empty. "He can't be more than an hour ahead of us. The fire's still hot." Buck Antonelli was nearing forty and wondered how long it would be before he had to hang up the badge. Would he know it was time? Not understanding it was time could get a man killed. It was a wise man, he thought, who understood his own limitations and wondered if he would be as wise.

Take a job as sheriff in a quiet little county, bust some drunk's head once in a while, cozy up to a pretty girl now and then, and drink good liquor. Not yet, Buck old son, not yet.

The wind had some serious cold in its gusts and Antonelli knew that a heavy snowfall would make it almost impossible to track Johnson. He had to get moving before Johnson got too far ahead, before the storm destroyed all the prints he would follow.

"I need you, Josh, but you need to think about something. If you ride with me, you probably won't have a job when you get back. That sheriff you work for ain't gonna welcome you back."

"I don't have anything to come back to, Marshal, and if I ride with you, I know most any other sheriff would hire me just cuz I did." He laughed through his slight embarrassment as did Buck. "What I'm tryin' to say is, yes, I'd be proud to ride with you."

"Mount up, then," Antonelli said.

SUNRISE WAS SLOW TO COME, fighting its way through heavy clouds, and slow to warm, having little impact on a bitter cold north wind. The small hunting party of Washoe Indians, having lived in these mountains for generations didn't give the conditions a second thought. Their fires were hot, and their blood was hotter after losing several members of the group to these white men.

They spread out across the face of the mountain and slowly made their way through the trees and brush toward the white man's fires. Calhoun was tracking a group to his left and Purdy was watching another group to his right.

Using hand signs, they let Morrison and the others know what was happening.

"Look back up toward where the fires were, Purdy. See that movement? That's another group that will hit us once we get really busy with these two coming toward us." Calhoun turned back toward the fire. "Morrison, did you hear that?"

"I did, Slim, and we'll keep a close eye on them. Better hunker down for a long fight, I think."

The wind was screaming at hurricane strength and carried several tons of snow along with it, hammering the mountains and canyon, bending trees, toppling some, when the Indians on the left of Calhoun attacked in strength. The screaming was muted by the storm, but the intent was clear.

Slim used his rifle for the first two shots and pulled that revolver for the next couple. He hit one man with a rifle shot and was sure he hit at least one more with the first two pistol shots. He could feel more than hear Purdy O'Neil firing as well. "Comin' from my side, too, Calhoun. Got two of them red devils."

The wind hampered their ability to take aim, the snow hampered their vision, and the Indians themselves did what they could to hamper them even more. They seemed to come in groups of three, and Bull Morrison could see wounded men try to get into cover. He fired his rifle with precision and knocked two off that fast.

The men behind were taking their toll as well, making every shot count. It was Bull Morrison who took two men out firing just one shot by shooting the man attacking then using the rifle like a club on the one following. The one that was shot fell and Morrison was on his feet, running through the snow, toward the advancing second brave.

Instead of shooting that second attacker, he charged

him, swinging his rifle like a war club, all but took the man's head off. Morrison was screaming louder than the attacking Indians, had his knife out that fast, and was waiting for the third man who didn't appear.

Morrison was howling, swinging his knife back and forth, stomping through the snow, daring one of the braves to come at him. There weren't any left to come and it took Slim Calhoun's laughter to slow the big marshal down. "You are one fighting man, Bull Morrison," he laughed and the two came back to stand near the fire.

As fast as the fight started it ended. "It's the silence that gets you," Calhoun said. "It's the silence that makes you want to stand up to count the dead, and that's what the wounded ones are waiting for. They'll play dead until you drop down to see if they are dead."

"Don't talk to me about that," Fitzgerald said, rubbing the wound across his face. "Damn fool move on my part."

"It's light enough to check 'em, though," Morrison said. "Nice and easy, boys, and we don't want prisoners."

They walked through the deep snow and found no survivors. There were indications that during their retreat at least two wounded men were dragged out of the area. "They'll be back," Calhoun said. "They'll lick their wounds and come back with a vengeance."

"That group holding back never did come down the hill," Martin said.

"They'll be attacking an empty camp when they do come. Can we get to that gold, Slim?" Morrison was motioning for Fitz and Cliff Martin to start packing.

"Me and Purdy are almost sitting on it, Bull. We'll dig it out while you load everyone up. We'll make this a running battle with these Indians. They don't seem to want to use their horses in battle."

"They kept right with us yesterday but attacked us this morning on foot." Calhoun remembered his fight two days before when the Indians were also on foot. "That might give us a bit of an edge, Bull."

"Yeah, these are mountain Indians, not plains Indians. They have their horses for work, not for battle. We can protect our flanks and keep moving all day, I hope," Morrison said. "Gonna be cold, too."

Slim and Purdy had the sacks of gold out from under the trees in less than ten minutes and brought them down to the horses. "The faster we can clear out of here and make time on that road the better. How's our prisoner holding up?" Calhoun saw Martin struggling to get Hawknose Mackenzie up on a horse and walked over to help.

"He's alive but we'll have to tie him to the saddle," Martin said, wincing as he got Hawknose into position.

"You're still hurtin' some too, I see. Everything working?"

"I'm hurt but not bad enough to not be able to ride and fight. I sure do like the way you shoot, like you don't even aim."

"Reflex, I guess," Calhoun said. "It's kinda like pointin' a finger," he said, quickly pointing at the young deputy. "Gotcha," he laughed. Martin didn't.

They had their horses, the mule, and themselves on the trail inside fifteen minutes and Morrison was looking back up the mountain as they rode out. "Fires are down, Slim. They're moving too. You and Martin ride out front, Fitz, you ride next to Mackenzie, and Purdy, you ride back here with me.

"We'll scatter in a semi-circle if they attack."

"You mean when, Bull," Slim chuckled. They moved down to the road from the campsite and Calhoun set the order. "Martin, we'll ride at a strong trot for an hour, then

back off and let the horses breathe. You okay with that Fitz?"
Calhoun turned to get a nod from Fitzgerald and put his
horse in a trot. All eyes were on the western flank of that
canyon, searching the trees for movement.

"Gotta watch hard, Purdy," Morrison said. "The best way
for them to even up the odds is to strike from behind. That
would be you and me. Take us out and move on Fitz and
Hawknose before Slim even knows there's an attack." Bull
Morrison had his blood boiling, almost smiling as he talked
about a possible attack.

"I've heard of that, Bull. Shame we can't ride facing backward," he chuckled. They rode for at least half an hour
before Calhoun pointed up and off to the west. Purdy O'Neil
spotted three riders pounding down the main road behind
them. He howled at the group, "Indians!" He pulled his
horse to a stop, jumping from the saddle, rifle in hand.
Morrison was right next to him and dove into the brush at
the side of the road.

Calhoun saw four more riders coming down the side of
the hill and he and Martin hit the dirt, crawling into the
brush. Fitzgerald let go of the lead ropes for the mule and
Mackenzie's horse and dove into the brush as well.

"Let 'em get close, boys, and take good aim. They might
have back up that we can't see," Morrison howled. The
Indians were screaming in their attack, the wind was blowing, and snow was falling hard. "Pick 'em off like they was
quail," he yelled, bringing his rifle to bear on a warrior
twenty-five yards from him.

The melee lasted less than a minute, but every weapon
was steaming hot as the bodies fell to the snow-covered
ground, dead or dying. Again, it was silent save for the
hurricane winds. "Sound off," Morrison yelled and each in

turn yelled they were alive. It was Fitzgerald who sounded wrong to Morrison.

The marshal ran to Fitzgerald and found the man suffering from a gunshot wound to his leg, the blood pumping onto the snow. "Damn, Fitz, you gotta quit getting in the way of these devils." He stretched the man out in the snow and ripped his pants leg open. "Better get this bleeding stopped quick," he muttered and motioned for Calhoun to hurry over.

"You're a better doc than I am, Slim. Help him." Calhoun could hear the anxiety in Morrison, could see it in his eyes. Morrison and Fitzgerald had been riding together for more than twenty years, were great drinking buddies, and each had saved the other countless times. "Help him," Morrison whispered, moving off to the side, making room for Calhoun.

Calhoun had been riding with Morrison for five years and felt extremely close to the chief marshal, knew that Bull felt the same way, and understood the closeness of these two. He wadded up the torn pants leg and pressed it hard onto the wound. "Hold that hard, Fitz while I apply some pressure up here," he said, pressing his fingers hard into Fitzgerald's groin.

"Damn, Slim, easy there, pard." Fitzgerald tried to squirm away, and Calhoun held him in place.

"No, no, Fitz, hold still and hold that rag in place." Calhoun watched as the blood flow slowed to a trickle and finally stopped. "Hold it tight, now," he said, easing pressure off from the groin. "Good," he said, and ripped more of Fitzgerald's pants leg and used the strip to tie off the bandage. "You're a wreck, old man," he chuckled, looking at the two leg wounds and the battered and still bleeding face.

"Thanks, Slim," Fitzgerald muttered. "Sage brush wasn't

big enough for me and that Indian bastard. He shot me after I shot him, damn it. Well, I shot him a second time, so I win."

"You been attacked twice by wounded Indians, Fitz," Morrison chuckled. "Gotta take better aim, son. Slow and true," he laughed," but Calhoun could hear how hollow the laugh was. Morrison had almost lost a long-time friend, a partner on the long trail, a man who meant something to him. Calhoun knew how hard it was for Morrison to reveal feelings but could also understand how the near-death of a friend could affect him.

Morrison scuffed some snow, smiled that terribly scarred smile of his at Fitz, turned, and walked over to see if Hawknose Mackenzie was still alive. "How does this guy survive? Look at that. He's half hanging off the saddle, been shot again, and still breathing. Well, let's get him patched up, retied, and get moving. Those bastards will surely attack again and soon."

The chaos that followed the brief, but bloody battle ebbed into slightly organized movement as horses were gathered, tack attached, and wounded patched. They were riding at a strong trot within minutes. Slim was again in the lead along with Martin, but Morrison was riding alongside Fitzgerald and Purdy was alongside Mackenzie who was tied tightly to the saddle, unconscious.

"Those Indians have no fear, Slim." Morrison loved a fight more than anything else in his life, and always analyzed how his enemy fought after a battle. "They don't have a full grasp of the power of their weapons, either. They just fire away and hope they hit something, and most of them carried battle axes and lances. All that to our benefit."

"Guns are still relatively new to them, Bull. We've had guns for many generations while they've had stone war clubs and wooden lances. They may not be very good with guns but you sure can't short them on aggressiveness or desire."

Morrison nodded and dropped back beside Fitzgerald. "Hang in there, Fitz. Once we're out of this canyon it'll probably be a little easier ride for you."

"We'll be out of this canyon and out in the flat desert before sundown if we don't have any more attacks," Calhoun yelled back. He looked over at Cliff Martin. "Think we can make Mormon Station tomorrow?"

"Not a chance, with this weather, Marshal," Martin said. "When we're clear of the canyon we'll probably be clear of the Indians. One of us could ride ahead, fast, and alert Mormon Station."

"If we weren't fighting both the weather and the Indians, I'd say go ahead, Cliff, but right now, we need your gun. This storm really slows us down, having to cool out the laboring horses regularly and giving the Indians that much of an edge. We'll talk about it in the morning, though."

CHAPTER 17

It was a steep climb out of the Carson Valley into the high Sierra Nevada, then down to the shores of Lake Tahoe, before another long climb out of that paradise. "Beartooth knows this country like the back of his hand, Josh, so we've got our work cut out. We need to stay hard on his trail. We need to move fast but not kill the horses."

This was the part of being a U.S. Deputy Marshal that Buck Antonelli loved the most. The chase. He could read trail as well as any Indian, could read his surroundings as well, also. How the mountains dipped and soared, whether one canyon would lead to others or end in a blank wall, how streams meandered through the various ranges. "Beartooth is a fine tracker, Josh, but I'm just as good or better. His advantage right now is that he knows this country better than I do."

They were riding through a forest of massive pines, firs, cedars, and aspen spread across flanks of granite that towered thousands of feet above sea level. It was late fall and they were above the seven-thousand-foot level and would soon run out of trees. By the time winter was over, this trail would be under twenty to thirty feet of snow.

Their horses were worn out from the hard climb and Buck Antonelli hoped that Johnson's horse was ready to give out, too. The weather was against them one way, that is, blowing snow and bitter temperatures, while on the other, they could plainly see Johnson's trail.

"That first snow is gonna help us, Marshal, if it doesn't snow hard again. There isn't much activity and his tracks are plenty obvious. Why did he attack the judge?"

Buck Antonelli had to chuckle before trying to answer the question. He spent ten minutes telling the story. "It all boils down to ego, Josh. The man is overwhelmed by his own self. The judge is a conniver, too. Beartooth wanted that badge in the worst way and the judge saw how he could get out of paying the bounty he offered."

"Sounds like Johnson has a good argument but not good enough to justify beating up Judge Chastain. When we catch up with him will he resort to firing on us?"

"I've been wondering that myself. Remember, Josh, he did more than beat up the judge. He murdered Duff Dorman. He's prideful as can be but I think he might listen before just trying to shoot us. Right now, I don't know if he is running away from us or just trying to get home. It'll be dark soon and these horses are done for today. Let's pitch camp under those trees. Those big slabs of Sierra granite will be good wind breaks. I gotta think Johnson is setting up his camp about now, too."

"I'll take care of the horses and gather some wood. You seem to know where this Beartooth fella is heading."

"He's pretty well known as a tracker around Placerville. I'd put my money on there. If the snow is heavy in the morning, I think it'd be best if we just ride for Placerville instead of trying to stay on his trail."

Buck watched Josh get the horses tethered in fair grass after kicking as much snow as he could out of the way. The horses would also kick it aside. He piled all the tack near where Buck planned the fire pit. "You've spent some time on the trail, I take it, Josh."

I came into this country for the silver, Marshal. Worked cattle in Texas, made three long drives and heard about the big silver strike when I was somewhere in Kansas," he laughed. "I never really knew where I was. It's kinda like that on the drives. Anyway, I learned right fast that working in a silver mine hundreds of feet underground ain't for me. Offered this job from Sheriff Rogers and found that I like carrying a badge but working for Matt Rogers ain't very good."

Buck Antonelli was laughing hard at the comment and whacked the boy across the shoulders. "Worst example of a lawman I've run into, boy. I've been riding with Bull Morrison and Slim Calhoun for several years now, and that Rogers is lucky that it was me he had to deal with and not Morrison."

They ate well that night and slept warm, finding a fresh coat of snow covering everything in the morning. Antonelli rousted Josh out before sunrise, had a fire blazing and coffee boiling before Josh Henry could get his boots on. "You'd be a good ramrod on a cattle drive, Marshal," the young deputy laughed.

"We'll join the main Johnson cutoff road shortly and I'll bet find Beartooth's trail. He probably figures he's being followed but with the snow won't worry about leaving sign.

"What we gotta watch for is him trying to sneak off the

main trail and disappearing in the wilderness. He ain't really the brightest tracker, but the thought might take hold."

The emigrant trail across the mighty Sierra Nevada was well used, from the earlier days of the forty-niners to the more recent rush of miners from California to the massive silver strike on the Comstock. "Won't find many folks out and about in this weather, Josh. That wind comes straight down from Alaska, I've been told."

Within the first hour on the trail they found where Beartooth had camped, and Buck Antonelli was almost dancing. "He ain't trying to run away, Josh. He's just riding home. We'll have him in our sights before the day is out. Let's push these horses a bit."

They rode as fast as the storm and terrain would allow, stopping only once to build a fire and warm up with some coffee and cold biscuits. Antonelli found some chunks of dried elk in his saddle bags and they softened them in their coffee. "We can see his trail fine despite the heavy snow, Josh. We're close. Keep your eyes open and be ready to defend yourself.

"If he gets scared, if we seriously frighten the man, he'll attack. I really want this man alive. Remember, he's already killed a man and he has to face up to that. What he did was commit a hanging offense and he's not gonna go down easy."

Josh Henry was fast to recognize what an education he was getting riding with a Deputy U.S. Marshal. *Sheriff Rogers would simply say that Johnson was a criminal, bring him in. If dead, so be it. Marshal Antonelli says Johnson is an outlaw but bring him in alive if at all possible. Little nuances of life as a good lawman, not just a badge carrying gunman.*

They were in high country, above the tree line, in massive slabs and boulders of granite, being hammered by intense winds and heavy snow when Buck Antonelli brought them to a halt. "Saw something, Josh." He pointed off to the right, into a stand of rocks that would shield someone from the wind. "Do you see a flicker of fire in the blowing snow?"

Josh Henry shielded his eyes as best he could and after just a moment or two nodded yes. "Looks like a nice warm fire to me, Marshal. You figure that's Johnson? I doubt that he's heard us."

"Let's tie these horses off, bring your rifle, and we'll walk very carefully into that little camp. Keep in mind that he is a dangerous, strong, wanted man. We'll do everything we can to bring him back with us, alive. If he feels trapped, he will be more dangerous than any bear protecting its young."

Buck didn't have to say anything about wanting to get back down out of that high country as quickly as possible. These early storms often laid the base for following winter storms and could bring as much as five or six feet of snow. "We need to catch him up and get down to the lake as quickly as possible. Sure don't want to get trapped up here."

They were near the eight-thousand-foot level and Lake Tahoe was near the six-thousand-foot level and there would be a drastic difference in the amount of snow each storm dropped. Buck could remember the stories told of the Donner party when it got trapped near Tahoe. It was a fall storm that created that disaster.

Using hand signals, Buck moved Josh around a boulder the size of a small cabin while he went the other way. He motioned to be quiet and slow and let Buck take the lead. Josh gave a nod and smiled back. *He's gonna be a lawman for a long time, I think,* Buck mused. As he moved around the rock it became obvious that Johnson had a large fire built.

Buck was almost on his knees as he carefully looked around the edge of the rock and saw Beartooth kneeling down at the fire, pouring coffee. His rifle was several feet away near a lean-to covered bedroll along with his sidearm. Buck Antonelli stepped out from the boulder.

"Mornin' there, Beartooth. Nasty storm, eh? How's that coffee?"

Beartooth Johnson spun around grabbing for his pistol which wasn't there and charged Antonelli. He came low and fast, like a griz saving a cub, and the two men rolled through the snow and rocks, each desperately trying to grab something, hit something, or kick something. Beartooth was larger than Antonelli but the deputy marshal was a bit younger and better trained in fighting.

Beartooth was on top but Antonelli had his arms wrapped around the big man and was hammering both fists down hard onto the man's kidneys. Buck could feel Johnson weakening from the brutal punishment and rolled over, getting on top of the tracker, slamming those fists into the man's face until Johnson simply quit fighting back.

Antonelli feared that Johnson was feigning, and was slow to get off the man, only to find Josh Henry standing there, his rifle pointed at Johnson's head. "So, that's why you quit, eh? Thank you, Mr. Henry," Buck said getting to his feet, jerking Beartooth to his.

"Now, about that coffee, then a hard and fast ride down to lake level before we get trapped up here. Oh, by the way, Mr. Johnson, you're under arrest." He walked to the fire while Josh escorted Beartooth at the end of his rifle. "Will you ride with us willingly, Beartooth, or will you force me to tie you tight and make this a most uncomfortable ride?"

Beartooth watched a calm and poised Buck Antonelli pour three cups of coffee, saw Josh Henry standing cautiously with a cocked and ready rifle, and decided it would be best to do as these two said, at least for the time being. "I'll ride with you, Marshal, but you ain't got no call to arrest me."

"You beat the hell out of a federal judge, Mr. Johnson. That's against the law, sir. Oh, and yes, you murdered Duff Dorman. Now, Dorman's murder isn't a federal offense, so the local sheriff will have to attend to that. However, beating up a federal judge is."

"That stinking judge stole my bounty money. He should be arrested, not me."

"Well, we'll let a jury decide that issue. Josh, bring our horses in, Beartooth, get yourself packed up. One stupid move Mr. Johnson and I'll whip you to a bloody mess and tie you to your horse, facing backward. Oh, and by the way, it would be my pleasure, sir."

They made it back to their first night's camp, but the snow was getting deeper and drifting because of the high wind. "We'll just warm up, Josh. We might have to ride well into the night. We don't want to get caught up here.

"Johnson, what kind of supplies you got?"

"Couple of pounds of venison, flour, and coffee, Marshal. Enough for two days."

"Good. Light a fire, Josh, and we'll boil some coffee, rest the horses, and be off."

The Johnson Cutoff was a reasonably easy road since wagons, coaches, and thousands of horses had carved it out, and even though the snow was drifting, the ride down to lake level was accomplished with little difficulty. They stopped at a lodge for the evening.

"We'll need a room with two beds, sir," Buck Antonelli

said, "and supper for three, in the room. I'm Deputy U.S. Marshal Buck Antonelli, this is my deputy, Josh Henry, and our prisoner. Along with supper, please bring a jug of whiskey."

The owner of the lodge welcomed them. "Not many people out and about in this weather, Marshal. The lodge is all yours, tonight, if you'd be more comfortable having your supper in front of the fire."

Antonelli had to think about that for a moment and looked about the place. There was a long roughly timbered table near the rock fireplace with benches along each side. A few rough-cut tables and chairs were also scattered around. What caught his attention immediately were the looks that passed back and forth between Johnson and the lodge keeper.

"I think we'll be more than comfortable in our room, innkeeper," he said. "Knock before entering or you might get shot. My young deputy here has been aching to kill someone all day, I'm afraid."

The innkeeper actually scampered off to the kitchen, returning with a large key. "It's the first room at the top of the stairs, Marshal. Yes, I'll knock. You'll find kindling and wood for the stove and I'll have fresh water for the bowl brought up."

Antonelli chuckled all the way up and into the room while Josh Henry prodded Beartooth up the stairs with is rifle. "Why did you say something like that, Marshal. I've not said anything about wanting to shoot somebody."

"Mr. Johnson and our fine innkeeper seem to know each other, Josh. I just wanted to let the gentleman know that we will shoot first, ask no questions, and protect our prisoner. The two made eye contact several times while we were talking about fireplaces and supper."

"You got a way about you, Marshal. I think I'll be sorry when this ride is over."

"I think you might want to think about joining the service, Josh. I'll talk to Bull about that." Josh Henry didn't even try to hide the smile that spread across his young face.

CHAPTER 18

"ONE MORE DAY ON THIS RIDE AND I'LL JUST SHOOT THIS Hawknose Mackenzie dead and we won't have to travel at the pace of a snail." Bull Morrison had been in a rage since sun-up, with two injured members of his posse and a badly wounded prisoner. Their camp the previous night had been a cold one, and because of the threat of continuing Indian attacks, he had not slept more than an hour or two.

"We should be in Mormon Station tomorrow, Bull," Slim said. "Cliff Martin left late last night and said he would ride hard into the village and bring help back to us. We'll have a hot meal with fresh meat tonight and sleep well." Slim Calhoun had taken care of multiple wounds suffered by Fitzgerald and done his best to keep Hawknose alive. Purdy O'Neil rode point since leaving camp and Morrison rode at the back.

"Don't you find it interesting that we haven't heard a word from Buck Antonelli?" Slim dropped back to talk with Morrison. "For that fool sheriff to not send people to help, I would expect, but why haven't we heard anything from Buck?"

"He was riding with Tracker-man and that smart nose kid, Slim. He's probably had more fun than we could even think of," Bull laughed. "Here we are, fightin' off Indians, capturing wild criminals, and he's been having fun in the big city."

"Somebody should have sent us word on the judge, at the least," Calhoun said. Bull could see the worry in Calhoun's face and understood his deputy's concern. They were on this trail because the judge's wife was kidnapped and murdered, and even though the judge should not have been involved, since he was, and injured, the marshals were responsible for his wellbeing.

"Now it's my turn to calm you down, eh?" Morrison laughed. "Do you think Mackenzie will last another night in this cold?"

"I can't understand why he's alive right now," Slim chuckled. "That man's foot is rotting right off the leg and he's suffering from two bullet wounds besides. Toughest hombre I've run into in a long time, Bull. He's more like you," Calhoun laughed, ducking a swinging rifle barrel and riding back to his patient. He could hear Morrison cussing for another full minute.

The ride across the rolling Pine Nut Range and down into the wide flat Carson Valley was uneventful until almost sunset. They were still a full thirty miles of so from Mormon Station and moving slowly when they spotted four riders coming up on them. "Looks like our welcoming committee," Slim hollered back at Morrison.

Cliff Martin led Hal Owens, Doc Trask, and one other up to the caravan. "Sure glad to see you," Purdy O'Neil said. He led the group off the trail and into a stand of cottonwood trees to set up camp for the night. "We got walking and not walking wounded for you Doc."

Martin rode to Slim and motioned to him to follow and rode back to where Morrison was. "All hell's broken loose, Marshal." His eyes were dancing as he told the story of Beartooth killing Duff Dorman, attacking the judge, and running off. He was still laughing about that when he told about Buck Antonelli and Josh Henry chasing Beartooth.

"Dorman's dead?" Calhoun asked and looked at Morrison.

"Where's this sheriff of yours?" was the only comment from Bull Morrison. He rode up to the nearest tree and stepped off his horse. "Let's get fires lit, bedrolls laid out, and the wounded taken care of. Wish you'd brought a wagon with you, Martin."

"Old man Potter is bringing a wagon and should be here first thing in the morning. Owens and I have fresh meat and potatoes with us, and the doc has all the medicine he could pack. The sheriff said there was no reason for him to be here."

"Good," Morrison said, spitting his chew ten feet, "cuz I'd shoot him sure as hell." He found a rock near where one of the fires was lit and sat down with his back to it. "Emerson? A complete loser, as a man and as an outlaw. Did he survive the ride to Mormon Station? Looking forward to seeing him and Hawknose swinging." He wasn't laughing or smiling.

The fire was started, and Calhoun slumped down near Morrison and Martin. "Tell me about this attack on the judge and the killing of Dorman. That kid had trouble written all over him, but this is a surprise."

Martin hollered for Owens to join them. "Owens was on the scene and can tell you better than me." Owens spent about five minutes relating how Beartooth attacked the judge when he found out there was no bounty, and then killed Dorman when Dorman demanded his share of the bounty.

"The sheriff wouldn't let me ride with Deputy Marshal Antonelli and said Josh Henry was fired for riding off," Owens said.

"Tell me more about Buck Antonelli chasing off after Beartooth Johnson. That Beartooth is a blowhard of the first order and Buck'll have him in irons in quick time. Who's the kid riding with him?"

"He's the only good deputy Rogers has, except for me," Martin said, not getting the response he hoped for from Morrison but getting a hard glare from Owens.

"Ain't saying a whole bunch," Morrison chuckled.

"Why is Buck chasing him and Rogers isn't riding with him? He is a federal fugitive, Johnson is, but also wanted for town murders. What a screwed-up sheriff's office." Morrison's anger hasn't ebbed a bit and Calhoun knew someone would get hurt before the night was over.

"Matt Rogers wouldn't go and wouldn't let Owens or Henry ride with Antonelli, but Josh Henry rode out anyway. Rogers said he would fire him if he came back." Martin got up to get some coffee and get some distance from Morrison who was getting more and more angry.

"I don't suppose any one of you were bright enough to bring a bottle along?" Bull Morrison snarled.

Doc Trask chuckled and brought one over to the marshal. "I brought two, Marshal. One for wounds, one for us."

"Us meaning, you, me, Calhoun, Purdy, and Fitz. The rest of you are on your own," Morrison chuckled. Or, was it more a snicker with an evil look to go with it. He scowled at Deputy Martin.

"Listen to me carefully, Martin. I have a wounded deputy

riding with me right now, and another deputy chasing a killer somewhere in the Sierra Nevada. That man is riding with a member of your department. I want a straight answer and if I hear the slightest bull crap coming from you, I might just shoot you.

"Is this Josh Henry a good lawman? Can Buck depend on him? Tell me the truth."

Cliff Martin had never felt more afraid in all his life. He saw death in Bull Morrison's eyes and knew for the first time what it meant to lead lawmen. Morrison was in command and had nothing but trust and respect for his men and from his men. He wanted to be sheriff because of what the position was and now felt small, unworthy, and knew he would not be running for the job.

"I would put my life in Josh Henry's hands, Marshal. He's as trustworthy a man as any I've ever known, strong, and willing to do what needs to be done."

Morrison snuffed once and passed the jug to Martin. "Mr. Purdy, will you come here for a minute? Slim, sit tight. Martin, get that fire good and hot, I need to talk with these others."

Martin knew he was simply being dismissed and headed out to get wood for the fire. Slim and Purdy hunkered down with Morrison. "I heard part of that, Bull. You thinkin' of sending me off to find Buck?"

"What I was thinkin' was askin' your opinion. Buck is a fine deputy. I have nothing but trust in the man, but if this Beartooth has become a killer, I'm wondering about this other feller, Henry."

"You put the fear of God in Cliff Martin," Calhoun chuckled. "I don't think he was lying or just talking. If what he said is true, I think Buck has some good back-up. Buck is more that capable of handling Beartooth. We'll be in

Mormon Station tomorrow and if you still have doubts, we can ride out."

Morrison looked at Purdy and got a nod from him, stood up and walked to the fire to stand with his hands out for the warmth. "Listen up," he hollered out. "We eat good tonight, sleep warm, and be on the trail at sunrise. Try to keep him alive, Doc. Fitz, you get yourself healed up, and Martin, keep that fire burning hot. After supper I'll take first watch, Slim, you take second."

SUPPER WAS bowls of lamb stew and sourdough biscuits along with a jug of whiskey brought to their room by the innkeeper. "You're my only guests, Marshal, so what time would you like your breakfast?"

Buck Antonelli noticed that Beartooth was paying close attention to what the innkeeper was doing as he set out the night's meal. For a bowl of stew and biscuits, why were there knives being included? Henry was watching Beartooth, turned and nodded at Buck. The innkeeper was positioning himself so to shield Buck's line of sight to Beartooth.

"We'll just take a passel of biscuits and be out of here at sunrise, thank you." Buck stood up and walked to the table and picked up the knives just as Beartooth made a lunge at Josh Henry, holding a large skinning knife. Henry let the rush come on and knocked Johnson's arm aside and drove his fist deep into Johnson's ribs, falling to the floor with the big man. Beartooth was fighting back hard and Josh Henry hit him in the face hard, twice, and made a grab for that big knife. Beartooth was a good knife fighter and Josh Henry was young and strong.

The table and bowls of lamb stew exploded as the men wrestled for the knife. Josh got on top of the big tracker and drove his fist into the man's face over and over feeling Johnson's strength begin to fade. In a desperate move, Josh wrenched the knife away and drove it back into Johnson's body. The big tracker slumped back, breathing hard.

Josh smashed him in the head as hard as he could and then grabbed rags from the bedding and what was flung to the floor and started working to keep Beartooth Johnson alive.

When the fight erupted, the innkeeper spun around with a revolver in hand and fired one shot at Buck Antonelli. Buck felt the bullet slice through his pant leg, drew his weapon and put two quick shots through the man's chest, driving him back against the wall where he fell to the floor, dead.

"I saw the looks that passed between those two when we were downstairs, Marshal. I guess you did, too. This wound isn't as bad as it looks. The bleeding is under control, but he's one strong sumbitch. We need to put him in heavy shackles."

"Wish we had something like that. Run out to the stables, Josh and bring ropes back with you. Yeah, I saw those looks, too," Antonelli said.

Josh was back in minutes and Beartooth Johnson was tied up like a hog for market, squalling like one, too. "Quiet down, Johnson or we'll let you spend the night in the stables with the other animals. I'm runnin 'out of being nice. You are also responsible for the innkeeper's death, and the charges are pilin' up and I'm 'bout ready to shoot you and call it fair." Buck Antonelli still had lamb stew splashed across his shirt-front, blood from the innkeeper on his boots, and was ready to kill just about anything that moved.

"Let's drag this body outside, Josh. He'll freeze up overnight. We'll try to find some kind of local authority in the morning and then head back off the mountain, if we can. I expect Bull and Slim will be there when we get back. I got some words for them," he snarled.

"I just bet you do," Josh chuckled, and Antonelli broke down and had to laugh along with him.

"These two must have been friends for some time for the innkeeper to do what he did," Henry said.

"S'pose so. Tight communities form in the mountains, son. Probably trapped and hunted together, may even have done some other little jobs together. Innkeeper was ready to fight for the old tracker so there was some kind of background I'm sure we'll never know. Let's raid the kitchen, get some sleep, and move out at dawn."

WITH THE SUNRISE and a pot of coffee in their bellies, Henry and Antonelli found a man working near the stables and sent him for who he called the justice of the peace, a grizzled-up gentleman who said he would take care of burying the innkeeper and forward Antonelli's report to the country sheriff.

"Had to shoot him," Antonelli said. "Never even heard his name."

"Kinkead," the judge said. "Theodore Kinkead. Pompous old bastard. Won't be missed much, I fear. Well, have a safe trip, Marshal." They were on the trail inside the hour.

"It hurts, Marshal. You can't make me ride my horse through these drifts with my hands tied behind my back and bleeding from a knife wound, too." It was a pathetic sight for Josh Henry to see, this big tracker almost crying like a baby, pleading to be treated nice.

"It was you come after me, Johnson and I whupped you good so shut your damn mouth and act like a man whats been bested." Henry had taken many a drunk to the cells but hadn't run into a man acting like a baby. "Maybe I shoulda stuck that knife some deeper."

Beartooth's attitude changed to that of a snarling animal, one that cussed like a muleskinner, and he started kicking his horse hard. Josh Henry used the knotted end of the lead rope and whipped Johnson two or three times before the tracker stopped kicking.

They were over Spooner Summit and working their horses down toward the valley. The storm had left several feet of snow that the wind had drifted. It would be a long slow ride off those mountains.

"You're a lucky man, Johnson," Buck Antonelli called back from his lead position. "If Bull Morrison was on this trail, you'd already be a dead man. He didn't much like you to start with."

The mumbling, grousing, and crying out continued all the way to the valley floor, several hours later. "That smoke yonder better be Mormon Station, Josh, or I'm just gonna shoot this jackass and leave the body lay."

CHAPTER 19

"WE'LL BE IN MORMON STATION SOON, HAWKNOSE," DOC Trask said, riding in the back of a large delivery wagon. Mackenzie was laid out in blankets situated so he was mostly stationary, despite the wagon's movements. The unconscious Mackenzie couldn't hear the man, but the doctor kept up a one-way conversation anyway. Deputy Owens was driving the wagon and turned with a questioning look.

"Always figured that they just might be able to understand that I was trying my best to keep them alive," the doc said. He was scowling and Owens turned back to driving. "All these men I'm riding with seem to take great pleasure in shooting other men, ripping flesh, and breaking bones. Oh, sure, Hawknose, they say they are doing that in the line of duty, and to keep the peace. You, sir, are a wanted outlaw, therefore they have a great duty to shoot you.

"And I'm the man who has to try to put you back together. Fit this piece to that, stem the flow of these fluids before you run dry, and keep you alive long enough for them to hang you. No man will try harder to keep you alive,

Hawknose." Mackenzie would have seen the saddest eyes ever if he'd been conscious.

Mackenzie's foot had to be taken off and the doctor was afraid that the infection had moved up into the leg. His bullet wounds were healing since the doctor was able to extract the bullets with some ease with Mackenzie being unconscious. The infection-driven fever wouldn't break, though. "I may have to take even more of his leg, Marshal, if this fever doesn't break."

Morrison was riding alongside the wagon to check on his prisoner. "We ain't stopping, Doc. We're just an hour or more from town and I got my own bone to pick with that sheriff, so keep him alive and you can saw away when we get to town."

"You're a hard man, Marshal. Yes, I know, this man is an outlaw, wanted for murder and more, but he's still a human being, and he's suffering." Doctor Trask was almost pleading, but Bull Morrison wasn't having any of it. Mackenzie was an outlaw who needed hanging.

"He'll get a trial, a fair trial, and hang, Doc. You have your job, I have mine."

Morrison was frustrated with the slow trip back and more than furious that Sheriff Rogers hadn't formed a posse to ride with Antonelli, that he even forbade his deputies from joining the chase. Morrison broke rules more often than most in the marshal service but was considered a top-notch lawman. "For a lawman to simply turn aside like that is more than I can handle." He called Slim Calhoun over, needed his best friend, his back up in every occasion, to help him understand. "I'm gonna do more than just kick some butt, Calhoun. You better be ready to keep me from shooting that fool."

"Or help you," Slim laughed. "Deputy Owens said that

Antonelli asked them to ride with him and the sheriff wouldn't let them. He said that Josh Henry decided to ride with Buck anyway."

"Good for Josh Henry. Fitz is bad hurt, and I can't just sit on a walking horse for another several hours. We need to be in Mormon Station, Slim. Do you think Martin and Purdy can bring this group on in to town? Maybe we could ride on ahead and have a chat with this so-called sheriff."

Calhoun called Fitzgerald over. "How you feeling, Fitz?"

"The doc did a good job on me, Slim. I'm sore, guess pretty damn ugly, too, but I'm fine. I heard what you were saying, and I can bring this group in. You and Bull go ahead on in. We'll be along. I think the Indian problem is over with."

"We'll have steaks and a warm bed waiting for you, Fitz," Bull yelled back as he and Calhoun put spurs to their horses. "Let's go, Slim, I'm itchin' for this fight."

"I don't think we've ever ridden into such a goofed-up mess as this one, Bull. Even the good guys are stinking thieves, and we're protecting a judge who was married to a soiled dove."

"What?" Morrison howled as their horses pounded their way west. "A dove? Chastain's wife was a working girl? Where'd you come up with that?" He was almost laughing, trying to get the picture in his mind. They were riding at a gentle lope and Slim slowed them down some so he could explain.

"When we were up on the side of the mountain, after I bashed his head in, Hawknose told me all about it. Told me how Mercer attacked Mrs. Chastain even though he didn't have to. She was quite willing since the two of them had some twenty thousand dollars to spend."

Morrison was laughing right out loud, listening to

Calhoun. Calhoun wasn't through. "Those horrible cuts on Mercer's face came from Abigail Chastain and another girl in Carson City. Abigail worked the saloons in San Francisco before she met our fine judge."

"You didn't say it, but I can hear it in your voice," Morrison laughed. "The judge don't know any of this, does he?"

"Not a word of it," Calhoun snickered.

It was several hours later the two riders came into Mormon Station, tired, filthy dirty, and sore from fighting outlaws and Indians, but looking for one more big fight before the day was over. Bull Morrison led the two up to the hitch rail in front of the sheriff's office, dismounted, and charged into the empty office. "Damn," the big man said, walking back out to join Calhoun.

"Probably at the saloon, Bull. That's his real office." They walked across the muddy street and saw three riders off in the south, walking their horses slowly into town. "I do believe that's Buck Antonelli coming in, Bull. Let's greet him before we pick a fight with the sheriff."

"No, I want my ten pounds of meat, Slim. Buck or that Josh Henry fellow will know where to find us. I want that man's blood, Slim," he growled, leading them into the Mike and Dan's House Saloon. In Bull's mind, Rogers sent Buck Antonelli out to catch an outlaw Rogers should have been responsible for, and without back up.

"Yes, Slim, I know. You don't have to say it. Beartooth Johnson is wanted for federal crimes, but Rogers failed in his primary duty as sheriff of this county and put one of my deputies in serious danger."

Sheriff Matthew Rogers was at his regular table toward the back of the place, having a game of cards with two others and spotted Morrison and Calhoun coming in. "This may be a problem, gentlemen," he said. "That's the marshal with the bad attitude coming this way."

"I'll back your play, Sheriff," Nate Daniels said. Daniels was a rancher who seldom spent much time at his ranch, letting his foreman handle the real work. Hobnobbing with the sheriff and county commissioners was more to his liking. He was about five feet and eight inches tall, neared the two hundred mark on scales at the feed store, and at one time was as strong as a Hereford bull. That was a few years ago.

"You're a piss ant who shouldn't be allowed to wear a badge, Rogers. My deputy asked for your help capturing a wanted criminal and you turned him down. Men have died, others are in serious condition, and all because you won't do your duty. You are honor bound, wearing that badge, and you are a failure."

Morrison was hovering over the pale sheriff, daring the man to defend himself when Nate Daniels jumped to his feet and charged the marshal. Both men were relatively short and very heavy, the difference being that Morrison was in excellent physical condition and Daniels wasn't. Morrison howled with delight when Daniels crashed into him, taking the two of them to the floor.

Morrison rolled with the man coming to his feet, knocking over the table where Rogers was still sitting, and in the melee, Morrison swung a massive fist at Daniels, missed by a mile, and smashed Roger's nose into a mass of bloody mush. Slim smiled seeing the little play and how Bull got his man.

Daniels came at the marshal again and Morrison swung that right into the man's face, followed with a left round-house to the man's heart, and watched Daniels fold up and fall back on top of Rogers.

It was very quiet in the bar for several moments before the loud voices started and Slim Calhoun pulled his coat to the side. "I'm Deputy U.S. Marshal Calhoun, that's U.S. Marshal Morrison. Just doing our duty, folks. Something your sheriff hasn't learned about. Go on back to your drinkin', everything's under control."

Morrison ripped Daniels to his feet, slapped him across the side of his head twice and told the man to go home. "You ain't good enough to play with the big boys, Mister. Get out of here before I arrest you." He reached down and got Rogers to his feet.

"Sorry about that, Sheriff," he snarled, his grin becoming even more grotesque around that long ugly scar. "Man ducked just as I swung. Get your scrawny butt over to the office. We have some business to take care of." He shoved the sheriff toward the doors, pushing some of the men lined up at the bar aside. He looked at Calhoun with a little boys grin on his ugly mug.

"Still got some fire in that belly, eh?" Calhoun joked. "Took two out and looking for more, are we?"

"You just never know," Morrison chuckled. They found Buck Antonelli, Josh Henry, and the trussed up Beartooth Johnson inside the office. Morrison shoved Rogers into a chair, walked around the desk and sat down in the sheriff's chair and looked at Antonelli. "Coffee, por favor, Deputy?"

Antonelli laughed and looked at Henry. "The marshal would like some fresh coffee, Mr. Henry, if you please. Nice to see you too, Marshal. Have a nice trip? You might want to hear about mine."

"You sure as hell don't want to hear about mine," Morrison growled. "Glad to see you got your man."

"He tried to give us a little fight, Bull, but Josh Henry here took care of that problem. You have a nice trip, did you?" The sarcasm wasn't as heavy as he intended but it did seep through some.

Morrison ignored the jab and turned his attention to Josh. "I've got a wagon load of injured comin' this way, Mr. Henry, and I hear that you're among the few in this town who knows how to get things done."

Henry looked at the sheriff, sitting quietly with a bloody rag pressed to his mashed-up nose. "Yeah, I guess I do," he stammered. He wanted to ask about that nose but had just enough common sense to keep quiet. It'll all come out, he thought, and poured coffee for everyone.

"You were chasing Beartooth Johnson," Slim Calhoun said. "I'm glad he didn't get away from you. Tell me all about his shenanigans and then I'll tell you about ours."

"No, Slim, he didn't get away," Buck Antonelli said. "What a mess. When he got back to town, he actually whipped on the judge and then when Dorman confronted him about that bounty, shot the boy dead. There's some think Dorman went after him with a knife, so it might not have been open murder."

"It wasn't murder," Johnson snarled. "Fool boy attacked me with a knife. I shot him in self-defense."

"We'll see about that," Buck said.

Bull Morrison pulled a flask from inside his coat and poured generously in his cup and handed the flask to Slim. "I want you to find a place where all these people can be tended, Mr. Henry. Doc Trask tells me there's no hospital or clinic in this town and his place is what's used. Hawknose is just barely alive, Fitzgerald has two gunshot wounds and a torn-up face, and Deputy Martin is wounded.

"There may be more to come," Bull chuckled, looking Rogers in the face. "Can you find something for these fine folks, Henry?"

"You're forgettin' two, Marshal," Buck chuckled. "Gus Emerson was moved over to the doc's house and I assigned an older man here in town to be with him. He ain't no threat to the judge who is also recuperating there. I don't think you want to put Hawknose in the same room with Emerson and the judge, though."

"No, I don't, and I don't want Hawknose and Emerson in the same place. They've already shot themselves once. We sure as hell can't keep the wounded in jail cells either."

"This probably ain't gonna sound right," Josh Henry said, "but the sheriff has the biggest house in town."

"No, no," Rogers started to say and was cut off immediately.

"Good, that will do fine. When that wagon and those riders come in, have Doc Trask set them up at Rogers' place." He looked at Rogers, smiled, and continued. "I thought I heard that Emerson died. He's alive?"

"Doc got his face all cleaned up and the bullet wound wasn't that serious either. He's still got a fever, weak as hell, but the infection is clearing up nicely." Josh Henry looked around the room. "Doc ain't gonna like half the wounded in one place and the other half somewhere else."

"You're probably right," Morrison agreed. "That ain't my problem. What condition is the judge in? That group should be here in the next couple of hours," he said, walking around the office. "Let's you and me head over to Doc's place and talk to the judge, Slim. Henry, why don't you bring Beartooth and join us. Buck, maybe you could ride out and hurry that wagon a bit."

CHAPTER 20

"That is one mean looking face you got going there, Fitzgerald." Buck Antonelli rode up on the incoming group to see if he could hurry things along. "Take on the whole Indian nation, did you?"

"Felt like it at the time, Buck. Good to see you. Doc's back there in the wagon tryin' to keep old Hawknose alive. That's why we're moving so slow."

"Gonna run out of daylight if we don't get things moving. Bull's in a real twit. Seems Emerson is still alive, the judge is fine, Beartooth's in custody and the sheriff is bleeding all over his jail."

"Sounds like you've been having almost as much fun as we have." Fitz sat back in his saddle and chuckled. "All the years I've been in the service, and these last many with Bull, I don't think I've even been on a chase that went in so many different directions. They ain't one of 'em, good guy or outlaw, that ain't an outlaw in some way."

"I Think that even includes the judge," Fitzgerald said. "What a raspy old bastard he is. I've seen that so many times. A man gets so much power that people are afraid to challenge him and then it goes to his head and he becomes a demanding bastard."

"I won't let that happen to you, Buck. I just won't," Fitz laughed.

They drifted back to the wagon, nodded to Owens, who was driving, and to Purdy, who was riding alongside. "It would be best if we get into town before dark, Doc," Antonelli said. "Marshal's got some of the wounded at your place and others at the sheriff's. Gotta keep some of these outlaws separated or we'll have more wounded and dead."

"You don't really care whether this man lives or dies, do you? I know the marshal doesn't."

"You put it that way, Doc, I guess I don't. He shot the stage messenger and left him for dead, kidnapped a federal judge's wife and let his partner murder her, and he attacked and tried to kill a U.S. Marshal. Nope, I guess I don't really give a damn whether this man lives or dies."

Doctor Trask shook his head, growled something that wasn't understood and turned his back on the riders. "You do what you have to do, Marshal and I'll do what I can to keep this man alive." He was still shaking his head as he felt the wagon move a little faster down the trail.

Antonelli turned to Owens. "Let's pick up the pace, Deputy and get this train moving."

Even with the hustle it was nearing dusk when the group rode into Mormon Station. "Purdy, I want you to help the doc get Hawknose settled at the sheriff's place and Buck, help Fitz get settled at the doc's. You stay there with them and keep Emerson and the judge separated. God knows what that fool Emerson might try."

"Or the judge," Calhoun snickered. "Owens, after you drop the doc and Hawknose off, get rid of the wagon and team and make the rounds of the town as county deputy.

Martin, I'm appointing you as acting sheriff until Rogers can resume his duties, and Josh, you and Antonelli spell the men at the hospitals."

"What are you gonna do?" Bull Morrison chuckled.

"I'm gonna join you at the saloon for a cold beer and see if we can figure this mess out. There've been a couple of hundred laws broken over the last couple of weeks and we don't even know about others, more than likely." He took a long look at Bull, had to laugh at just how dirty the man was.

"I think I'm gonna send a bunch of wires to San Francisco, to Hank Churchill and to the attorney general's office, then we can have those cold beers. A hot bath wouldn't be out of the question either."

Buck Antonelli rode out to the doc's farmhouse and asked the old man who had been assigned to watch over things to help him get some hot water in a large wash tub in the kitchen. Peter Krebbe was nearing seventy, had come west well before the gold rush to California, worked as a buckaroo, deputy sheriff, hard rock miner, and bartender over the years.

"No problem, Marshal. You look like you've been in those duds for a couple of months."

"Not quite that long, but you're close."

He was still laughing as he sat in a chair next to the judge's bed. "You look like you're feeling better, Judge. You'll be glad to know that we have both of the men that kidnapped and killed your wife. They are in serious physical condition, may not live to stand trial, but they are in custody."

"I want those men hung as soon as possible. Strung up in front of me. Tomorrow morning would be too late as far as I'm concerned." Antonelli wondered if the man had any other temperament than rage. "I demand it, Marshal."

"You know as well as I that ain't gonna happen. After they get well enough to travel, they'll be moved to a federal holding facility for trial. That's gonna be a mess. The abduction took place in California, and the murder happened in Nevada Territory. Two jurisdictions.

"Coupled with all that, there are numerous local crimes committed in several jurisdictions. All that will have to be sorted out before any trials can take place. Will you be able to travel back to your home soon?"

"I'll not leave these foul creatures until I see them hung, their rotten bodies shoved underground, and only then will I be satisfied." He was shaking in his anger, his eyes burning holes in Emerson, who was in a bed at least fifteen feet away.

Sanctimonious bastard probably means that, too, Buck thought, trying to hold back a smile. *I see why Slim wanted me over here. That fool might just try to be judge, jury, and hangman all in one.* Another thought came to mind, one about how a man like Chastain even gets to be a federal judge. Buck Antonelli smiled and just let the thought fade away. Thoughts rumbled around and one particular one, from his mother, he thought, stuck out. *Don't try to change something you can't change or fix something that ain't broke.* He smiled. *I sure can't do nothing about this judge.*

"You and Marshal Morrison can work out those details, Judge. I think it would be best, since your injuries are almost healed, that you move from here to a hotel room in town."

"I'll not budge from that evil man's side," Chastain said, pointing at Gus Emerson who had been sat up, listening to the harangue. "You will hang," he howled across the room. Chastain stood up and started to walk toward the still seriously injured Emerson and Buck stopped him with an extended arm.

"Hold on there, Judge. We'll have none of that. Settle down, now."

"Don't you put your hands on me. Do you remember just who I am?" He shook Antonelli's hand off his arm, brought himself to full height and glared at the deputy marshal.

"I do know who you are, judge, but I also know that you know better than to interfere with a federal prisoner. Now, calm down or I'll be forced to do something I really don't want to do."

Chastain looked Antonelli over from head to toe and slowly allowed himself to be sat back down on his bed. He saw an older man with several days growth of beard, dirty from a long trail, eyes that said he would do what needed to be done, and hard hands capable of serious damage if called on.

He remembered that those were the hands of a U.S. Deputy Marshal, a man dedicated to his protection, dedicated to working for the court. Protector of the federal judicial system. But the rage wouldn't go away. "That man abducted and killed my wife," he all but screamed before slumping onto the bed.

"I know," Buck said, softly easing the judge down. Krebbe picked that moment to say the Marshal's hot water was ready. Buck motioned Krebbe back into the kitchen. "Keep a close eye on those two, Mr. Krebbe while I take a quick and needed bath. Chastain is almost out of control and he just might try to kill Emerson."

"There's something lacking in that man, Marshal. He thinks very highly of himself but has no thoughts for anyone around him. Everything is a demand, nothing is a request." Krebbe shook his head and walked into the ward area to keep the two men separated at all costs.

"I UNDERSTAND there might be a reason to keep these men separated, Marshal, but neither one is capable of doing anyone any damage." Doctor Trask was pleading to keep Emerson, Hawknose Mackenzie, and Purdy O'Neil in the same place. "It doesn't matter to me whether it be my home or the sheriff's, but they all need constant care and I can't be spending most of my day riding a horse back and forth between the two places."

"It's a fine argument, Doc," Morrison said. "I think you agree that it's too late today to worry about it. Which place would you prefer the most wounded be?" Bull Morrison rarely changed his mind, but the doctor's pleading made more sense than his argument.

"My place would be best. Move the judge into the sheriff's house along with the wounded deputy and anyone else that needs help."

"That would be Beartooth Johnson," Morrison said. "Okay, then, we'll make those changes first thing in the morning, depending on who is still alive. You must take into account the fact that we're dealing with men who are murderers, Doc. You only see them as human beings, but they would kill you in half a second if they thought it would help them escape."

"Yes, I prefer saving lives, Marshal, and I suppose you know more about outlaws than I ever will." He had the slightest smile, shook hands with Bull, and walked out of the sheriff's office to wend his way home. Morrison watched for a minute, grabbed his old hat and headed across the street to the saloon and supper with Slim Calhoun. A stop at the telegraph office took fifteen minutes. *Old man Churchill ain't gonna believe any of this.* He was chuckling as he wrote out his wire.

"GET the doc and our patients all straightened out?" Slim asked when Morrison joined him.

"He's a good man, Slim, but he's about as dumb as a chicken when it comes to outlaws. We'll move Hawknose in with Emerson, leave Buck Antonelli and Fitzgerald at the doc's to keep the prisoners under control and get Fitz fixed up, and move the judge over to the sheriff's place first thing in the morning. That's where I'm staying, too. At the sheriff's invitation," he chuckled.

"I bet," Calhoun laughed. "Invited while looking down the barrel of you revolver. I'll bunk up at the doc's, with or without an invitation. Are you sure you want Beartooth and the judge in the same house? This is a dilemma, eh? Keep Emerson and Hawknose apart. Keep Emerson and the judge apart. Keep Beartooth and the judge apart. Most of them too wounded to simply put them in jail cells where they all belong.

"How many wires did you send out?"

"Half a dozen. We'll have transportation coming in the next few days. Boys from Sacramento will take charge of the prisoners and get them moved. I'll be damn glad to get rid of the bunch.

"I'm also meeting with the territorial attorney in the morning. Most of what we've been through the last many days would not have happened if that sheriff had done his duty, and I'm filing charges in the morning."

"You've come a long way, Bull Morrison. Just a day or two ago you would have simply shot the man."

"I still might," he chuckled. "Pour me a glass full while I think about something you just said."

"About what?"

"About jail cells. Emerson and Beartooth are both well enough to be put in jail and Hawknose must be tended often, so he could stay at the doc's. Fitz needs care but doesn't need to be bed-ridden or anything like that. The judge is certainly well enough to be on his own. Hell, Slim, you just solved our biggest problem.

"Now, about that drink," he laughed.

CHAPTER 21

"YOU ARE NOT MOVING ME, MARSHAL. I WILL NOT BE TAKEN from those two killers. I'll not leave them before I see them hung, their necks broken, their final breaths taken." Judge Chastain was more than adamant, he was boiling with rage on a beautiful fall morning in the ward/living room of Doctor Trask's farmhouse.

"This isn't a request and it isn't your decision to make," Bull Morrison was just as adamant as the judge. "Emerson and Beartooth Johnson will spend the next several days in the Mormon Station jail, and you, sir, can stay where ever you wish. The doctor says you are more than well enough to fend for yourself. There are rooms at Mike and Dan's House and Saloon.

"The only people staying here are those seriously wounded and deputies to protect them. This is not open for debate. Now, sir, pack your things and make your arrangements in town."

Doctor Trask saw the impasse and tried to ease the situation. "Maybe you'd join me for a cup of tea, your honor, and we can have a little conversation. You're upset at losing your wife in such a brutal manner and it's more than under-standable." He looked at Morrison as if to say, back off now, and maybe I can get the old coot out of my house.

Morrison stood up, nodded to the doctor and walked over to where Slim Calhoun was chatting with Fitzgerald. "If I never see that man again," he said, sitting on the edge of the bed. "How you comin', Fitz?"

"I'm gonna live, Bull. No infection on the sliced-up cheek, bullet wound is healing, and it's only my pride that's wounded bad. I walked right up to that Indian like a damn fool, Bull."

"Aw, hell, Fitz, every single one of us has done some-thing like that at least once. Besides, think of how many really good stories you'll be able to tell about that scar." He looked around the room and ran his fingers slowly down the length of scar on his own face. "Speaking of stories, Slim, how is Beartooth doing?"

"He's in jail, so we don't have to worry about him. Figured out how to get the rest of today worked out? Still planning on putting Emerson in jail before moving Hawknose over here?" Morrison could see worry in Calhoun's face and hear it in his voice.

"That's the plan. Just as soon as we get the judge out of here, I want you, and Buck to escort Gus Emerson to the jail. Emerson is well enough to ride but I want you boys to walk him over. He's just stupid enough to try an escape. We'll have to move Hawknose by wagon, though."

"Where's Buck now?" Slim Calhoun asked.

"He's at the jail with Josh Henry and Owens. Cliff Martin is meeting with the county commissioners and I have to meet with the attorney general and then talk with the commissioners. All of this because one man would not do his duty. None of this would have taken place if Rogers had formed a posse and chased Emerson down after he killed that man in Carson City.

"Well, so much for that," Morrison snickered. "I'm off. Keep me informed, Slim. Buy me whiskey if you hear a ruckus downtown." He was laughing as he headed out the door. "We're meeting at the jail, by the way."

IT TOOK some fast talking but Doctor Trask had Judge Lemuel Chastain calmed down enough to get him to the hotel. "You'll feel much better, Judge, after a good meal and a taste or two of brandy. The marshals are very good at what they do, and justice will be served."

"Thank you, Doctor. I'll not forget your kindness." He had sat quietly at the kitchen table drinking the good doctor's tea, planning how to make sure those killers got their due, that is, a hangman's noose. *I don't trust that Marshal Morrison for a second and I want those men hung, their necks stretched past the breaking point.*

He had a slight smile on his face as he shook hands with Trask and stepped toward the buggy the doctor provided. "I'm sure I haven't been the easiest patient you've ever had, but I want you to know I appreciate your fine work."

If either Bull Morrison or Slim Calhoun had been there, either or both would have known the judge was up to something. He had acquiesced to the doctor's suggestions with a slimy ease, they would have said.

Doctor Trask helped him into the buggy for the short ride to Mike and Dan's House and had two men to help get the judge and all his belongings settled there. Trask wondered, as he drove the buggy back to his place how it was so easy to convince the judge to make this move. The judge was either angry to excess or calm as the eye of a hurricane. It was the calm that predicted danger, not the anger.

"One minute the man was in a wild rage and the next he was fully convinced that the move to the hotel would be the best." The murmuring continued all the way home and in to the kitchen where he poured a cup of tea for himself. "That man's an enigma," he said, sitting down at the table.

"Got a problem, Doc?" Slim said, coming in for some coffee. "I'd think you would be ecstatic getting that man out of here."

"I should be, yes, Marshal, but I'm not. He was a blustering fool one minute and then acquiescent as a kitten the next. Judge Chastain, I'm afraid, is a very disturbed man." Calhoun had to agree.

"I'm not sure how I would behave if I had a loving wife abducted and murdered by the likes of Emerson and Mackenzie. Bull has suggested from time to time that my fuse is mighty short," he laughed.

The doctor laughed right out. "He would certainly be the man to know about short fuses, my friend."

"THOSE MARSHALS ARE NOT GOING to do their job. They are not going to hang those two men who ravaged and killed my wife." Judge Chastain thundered the words through the saloon. He was standing at the near end of the long bar, challenging the drinkers of the town to do the right thing. The barman was enjoying the spectacle, pouring more drinks than he had in some time.

The muttering started with his first drink of brandy, and with each sip through that first glass, got louder and louder. Judge Chastain was on his third glass of brandy, the muttering evolved into long, loud rants, bringing most of the mid-day crowd to his end of the bar. He talked directly to them and within a short of amount of time had them convinced that they were his only answer to getting the job done right.

He was fearless in his accusations, telling in great detail the abduction of his beautiful and loving wife, the horrible things those two men, devils incarnate, had done to her before brutally killing her.

"Those two men robbed me of the one thing in my life that I cherished, my dear and precious wife, Abigail. Those villains need to be hung, not well cared for in some heated jail cell. Strung up by their necks until dead." He thundered the demand, thumping the bar with a ham sized fist.

The crowd was answering him back, loud, strong, giving it back to him.

"Hang the bastards," rung out, chorus after chorus. "Hang the murdering fools," could be heard throughout the large building. The judge didn't let up, either, bellowing out, time and again, "These men need to be hung, today."

He had them riled, had their blood burning as his was, and knew that he could march them to the jail and do the justice that sorely needed to be done. "One at a time, he yelled, those fiends will hang from the giant cottonwood tree that stands in front of this very hotel."

The crowd, well-fortified with strong liquor, was ready to march on the jail. "We'll take Emerson first," Chastain yelled out. "Then march on the doctor's and hang Hawknose Mackenzie, too."

The barman had seen ugly crowds before, knew this was not going to simply die out, that men would die and soon. From the glee of selling drink after drink to the knowledge that men would die, he had a change of heart. He called one of the working girls over and sent her to the jail to get help.

"Hurry, Mabel, hurry," he whispered, aiming her for the back door.

"I'll get ropes," one man called out, "and a wagon. We can hang them both from the big cottonwood in the center of town." A great cheer went up and several of the men started for the door.

"Let the judge lead us," someone called out. "That sheriff is so cowardly he'd never shoot a judge. Hell, he won't even shoot murderers."

Laughter and cheers echoed through the building, and Judge Chastain, shaking his fist in the air, bellowed, "Follow me."

MABEL CONTRERAS RAN AS FAST as her fat little legs would let her and burst into the jail completely out of breath. Deputy Owens jumped from the chair behind the sheriff's desk. "Mabel, what's wrong?"

"They're going to kill him," she shrieked, grabbing Owens and trying to get him to run out the door."

"Who's going to kill him?" Who's going to kill who?" He was stammering.

Bull Morrison and Buck Antonelli were back in the cell areas with Emerson and heard all the commotion. "What's going on?" Morrison yelled, and the two came running into the office.

"Calm down, Mabel. Please, calm down," Owens said. "Calm down and tell us what's going on."

"That judge, he's coming here to kill the murderers. He's bringing everyone with him." She was shaking in fear, breathing hard from her run and slumped into a chair. "They're coming here."

"Oh, my God," Morrison said. "That damned fool.

Owens, take my horse and hightail it to the doc's and bring Slim and Fitz back here on the double. Buck, let's you and me grab some shotguns and stand our ground."

"With you, Bull," Antonelli said walking to the gun cabinet to get guns and shells. "We should have anticipated this, I guess. That man's completely out of control."

Owens was out the door and off to the doc's on Morrison's horse, and Bull and Buck were standing just outside the jail house door, shotguns in hand. There were at least ten men, yelling and screaming, boiling out of the saloon, led by Federal Judge Lemuel Chastain.

"Let's stop them when they're in the middle of the street, Bull. It'll give us room to control them."

"Good, and let's not let them get any closer than fifty feet from us. These scatter guns will get a good spread at that distance. Won't kill 'em but sure will stop 'em," he laughed. They spread out about fifteen feet from each other and held their weapons at the ready. "I can't understand most what's been going on," Bull mumbled, "and what's happening right now surely takes the full bottle. A federal judge leading a vigilante attack on federal marshals.

"Do you know what's even worse? " he said to Buck, "we're supposed to be here to protect him and one of us might have to shoot the judge we've sworn to protect." Buck just shook his head, tried to concentrate on the crowd moving slowly toward them, noisy, drunk, and dangerous. Bull Morrison was cussing a blue streak, using words Buck hadn't heard since the Mexican war in Texas.

Then, Morrison got quiet. "When I left the doc's," Morrison said so softly Buck had trouble hearing. "That fool was drinking hot tea with the doctor, telling him that he was fine, knew the law would take care of the killers, and not to worry. You're right, Buck, I should have anticipated something like this.

"No matter what else happens in the next few minutes, Buck, don't let me kill the judge. My God what a mess and all because of that damned fool sheriff. It'll be okay, Buck, if I shoot the sheriff. Remember that." He was growling by the end of his little speech and took a step off the boardwalk and onto the muddy street, shotgun cocked and ready.

"That's far enough, Judge," he bellowed at the crowd. "Stop!" He pulled the shotgun up to his shoulder and let the barrel swing slowly back and forth, left to right, across the crowd. Every man got at least one glimpse of the gun pointed directly at him. "The next man to step forward is a dead man."

The shouting and yelling quieted down immediately. There's something about looking death square the face that tends to sober one up. "Judge, you're making the biggest mistake of your life, if you take one more step toward me." Bull Morrison was snarling mad, that scar across his face crimson and ugly.

"You men go home. Go back to your drinking. Get off this street now," and he lowered the shotgun and fired off one barrel at their feet. "The next round goes into you, gentlemen."

Buck Antonelli stood slightly separated from Morrison and had his shotgun to his shoulder, moving it as Bull had, aiming into the faces of the men, while Bull ejected the spent shell and reloaded.

"You won't shoot me or any of these men, Marshal. We're going to see to it that those killers get their just due. You won't do your duty, Marshal, which is to hang those murderers, so step aside and let us do what needs to be done."

Judge Chastain thundered and shook his fist at Morrison, opened his frock coat to show he was unarmed.

"Hang those men!" He screamed the words, and the crowd surged a step forward. Buck Antonelli fired one round at about ankle level into the left side of the crowd, watching three men scream in pain and fall to the muddy ground, writhing in agony.

Except for the injured men's crying in pain, the main street of Mormon Station was as quiet as death itself. Morrison took a step forward and slapped Judge Chastain across the side of the head, sending the man sprawling into the mud, next to the wounded men. "Fomenting a riot is against the law, Chastain."

He stepped back, saw that Buck still had that scattergun to his shoulder and waved his back and forth. "You men have broken the law at the behest of a federal judge, and several of you are wounded because of that. If you are not wounded, get off the street now. If I see anyone on the street two minutes from now, I will shoot him dead."

The men saw their compadres shot down, saw their leader slapped up the side of his head, and saw a U.S. Marshal willing to shoot. They broke ranks and stampeded down the street, some into the saloon, most heading for anywhere they couldn't be seen.

"You, sir, come with me," Bull Morrison said to Chastain. Buck Antonelli swore Morrison was almost crying as he said it. He watched a U.S. Marshal slap a man down, a man he was dedicated to protect. Morrison reached down and helped the judge to his feet and walked him, gently, to the jail.

Slim Calhoun and Fitzgerald came riding up from the doc's in time to see Morrison escort Chastain into the sheriff's office. Buck was standing in the middle of the street, prodding three men with bleeding legs and ankles toward the jail with his shotgun. "Let's help those men, Fitz. We're right behind you, Buck," Calhoun called out, jumping down from his horse.

"Anything else you can think of that might go wrong, let me know," Fitz said. His face hurt like hell, but it didn't slow him down any and he jerked two of the wounded to their bleeding feet and urged them into the jail. Calhoun had to help the other who was hurt more seriously.

"Put those men all in the same cell back there," Morrison said. "Well away from Emerson. They can doctor each other for all I care. I ain't calling the doc." He had Judge Chastain sitting in a chair and pulled one up directly in front of the jurist. "Vigilante justice, your honor? I don't know whether to lock you up or shoot you." He pulled his coat aside to flash that big U.S. Marshal's badge in the judge's face.

"See that? President George Washington created this service and gave it the job of protecting the judicial system including members of the judiciary. You, sir, are a disgrace to that judiciary. And yet, I will honor my duty to you." No one in that room had ever seen Bull Morrison that humble, almost beaten. So dedicated to his profession and having it flung in his face as filthy dung might.

Slim, standing next to the pot belly stove was sure that he could see tears forming in the marshals eyes and had to look away. "I've never felt so low in all my life as I do at this moment," Morrison whispered. "I have ridden for some of the finest, strongest, most honest jurists in the world, and now, have been forced to knock one to the ground and threaten the man with arrest."

Chastain hadn't moved since being roughly seated, and just stared into space. Did he hear what Morrison was saying? Did it register that what he had done was a flagrant violation of, not just the law, but his own office? No one in that room could tell by looking at the man. Was he mad with power or had he simply lost his mind from the grief of losing his wife?

Marshal Bull Morrison bowed his head, his chin almost resting on his massive chest and took three deep breaths. Finally, he stood up and walked across the room to look out a window facing the main street. "What do we do, Slim? He's a disgrace to the system, should be removed from his position, but I can't bring myself to arrest him."

This was a side of Bull Morrison that few men had ever witnessed. The soft side, the part of him that made him human. Compassion, heartfelt feelings, not for Chastain the man but for what he should stand for, now a fallen idol. "He has put all of us in danger, Slim, the men we arrested because they assaulted and killed his wife are in danger, even those innocently walking the streets of Mormon Station are in danger.

"Some fool, believing this old codger could start shooting up the town, Slim, shooting into the jail, into Doc's place. I can't bring myself to arrest him and I know that's what needs to be done."

Morrison stood up and walked back to stand in front of the judge. "Damn you, Chastain. Damn you." He walked behind the desk and opened the drawer where that flask sat waiting. After taking a mighty pull, he sat back and stared at the judge.

Slim thought that if anyone did anything the least bit out of line right now, Bull would beat the hell out them first and then shoot them with fifty or more rounds. "Take another pull on that flask, Bull, and then let's sort this out."

Calhoun had to change the mood, get back on target, bring Bull back to the raging terror he normally was.

"Emerson is safe until the escort detail gets here. Doc insists on keeping Hawknose Mackenzie at his place, making him unsafe. That dumb tracker man is locked up safe, too. Fitz is well enough to move around and fight, and that deputy Martin wasn't that badly wounded to start with. Let's bunker up at the doc's.

"We can have Antonelli, Owens, and Josh Henry here to protect the prisoners, and you, me, Fitz, and Purdy O'Neil at the doc's protecting Hawknose and the judge. That escort should be here in three days. I don't think there's any threat from those townsmen. I think the judge got 'em drunk and riled and it's over."

"Good, Slim." Morrison was sitting up straight in that old cane-back chair and poured another shot into his cup. "I think you're right about those in this village. I want you and Fitz to take the judge back to Doc's and send Martin and Henry back here. Buck, I want you and Owens to hold the fort till they get here then bunker up."

"Where are you going?" Slim knew Bull had something in mind.

"First, I'm going to the saloon and lay the law down. Then I'm going to walk this town, street for street, and then I'll meet you at the doc's." Slim just nodded, smiled some, and nudged the judge to his feet.

CHAPTER 22

"Bull's in trouble, Marshal." The deputy brought two wires to the chief Marshal of the Pacific division. "He's in Nevada Territory and I think he needs help. It looks like the first one was sent several hours before the second."

Chief Marshal Hank Churchill, a twenty-year veteran of the service, took the wires and read them both. He put them down and looked at Deputy Marshal Terry Mulvaney, then turned his attention back to his desk. "We've seen this coming, Terry. Bring me the open files on Judge Chastain and send a wire back to Bull, telling him to take whatever steps are necessary to control the situation."

Terry Mulvaney hustled out of the office and Churchill wrote out an order to place Federal District Judge Lemuel Chastain in custody. Mulvaney was back with the thick file in minutes. Churchill looked through a few of the pages.

"There are still questions concerning the selling of those Spanish Grant lands near Santa Cruz that haven't been answered, but forming a vigilante group, causing a near riot, is more than I can accept. Take this order to the U.S. Attorney along with copies of the wires from Morrison.

"There isn't anything we can do about that county sheriff, that's purely a local matter, so send another wire to Bull to make sure he understands that. I understand his strong feelings on the matter, but he can't simply remove the man from office. He knows that, he just needs a little prod from me," Churchill chuckled. "I rode with that man for more than a year, Mulvaney, and, my friend, I survived."

BULL MORRISON'S boots were thumping as he strode down the main street in Mormon Station, walked around a massive cottonwood tree and into Mike and Dan's House Saloon. "Barman, pour me a glass of whiskey and then close this saloon until further notice."

"You can't do that," Spike Jensen said. He walked down to where Morrison stood. "You don't have that kind of authority, Marshal."

Bull reached across the bar and pulled Jensen across, dumping him on the filthy floor. "Yes, I do," he barked. He walked around the bar and poured a glass full of whiskey, laid a cartwheel on the wooden plank, and stood staring at three men standing at the bar. "Out," he said, and swiped their glasses away, letting them break on the floor.

"You three, at the tables back there, out," he commanded. "Now, Mr. Barman, do you understand my authority?"

"I do," Jensen whimpered.

"Good. Lock those doors until further notice. If I should find someone inside this saloon, I will shoot him dead. Understand?" He drank the glass of whiskey in two gulps and walked out onto the street, a broad smile across his scarred and ugly face. It was a long walk to the courthouse on the north end of town, and back south to the sheriff's office. He didn't see a soul on the street and turned to walk to the telegraph office.

"Glad you're here, Marshal. This just came for you. Looks like that blow-hard judge is in trouble. He still owes me for his last batch of wires he sent."

"Thank you, Mr. Peters. He owes more than that, I'm afraid." Peters watched Morrison's face change to almost friendly as he read the wires. "Thank you very much." Morrison walked back to the jail to have a chat with Chastain.

"I want you to read this yourself, Chastain. It's from the U.S. Attorney in San Francisco authorizing me to place you under arrest for these shenanigans. A detail has been sent to escort you back and hold you for trial." He handed two telegrams to the judge and wandered back into the cell area, took a turn and came back into the office.

"Can't put you back there," he snickered. "Emerson in one cell and Beartooth in another, either one willing to kill you on sight. The other cell taken up by the three hooligans who got themselves all shot up believing your nonsense." Chastain had not said one word since being brought into the office several hours ago and simply stared straight ahead.

"For a man who rants and raves at the slightest provocation, you're mighty quiet, Chastain. I hope you're giving thought to just how much trouble you're in. I understand how angry you were at losing your wife to these outlaws. It's a horrible loss for any man, but it certainly doesn't justify what you've done. Every federal judge will feel the impact of your behavior. You know that, don't you?"

Morrison's anger was building as he talked, and he knew he had to calm himself, remain rational, and simply do his duty. He couldn't help wondering why the judge was so quiet, almost as if nothing around him existed. Morrison poured some coffee and stood in front of the judge, staring but not glaring.

Chastain had been a devious man his entire life, never working things in a straight line, always edging off to the side for a hidden benefit of some kind. That's how he got around having to pay Beartooth the bounty he had promised. Was he being quiet for a reason? Did he have yet something else in mind to hurt or kill these outlaws who abducted, defiled, and killed his wife?

"I was wrong, Marshal. I'll not say anything more."

"We'll be taking you to Doctor Trasks for safe keeping until your escort arrives. You are a prisoner, sir, and you will do exactly as you're told. It pains me more than you would understand, but you will have to be restrained at all times. Stand up, please," Morrison said and put Chastain's hands behind his back and attached handcuffs. "Any attempt to escape or create confusion will bring immediate response from my deputies. Is that understood?"

Chastain simply nodded, stood rigidly erect, and let Morrison lead him out onto the office porch where Owens had the buggy drawn up. He helped get the judge up onto the seat, walked to his horse and mounted for the short ride to Trasks' place. "Follow me, Owens, and keep your eyes wide open. I don't trust anyone in this town."

Deputies Martin and Henry met them on the ride. "Everything set at Doc's?"

Josh Henry nodded. "We'll lock up the jail. Tight as possible, Marshal."

"While we're all here, I want to make this perfectly clear. We're using county facilities, but you members of the sheriff's office are under the command of the U.S. Marshal. Me. You will do what my deputies tell you to do. Henry, you've been working with Buck Antonelli and he has high praise for your work. You stick close to Buck and be his number two."

"Yes, sir," Henry said, and Morrison noticed the frown from Martin but didn't say anything. "All right, Owens, let's get moving."

BUCK ANTONELLI WALKED BACK into the cell area to check on the prisoners and found one of those suffering shotgun wounds to be crying out in pain. "What's the problem here?" He stood outside the steel bars and spoke to the man's cell mates.

"I think one of those deer slugs broke a bone, Marshal. He's in awful pain."

How many times has Buck Antonelli seen this little act play out? Open the cell to inspect the man's wounds, get attacked by his compadres and lose all your prisoners and maybe your life. "Shoulda thought about that before chargin' at me," Antonelli said. "You, cryin' boy, stand up."

The man eased up with his moans and groans, sat up on the little cot, and tried to stand up. Antonelli saw the pain cross the man's face and watched him fall back onto the straw mattress. "All right, as soon as Owens get back with that buggy, we'll work on getting you to the doc. One false move from either of you two," he said, pointing his finger as a gun, "and it will be all over. Bang, bang."

Martin and Henry came in to report to Antonelli. "Marshal says you're the boss," Josh Henry said, and I'm supposed to work close with you."

"Good. Old Beartooth giving them hell out there?"

"Same man tellin' the same stories," Henry laughed.

"We got a hurt man back there or we have three

conniving outlaws looking to make an escape. Here's what we do, gentlemen. Martin, you will leave your weapon out here and while Josh and I stand guard with our weapons drawn, you will bring the injured man out of the cell and into the office. Questions?"

"How'd he get injured?" Martin asked.

"I shot him," Antonelli chuckled. "We'll send him out to doc's place when Owens gets back. Let's go."

Antonelli waved his revolver around a bit, moving the two prisoners away from the one with the broken leg. "Just one little move is all it'll take and since all three of you have already been shot by me once, you know I ain't joshin'. Move back now."

If there had been an escape plan, Buck's moves eliminated the idea and the wounded man was moved to a chair near the wood stove in the office. "You got a name other than stupid?" Buck was down on one knee looking at the wound, just above the ankle. "Looks like two of those chunks of buckshot hit your leg bone at the same place."

"Name's Adams, Charley Adams. You didn't have no call to shoot me, mister."

"First off, Mr. Adams, I ain't a mister. I'm Deputy U.S. Marshal Antonelli. Don't forget that. And second, you were told not to move and instead you charged right at me. I'll stick with stupid, I think. Got a family?"

"He's married with two children," Josh Henry said. "They live on the Frankmore property, north of town. Adams does pick-up work around town and Mrs. Adams cooks for the Frankmores."

"Deputy Martin, why don't you run out there and tell Mrs. Adams that stupid here won't be coming home for supper for some time." Antonelli didn't say so but wondered if maybe Mrs. Adams might just like getting that message. "How about those other two back there? They got families?"

"I never saw the one with the black eye and beard. The other one works cattle for the Dreyfus ranch. He ain't married that I know of," Martin said.

"All right, then, get out to Frankmore's and keep an eye out for any kind of trouble that might be brewing. Damn that judge," Antonelli said.

JUDGE CHASTAIN HAD manacles on his ankles and around a table leg in the kitchen and was having a cup of hot tea, planning his next move. He lost an opportunity to have Emerson killed by that mob but was now within striking distance of Hawknose Mackenzie, the man who was so rude to Victoria, so vicious during the hold up. If he could keep his temper under control, maybe he would find a way to drive a knife deep into Mackenzie's heart.

"It isn't really necessary to chain me up like this, Doctor. I'm an old man, surely you know I couldn't possibly run away." The words poured like honey from a bucket, and the man's eyes seemed to plead for mercy. "It's most uncomfortable."

"I'm sure it is but what Bull Morrison says goes around here, Judge." Doctor Trask looked over at Purdy O'Neil for verification. "Isn't that right, Mr. O'Neil?" Doc Trask was more than happy to have Purdy in the kitchen with him after hearing about Chastain leading a vigilante mob.

"My orders are plain as day, Doctor," Purdy smiled. "One stupid move by the judge and I shoot him. This is gonna be a long three days I'm afraid. There was mention of another storm coming down from the north and I sure do hope it don't slow those boys down that are coming to pick you up, Judge."

Chastain sat quiet and watched Doctor Trask boil bandages and hang them to dry, watched Purdy add wood to the stove and make fresh coffee, and saw Deputy Owens leave for his ride back to the jail. There would be time, he thought. He'll have three days in which to figure out how to get a knife deep into Hawknose Mackenzie.

Owens got back to the jail about the same time that Martin and Mrs. Adams arrived. "Hello, Mrs. Adams," he said, stepping down from the buggy. "Martin? What's going on?"

"Charley's one of them got shot and Mrs. Adams wants to see him. You'll probably be making another run out to Trasks place." Martin escorted Mrs. Adams into the jail and was followed by Owens.

"Mary-Ellen, what are you doing here? You shouldn't be here," Charley Adams said. She rushed to his side and Buck Antonelli stepped in front, holding her back.

"Whoa up there, lady." He spun on Deputy Martin. "Who is this?"

"Mrs. Adams insisted on coming to see her husband." He stood there shaking his head, almost wringing his hands. "She insisted, Marshal."

"You don't know how to say no? Damn." Antonelli took the woman by the arm and walked her to the door of the jail. "Go home. Your husband is under arrest for attempted murder among other charges. Go home." He led her off the wooden porch, turned and came back onto the porch.

"Where will you take him?" She asked, tears running down her cheeks.

"He's been shot and will be treated at Doctor Trasks and then brought back here and held for trial. Go home and take care of your children." Antonelli was an old-line marshal who felt prisoners were to be kept isolated at all times until their trial. To bring the man's wife to the jail was out of line.

"That was stupid, Martin. Did you even check to see if she had a weapon?" Antonelli was angry and frustrated with what was happening. *Now I know why Bull acts the way he does. We have a jail full of stupid people and half of them are deputies.* He had to chuckle and walked to the stove for some coffee.

"All right, then, let's get this yahoo trussed up and in the buggy. Owens, I want you to drive him out to the doc's place. Martin, I asked you to keep an eye open for problems. Anything?"

"No," is all Martin said. He rode with the Marshals, helped bring Mackenzie in, fought off Indians with the marshals, and was being treated like a little kid by this Marshal Antonelli. He walked to the cell area to get Adams's coat and hat and came back with a sullen look on his face.

Owens was on one side and Josh Henry the other, and they manipulated Adams out the door and down off the porch. He helped himself climbing into the buggy. He hadn't said a word after seeing his wife hustled out of the office. "What will happen to Mary-Ellen?" He asked, his eyes were teared up and his voice choked.

"I understand she's cooking for a family, has a place to live." Antonelli kicked some dust around, and finally just let it all out. "That, my stupid friend is what you should have been thinking before listening to that fool judge. Your wife and children should have been more important than joining that damn mob. Stupid!" He found himself shouting in the man's face and turned and walked away.

"Get him out of here before I shoot him." He had to

snicker walking into the jail. *I'm even sounding like Bull. Fitz is looking like Bull and I'm acting like him. I'll sure be glad when this damn job is done.*

"Looks like Owens is coming back, Bull." Purdy O'Neil stuck his head into the ward area. "Has someone with him."

Bull Morrison nodded, looked to Fitz to back him and stepped out onto the porch. Martin stepped off his horse and helped tie off the buggy before helping Charley Adams down. "Gonna need help getting him in, Marshal. Has a broken leg."

Morrison turned and nodded to Fitz that everything was okay and helped Owens and Martin get Adams in and laid out on the so-called operating table. "Got another one for you, Doc," Morrison called out. "Purdy, you stay with the judge and keep that coffee coming our way."

"I hope you boys get the hell out of this area soon," Doc Trask mumbled, ripping the pants off Adams. "I've never worked this hard in my life." He spent several minutes cleaning up the nasty wound and in one quick move that brought a howl from Adams, set the bones back in place.

"Would have been nice if someone had put a splint on this," the doc growled. He made up a mess that turned out to be a cast for the leg and told Adams not to put any pressure on that leg if he wanted to keep it.

Martin, Owens, and Fitz moved him onto a bed and cuffed him to it. "What did Buck say about him?" Morrison stood at the foot of the bed looking at one sad outlaw.

"Deputy Antonelli said he was charged with contributing to a riot and attempted murder," Martin said.

"You're sounding rather stiff, there, Martin. Something in your craw?" Morrison's thoughts on the man hadn't changed from the times in the canyon. That lack of confidence hadn't left him.

Martin didn't answer, just walked out to join Owens. "Let's get back to the jail," he said mounting up.

Judge Chastain was brought back to his bed and cuffed to it. "It isn't necessary to do that," he said. "I can't possibly escape."

"You're right. You can't possibly escape," Bull Morrison chuckled. "Fitz, you and Purdy keep a close eye on these yahoos. Me and Slim got some work to do down at the jail. Hawknose and this idiot with the broken leg won't give you no trouble but be very careful of the judge.

"Come on Slim, we got some training to do

CHAPTER 23

"JUST WHAT KIND OF TRAINING DO YOU HAVE IN MIND, BULL?" The two were riding slowly back into town, feeling the wind picking up and the temperature falling. "You're worried about something, eh?"

"Yeah, and I can't put my finger on it. Chastain is being cagey as hell and he'll do something before his escort arrives, but that ain't what's on my mind. It's the sheriff that's got me riled right now. We haven't heard a peep from that man since I sent him home. Hank Churchill reminded me that I can't simply fire the man or even relieve him, so after we have a talk with Antonelli, we need to visit Matt Rogers."

"He doesn't strike me as the kind of man who would willingly get Involved in something, legal or otherwise. He likes the title as long as there isn't any work attached."

Morrison laughed right out. "He sure ain't. I'm wondering if he hasn't said something to either Martin or Owens. Those two are doing what we ask and nothing more. They are not willingly doing their jobs as lawmen in this county."

"They've been working for Rogers too long, Bull. Owens is a slacker all the way and Martin wants to be sheriff so bad he's willing to slack off to make Rogers look bad. They'll not do anything they aren't first told to do. Rogers wouldn't form a posse to chase Emerson, wouldn't help in our chase to catch Emerson and Mackenzie, why would you think his deputies would volunteer to do something?"

"That's why you work for me, Calhoun. Smart," he said. "We've got at least three days before the rest of the gang shows up to relieve us. What would you suggest?"

"You're the Marshal, Bull, but if it was my play, I'd put the sheriff back at the jail with Martin and Owens. They would be holding Emerson, Beartooth, and the two wounded fellers. Pull Antonelli and Henry back with us at Doc's place. I think Judge Chastain is our biggest worry, not Martin or the town people."

"I think you're right. That Martin can get in my craw just as fast as that sheriff, and I would bet he wouldn't be good back-up."

"You gotta remember that he was, back on the trail." Slim Calhoun smiled, remembering that Martin took a bullet back then as did Fitzgerald. "He fought hard, Bull."

They pulled their horses up to the rail and stepped down. "He's just spent too much time with Rogers," Slim said. "You expect everyone who wears a badge to be up to your standards, old man. There're only a few like Buck and Fitz around, you know."

"And you, Calhoun. Don't start that crap." They walked into the office and Slim saw the grim look on Bull's face and knew it would be a short meeting. Morrison looked around and saw that Antonelli was back in the cell area with Josh Henry and Martin and Owens were playing cards near the wood stove.

He nodded at the two and walked back to find Buck Antonelli. Slim walked to the stove, found a cup and filled it with boiling coffee. "Anybody walked the streets recently?"

Neither man responded in any way. Slim took a step back and kicked the table hard enough to send cards, coins, and coffee cups sailing. The table didn't splinter but it did tumble across the floor. Both men jumped to their feet in surprise, which turned to anger quickly.

"What the hell you do that for?" Martin barked. "Damn fool thing to do."

"Just a few hours ago there was a rowdy mob outside that door there," Slim barked right back at him. "and it wasn't controlled until at least three men were wounded by gunfire. You two are supposed to be the law and order in town, not lazy damn card sharks shucking your duty.

"Your jail, Mr. Martin, is holding two federal prisoners and two local prisoners who are also wounded. You want to be sheriff but you ain't no better than the lazy dog holding that office right now. Get your act together, son, or turn that badge in so a real lawman can wear it."

"Ain't no call to talk to me like that," Martin snarled, and his hand moved toward his sidearm. Before his fingers made contact, he was staring down the barrel of Calhoun's.

"Don't ever make that mistake again," Slim said, uncocking his revolver and slowly slipping it back in its leather. "Now get your skinny butt out there and walk those streets. Owens, clean this mess up and when Martin gets back you take your turn around town. We gotta keep the lid on this until the travel detail arrives. Don't make me say it again."

Martin slipped into his heavy wool coat and slunk out the door while Owens put the table back upright and started picking up the mess on the floor. Calhoun hid a little smile and walked back into the cell area. *Made that a little stronger than it needed to be but damn me, I've never seen lazy men like there are around this town. This town needs about fifteen pretty, single, girls walking about. These boys would be mighty busy trying to get their attention.* He was chuckling some when he found Morrison in Emerson's cell.

"Is there a problem?"

"No, I'm just trying to get the full story on the holdup and their activities afterward." Bull stood up, nodded to Emerson, and came out of the cell. "Ain't no way we could have saved Mrs. Chastain. They were that far in front of Al Bellows. Emerson killed her, then killed that man in Carson City. It was Hawknose that shot the messenger and then killed the miner here.

"They're gonna have to be hung two or three times, each. What was all the commotion out front?"

"Training the men," Calhoun snickered.

"Let's go find the sheriff and bring him back here. Buck, you and Henry be ready to come with us to Doc's place."

Antonelli nodded, smiled, and muttered, "Training, eh?"

"SHERIFF," Morrison hollered through the door. He had banged on it a couple of times without any response. "We need to talk, Sheriff, now answer the damn door." He stepped back and Calhoun was sure he was about to kick the door into splinters when it slowly opened.

"Yes, what is it," the tiniest little voice asked. The door was opened just a crack and Bull reached out and pushed it fully open, giving him a look at a lovely girl of about fifteen or so.

"Pardon, us, ma'am," he almost stuttered. He stepped

back, doffed his hat, and looked like a little kid in trouble. Calhoun laughed and Morrison scowled at him, getting back under control. "I'm Marshal Morrison and we're looking for the sheriff."

"He's probably down at the saloon, Marshal."

"Thank you, kindly," Bull said, a slight bow, and he turned on his heel motioning Slim to follow. "He say anything to you about having a daughter?"

"Nor a lovely companion," Slim laughed. "I think if a charming lady like that was at my home I would not be at the saloon. I thought you said you closed that place."

"I thought I did. Mr. Jensen probably just assumed the sheriff could reopen what I closed. Don't let me shoot the sheriff, Slim."

"We still on the same plan?"

"Far as I'm concerned, we are. We'll tell him to take his office back, to keep control of our prisoners, pick up Buck Antonelli and Josh Henry, and go back to Doc's." He snickered. "If I can control my temper."

Along with the sheriff, there were probably ten men having drinks at the bar or playing cards at one of the tables when the two marshals walked in. "Thought I told you to keep this place closed, Jensen," Morrison growled.

"Sheriff said to open it up, Marshal. That would be between you two. You can kindly leave me out of your problems. Whiskey is it?"

"Yes, it is and fill the glass." He took his glass of whiskey to the back of the saloon where Sheriff Rogers was holding down a table. "Like to have a word with you, Rogers."

Rogers nodded to an empty chair and pulled a cigar out to light. "Sit down, Marshal. Heard that judge gave your boys a bit of trouble."

"Not as much as your boys have given me," Morrison said. "Got word from the chief marshal in San Francisco that you should remain sheriff until the county commission decides what to do about your incompetence. I'm pulling Antonelli and Henry and leaving you, Martin and Owens.

"I have a troop of marshals due in in three days to escort my prisoners to a federal holding facility. I'm making you responsible for the safety of Emerson and Beartooth Johnson. Do you understand?"

Rogers looked around the saloon and saw that most eyes were on their table. Many of those present were on the street just hours ago, had been fully behind the judge, willing to whisk Emerson out of that jail and string him up. The sheriff played his hand.

"I've understood you right from the moment we met, Marshal. You're a bully who struts and demands and it's your boys that do the work. I ain't putting my boys at risk to protect your prisoners." He looked around the crowd, got a slight smile on his face, nodding to one or two of them. "If some of these men decide to see to it that justice is served, well, that's how it is. Why don't you just haul your prisoners out of my jail, out of my jurisdiction, for that matter."

Slim was standing off to the side and took two fast steps up to the table, his revolver in hand. "That's called inciting, Sheriff." He turned to the crowd at the bar. "Any man make a move on one of our prisoners or one of the Deputy U.S. Marshals, will either die or spend years in federal lock-up.

"Would you like to recant some of what you just said, Sheriff? Maybe some of those words didn't come out quite the way you wanted them to." Calhoun took a quick look at Bull Morrison and knew that he just saved the sheriff's life. Morrison was easing himself back into his chair, easing his sidearm back in its leather, and the hatred in his eyes burned like coal embers in a hot stove.

"No, I don't think he does, Slim." Morrison sat motionless for a moment, then stood up and slowly turned to the crowd. "Charley Adams will be leaving his wife and children shortly to spend several years in a federal prison. Two other men, they too may have wives and children, I don't know, are sitting in that jail over there, and will be joining Mr. Adams.

"Mr. Emerson is going to hang for his crimes, but not before he gets a fair trial. The evidence is overwhelming, but that man will get his trial. We have before us, then, another slight predicament. How many of you men are willing to join Mr. Adams? Think very carefully about that. Think of your family, your wife and children, think of your business, or the company you work for.

"One stupid move on your part can destroy more than just your worthless life. My prisoners will remain safe, and many of you may end up as prisoners or be dead."

Faster than Slim Calhoun had ever seen him move, Bull Morrison jerked his revolver out and slapped Sheriff Rogers across the side of the head, sending him sprawling onto the filthy floor, bleeding, and crying out. "You, sir, are under arrest for attempting to incite a riot. Threatening the lives of federal prisoners is a nasty thing to do, don't you agree, Marshal Calhoun?"

"I do, indeed, Marshal Morrison. Mr. Jensen, sir, would you be kind enough to ask your customers to leave, and then lock this place up?" Calhoun's weapon was still out, and he was wagging it about, walking toward the crowd at the bar. "Rogers called Bull a bully," he laughed. "You folks ain't seen half of it." He put two shots through the ceiling and leveled the sights on one of the men still standing at the bar. His knees weakened, his face took on the pallor of a dead man, and he wheeled for the door at a full run. The barroom was cleared out in seconds.

"Well done, Slim. Well done," Morrison said, pulling Rogers to his feet. "You really did it this time, Rogers."

CHAPTER 24

"How many times do we have to change our plans, Slim?" Morrison was actually chuckling as they pushed Rogers through the door of the jail. "The current one ain't working." He shoved Rogers into a chair, found his flask, and took a long drink. "Damn you, Rogers."

Martin walked in from back in the cell area. "Sheriff," he exclaimed. "What the hell happened to you?"

"He ran into a gun barrel, Martin. He is also under arrest for being stupid. We have us a little problem that needs a full discussion. Lock this fool up and come back out here. He is a federal prisoner as of this moment, so don't play any more damn games with me."

Morrison was strung tighter than Calhoun could remember seeing and hoped the man could hold his anger for just another short while. Martin took Rogers by the arm and led him back into the cell area and came back out. "I need to sit down," he said and slumped in one of the hard-back chairs in the office. "What's happening around here?"

"This is what happens when a man is elected sheriff and has no idea what the job is, he just won." Calhoun reached across the desk and poured he and Martin a healthy dose of whiskey in their coffee cups. "Rogers just tried to take up where Judge Chastain left off."

"Which brings us to this predicament, Mr. Martin," Bull said. "This little town of yours could very well blow up in our faces. We could have a full-scale riot on our hands in a matter of hours or less, and what's standing between my prisoners and certain vigilante death is us."

"He means, you, Owens, and the marshal service. If you're going to continue wearing that badge you must make the decision to do exactly what Marshal Bull Morrison tells you to do, without question. Where is Owens?" Slim Calhoun walked over to the stove to warm his hands and pour more coffee.

"He's supposed to be walking the streets, Marshal. Like you said for us to do. He and Marshal Antonelli left half an hour ago."

"That's a good thing," Bull chuckled. "Here's the situation, Martin. There are maybe ten, fifteen, men who are looking to hang Emerson and Hawknose Mackenzie because of Chastain's ranting and your sheriff's poor choice of words. Emerson is here and Hawknose and the judge are at the doc's. If we try to move Hawknose, he'll die. If we bring Emerson to the doc's, God knows what Chastain will try to do. We're already sure he'll try to kill Hawknose."

"That's it, Bull." Before Morrison could continue, Calhoun said, "I think that's our only choice, Bull. I really do. Hawknose can't move, so we chain Emerson to one bed and Chastain to another and set up a defense in case the local men do try to attack."

Morrison sat back in his chair, a smile slowly crossing his ugly face. "That's why I hired you, Slim. Damn me, but it is.

"Are you going to continue wearing that badge, Deputy Martin?" Bull Morrison's jaw jutted forward, and the angry eyes demanded an answer.

Martin, to Bull's almost surprise, stood straight up, almost saluted, and said, "I am, sir. You and I haven't gotten along like we should, I've fought you some, but I am a trained lawman, and I understand my duty."

"Glory be," Bull hollered. "I'll just be damned. All right, then, Deputy Martin, we'll leave Owens here to keep the two wounded prisoners, and we'll make the move to Doctor Trask's. Go get a wagon and team."

"BUCK SHOULD HAVE BEEN BACK some time ago, Bull. We need him and Owens, sure can't make our move without him."

"As soon as Martin gets back with the wagon, we'll take a walk around and find him and Owens. He's probably worked Owens half to death and loving' every minute of it."

He hadn't taken a breath and Antonelli walked through the door. "Glad you're here, Bull. I think we may have us a little problem comin' down the street."

Bull and Slim jumped up and ran out onto the porch with Buck. "Is that Owens coming with those men?" Slim Calhoun shaded his eyes from the bright afternoon sun, shaking his head. "What's next?"

Bull slipped back in the office and came out with Slim's rifle and carried his double-barrel ten-gauge scatter gun. "It ends now," he growled, tossing the rifle to slim. "Spread out, I'll take the middle with this killin' beauty, and shoot to kill. No more tryin' to be nice to these idiots."

Antonelli spread out to the left on the main street of Mormon Station, Bull stood in the middle of the street, his legs spread some, that mean shotgun poised and cocked, while Slim Calhoun took the right side. The group of men, led by Harold Owens, stopped about a hundred feet from them.

"Glad to see you took the badge off, Owens," Bull yelled out. "You ain't man enough to wear it. Sheriff's in jail, his head bashed in, arrested for incitin' a riot. You men are hereby arrested for attempting to Lynch a federal prisoner. Drop your weapons and come forward peacefully."

Slim couldn't hold back the chuckle and got a quick smile from Bull. *That man's got a way about him. Don't tell these fools to go home, hell no, arrest them. There's ten guns against our three, so he figures the odds are in our favor. I love that man.* "Game's over, Owens. There'll be no ankle shooting this time. Drop your weapon and come on in."

The town's men didn't budge and looked to Owens for some kind of order. Owens in turn looked around to see if they were with him. "We're gonna hang Emerson and then Mackenzie, Marshal, and you ain't gonna stop us. What a horrible thing they did. Kidnap, rape, and kill the judge's wife. You won't hang 'em, we will," he hollered. The men behind him shouted out and the group started to surge forward.

Bull Morrison brought that shotgun up and every man had a chance to look straight down those wide barrels. Before he could fire there was loud screaming and Martin came with the wagon and team at a full gallop around the corner and right through the mob.

Horses hooves churned up the muddy street and men went flying or fell before the onslaught. Owens was smashed between the lead team, other men were kicked or run over. Many dove for safety. Bull, Slim, and Buck didn't hesitate and ran to the melee, knocking those still with it unconscious, grabbing weapons and slinging them aside, and bringing the situation to an immediate halt.

Martin got the teams slowed and turned back to where Bull had Owens up on his feet. The man was badly injured, and Bull whacked him hard across the side of his head, letting him fall back in the mud. "Damn fool. All right, let's get these men down to the jail. What a mess."

"Looks to me like another set of plans coming up, Bull," Slim snickered. "Let's just take the whole bloody bunch to the doctor's and sort it out from there." He watched Bull walk over to the saloon and rattle the door. In a minute the door was opened, and Bull walked in and was back out with three bottles.

"Now, let's get this mess loaded up and moving before something else stupid happens around here."

Most of the men were conscious enough to help themselves into the wagon, the others were laid out in the rough wooden bed. "Buck, stay at the jail until we come back for those fools," Slim said. "There can't be enough stupid men left in this town to give you any trouble."

"I DON'T HAVE this kind of room, Marshal. My God, man, you've brought fifteen more people out here." Doctor Trask wasn't angry so much as he was overwhelmed.

"They don't have to be comfortable, Doc. Besides, there's only ten of 'em. They just have to be where I can keep an eye on them and not have more problems with town folk. They brought it all on themselves, so I got no pity. Let 'em sleep in the hog shed for all I care. I just have to keep 'em all in the same place."

Slim Calhoun and Buck Purdy O'Neil were separating the men involved in the vigilante mob from those involved in the murders and robberies, and most of all keeping a close eye on Judge Chastain, Gus Emerson, Hawknose Mackenzie, and Beartooth Johnson. "These men must be chained to their beds at all times, Doctor. I know this is a real problem for you, but they must also be separated. Chastain is plannin' all the time and you can bet so is Beartooth.

"Emerson is just a scared little boy at this point and Mackenzie, one leg already gone, is barely alive. We'll give you all the help we can."

Morrison called the men together. There were his deputies, Calhoun, Fitzgerald, and Antonelli that he knew he could count on. There was also Purdy O'Neil and Josh Henry he could count on. And then there was Martin. Could he count on him? He sure did come through with that wagon. He did take a bullet on the trail. Maybe, Bull thought, it was time to accept the man for what he had shown himself to be. A fighter and a lawman.

"We got to keep this little party alive and under control for another two days, gentlemen. I don't expect any more trouble from town. That's over. Hell, there ain't anyone left. Won't be no trouble from this rowdy bunch here, I do believe. We'll be in squads of two. One marshal and one non-marshal in each, and one of the squads always resting or sleeping. Slim, you put it together. I'm gonna work with the doc and see if I can make it easier for him."

CHAPTER 25

"One more day, Bull. I think we're gonna come out of this one, finally." Slim Calhoun hadn't slept in more than thirty hours, seeing to it that all the deputies were on duty, seeing to it the prisoners were fed and had water, and most of all, keeping a close eye on Chastain and Beartooth. "Those boys coming up from California should be here tomorrow at the latest."

"You need some sleep old man. I'll take over what you've been doing. Doc has one more cot set up near the fireplace. Grab something to eat, take a healthy slug of rot-gut whiskey, and go to bed."

"We're worried about Beartooth going after the judge again, and I agree, we should be, but what about Emerson? Chastain should be going after that bad man and the other way around." Calhoun was shaking his head some.

"Chastain is chained up, Slim. And our little boy bandit doesn't have a gun in his hand. He's just a young kid with a gripe -not a bad man without that gun or men behind him. Just a pitiful little kid. I'm going to enjoy watching hang."

. . .

"You sound like my old Pa, Bull. No. I'm wrong, you sound like my old Ma," Calhoun chuckled and had to duck a roundhouse right. A good sleep and Calhoun was ready to joust with the boss. They were both laughing and jabbing at each other before Calhoun got serious.

"Chastain hasn't said a word to me for more than a day. He's planning something, for sure. Why did you let Charley Adams wife stick around?"

"She and Doctor Trask made an arrangement with the ranch she cooks for to have food available, at government expense, I might add, and she's been helping with the injured, too. Is there a problem? I thought it was working out," Bull Morrison said.

"She's been spending considerable time with Chastain, and they get very quiet when one of us comes near. I know that old bastard is up to something. How the hell did he ever get appointed federal judge?"

"That, dear sir, is the question of the ages." Morrison sat down at the kitchen table, poured the two of them another cup of coffee, and laced Calhoun's rather heavy with whiskey. "You're asking politicians to use good judgement in making appointments to the judiciary, Slim. Take politics out of the courtroom and we'd be living in utopia, my friend.

"Chastain isn't alone in being less than worthy of his office, and politicians will make grave mistakes in their appointments for many years to come, I'm sure. Some of those mistakes can be corrected early, while others, such as our fine Judge Chastain, will linger and cause problems. According to Hank Churchill, Chastain is under indictment for land fraud." He took a long drink of well laced coffee. "It's our job to keep order among the troops."

"Nice speech, Bull. You should be on a wagon traveling town to town selling snake oil. This whiskey is having a fine affect, sir. Wake me when you need me and feed me half a buffalo."

Morrison was still chuckling when he walked up to Chastain's bed. Mary-Ellen Adams was sitting on the side of the bed in deep conversation with the judge, just as Calhoun predicted. What could she do to help the old codger? Morrison wondered. More to the point, what is it he might want her to do?

"Mrs. Adams. Judge. Having a little mid-day discussion of the weather, are we?" Morrison glared at both of them. "I'd like to have a chat with the judge, Mrs. Adams. If you'll excuse us, please?"

"Of course," she said. Her actions around Bull Morrison told him in no uncertain way that she could live the rest of her life without ever seeing him again. She flounced her way toward the kitchen and her Dutch ovens full of beef and lamb. He had to hold back a serious chuckle at the display.

"Marshals from Sacramento should be here tomorrow, Chastain. I've filed all my reports on what's transpired over the last few weeks and the word from the U.S. Attorney is you will be transported in chains. Any nonsense on your part will be answered with force. Are we clear on that?"

"I have nothing to say to you," Chastain said, almost with a smile, and turned his back to the marshal. Morrison chuckled, stood up slowly, and walked away.

Calhoun's right again. That old man has something up his rotten sleeve. He walked out to the barn area where most of the prisoners were being held, at least those who didn't require considerable medical attention.

Purdy O'Neil and Buck Antonelli were sitting on empty

crates, watching over the bunch. "Anyone looking like they know something they shouldn't?" Morrison asked. "Chastain's got something in the fire and Mrs. Adams is probably a part of it. She come out here to talk to anyone?"

"Charley's still bed-ridden, Bull" Antonelli said. "She's with him often. Otherwise she only comes out here with food and water or to help the doc. Most of these men seem pretty upset over what they've gotten themselves into."

"I'll bet they are," Morrison chuckled. "I'm gonna go have a talk with Beartooth. Keep your eyes open. Something's sure to happen."

"Find Josh Henry, Bull. He knows everyone in this town. He would know the serious trouble makers. He's a good man, Bull. I'd like to see him in the service."

Bull nodded and walked back into the main house and to Johnson's bed. *Interesting, now that I think about it. Martin should know all these people, too. He should be offering his thoughts.* Morrison was shaking his head walking up to Beartooth's bed. The old tracker was chained down and not happy about it. "Ain't no call to chain me up like a dog, Marshal. You got yourself a real mean streak."

"Thanks, Beartooth. Yup, I surely do have one of those. Your friend the judge is planning something, and it probably is gonna involve you and Emerson, there." He nodded across the room to Emerson's bed. "Course, being chained up like a dog, you won't be able to do much about it. Just thought I'd let you know," he laughed and walked across the large room to find Henry.

"WE'RE MAKING GOOD TIME, John. Should be in Mormon Station before dark. That storm they talked about didn't amount to nothing." U.S. Marshal Gerald Hoover had a team of four leading the way into Nevada Territory. Behind them by about twelve hours were two more deputies guarding two prison wagons to transport the outlaws back to federal court.

"Last time I was through this country it was about knee deep in mud and the time before that the snow was higher than my horse was tall. This is almost a pleasure trip," he laughed.

John Peters nodded, looking out across the broad Carson Valley from the heights of the tall Sierra Nevada. "Beautiful Country, Gerald. We'll need to rest these horses for a day or two before heading back. We've pushed 'em hard."

"It'll be a long slow ride back, Peters. According to Churchill, Bull has arrested about half the population of Nevada Territory."

"Last time I rode with that man he shot half our prisoners. Listening to Churchill, he and Slim rode into a real mess, with a judge inciting a riot, a sheriff who simply didn't give a damn, and assorted other outlaws. He always gets the best assignments," John Peters laughed. "It'll be good to see that old bastard again."

"I'm hoping we can leave about half the prisoners behind with local charges instead of federal. Some of the federal charges will be within territorial jurisdiction and some in California jurisdiction. Churchill was supposed to have the territorial attorney general work it all out."

Riding behind Hoover and Peters were deputies Sam Reynolds and Ramon Sanchez. All four of them volunteered for this assignment, looking for the chance to spend some time with Morrison and Calhoun. Sanchez transferred north from New Mexico Territory recently and had only heard stories about Morrison.

"He can't really be that much of wild man," he said. "Can he?"

Hoover laughed and nodded. "He sure as hell can be, Sanchez. If his prisoners won't give him trouble, he'll provoke a fight. The man loves to fight and doesn't care who his opponent might be."

The four dropped down to valley level and made the ten miles from a hot spring north to Mormon Station just as the sun was falling behind the tall granite peaks. "I think the county jail is gonna be on our right," Hoover said, wheeling his horse onto the main street.

They rode up to the jail and dismounted. "Let's just tie off for right now. I'm not sure that Bull and Slim will be here at the jail." Hoover led them into the sheriff's office and found Martin stoking the fire.

"Evening. Name's Hoover, U.S. Marshal Gerald Hoover. Bull Morrison around here?"

"Marshal," Martin said. "I'm Deputy Sheriff Martin. I'll take you to the marshal. He didn't expect you'd be here before tomorrow." He called to Peter Krebbe in the back and told him to hold down the fort. The ride out to Doctor Trask's place was short and quiet. Hoover had read the initial report from Morrison and knew the name, Martin, and wondered if he was being led to an ambush.

"You rode with Marshal Morrison on the capture of Hawknose Mackenzie?"

"Sure did," Martin said. "That man scares me more than any outlaw ever could. I don't think he's afraid of anything."

Hoover had to chuckle. "The only thing Bull Morrison is afraid of is a woman crying real tears. He turns into a puddle of melted butter when that happens." Hoover's worries ended as they rode up to the barn.

"Hoover," Buck Antonelli yelled from the barn as the group rode in. "Well, damn me, old Churchill finally got you out of the office. Sure glad to see you boys. What a mess we've got here."

"Good to see you, Buck. Help these boys get settled and aim me toward Bull and a hot cup of coffee."

"He's in the main house there. Come on John Peters, you scamp, let's get you boys all settled. You're gonna make old Slim Calhoun happy being here. There ain't enough of us to take care of everyone we have in custody."

Hoover walked up to the house and found Morrison in deep talk with Josh Henry. "Bull, looks like half of Nevada Territory is under arrest here."

Morrison grabbed his old friend and gave him a big hug. Glad to see you, Gerry. Seems like old Judge Chastain got everybody in this valley riled some. Tried twice to hang Gus Emerson and Hawknose Mackenzie. Damn me, but we got us a mess, Mr. Hoover.

"This is Joshua Henry, about to make the transition from deputy sheriff to Deputy U.S. Marshal. Josh, say hello to Marshal Gerald Hoover. You'll be answering to him over the next several years."

"I don't think so, Bull. I'm rolling it over. Bought a little place near Placerville and some cattle, and I'm gonna retire next year. I hope Sam Reynolds, who is with me on this trip, will take my desk. Good to meet you, Henry. Welcome to the service."

"Let's go in the kitchen and cozy up to a pot of coffee and a jug. I'll bring you up to date. Don't know when, but this place may explode at any minute," Morrison said. "Josh, send Calhoun and Fitz in here, then bring those boys with Hoover up to date."

· · ·

MORRISON AND HENRY had talked over what might happen, who might be involved, and whether or not there would be a general uprising if something did get started. "I'm sure that Judge Chastain has Mrs. Adams working with her husband on something," Josh Henry said. "She's damn near as sneaky as the old judge and Charley is pretty stupid in most ways."

"Whatever happens, the initial target is going to be Emerson or Hawknose. They are the ones responsible for the death of Mrs. Chastain. We've spread the word that everyone will be on the road the day after our relief gets here, so whatever the plan is, it will begin when they arrive. You and Buck Antonelli need to be with Emerson and Mackenzie from that moment on."

Henry hurried to the barn, found Buck and the other marshals stowing gear and tending animals. "Bull has a plan, Buck," he said. He gathered the marshals around and explained how Morrison thought things might develop. "With us being with the main targets, everyone else can be spread out among the rest of the prisoners."

Buck led everyone to the main house, assigned two to stay in the barn, let the others roam about. "Let's get Mackenzie and Emerson in beds next to each other," he said. "Mackenzie is nearest the fire, so let's push Emerson's bed right up next to him."

Purdy O'Neil helped push the bed over and opted to stay close, and Ramon Sanchez said he would find Mary-Ellen Adams and stick close to her. "She's devious, Ramon. I'm glad I'm not married to her. Be wide awake and aware," Antonelli said.

Adams had been in the barn nursing his broken and gunshot leg but was brought in and was chained to a bed. Antonelli told Sanchez to not let Mary-Ellen spend too much time with him. "Adams can't move very much but he does know how to stir the pot, so keep them away from each other. There are two others we need to keep track of," he said.

"Yeah," Josh said. "Harry Saunders and Loren Mason have been trouble makers in town for a couple of years and I've seen Mary-Ellen chat with them regularly these last few days. Both men are in the main house and near Adams. The men here in the house are all wounded or injured to the point that they can't move around much. Those in the barn can and will if something gets started. That old judge really got this group fired up."

"I'll got out with the marshals in the barn," Purdy O'Neil said. He walked out to the barn, to join with Reynolds. "Fitzgerald will be back shortly. They are expecting something to happen soon, I think."

"If anything's planned, it'll take place while supper's being distributed," Reynolds said. "We got seven people out here, three of whom might cause trouble, and the woman that brings the food is trouble. If I was Morrison, I'd send her packing and make these men go without supper tonight."

"That's what I'm about to do," Bull Morrison boomed walking in the door. Trouble is, I can't find the witch. Hoped she'd be out here."

"Ramon Sanchez was supposed to keep track of her," Purdy said.

"He couldn't find her and came to me. We don't have enough people to go on a search for the woman." Morrison sat down on a crate and stared at the ground for a minute. "This separation from the barn to the house ain't good, so let's cuff all these boys and bring them in."

"Good," Purdy said. "You already have Mason and Saun-

ders cuffed to each other, I saw, and cuff Adams to somebody Josh Henry says we can trust. You don't suppose that
woman is out trying to round up some help, do you?"

"That's just one more good reason to get all these people
in the same place. That way, all of us are in the same place
too," Morrison chuckled.

The move into Doctor Trask's main farmhouse took
about half an hour and it was late night before everyone was
settled. Men were cuffed to each other and to the beds of the
wounded and injured, angry voices were heard during the
process and all the marshals were primed for a fight.

"Where's our damned supper?" Loren Mason demanded
in a loud voice, bringing cries for food from around the
main room. There was a bit of foot stomping and other cries
of a vile nature from the men.

Morrison stood near the fireplace, pulled his revolver
and fired two quick shots through Trask's roof. The silence
was deafening. "Ain't no supper tonight and if you don't like
it, too bad for you." He let the barrel of that big gun move
about through the crowded room and every man saw that it
was cocked, and the marshal had his finger on the trigger.
"Damn me but I love the silence," Morrison chuckled,

Calhoun smiled and nodded, and all the marshals
pulled their guns and cocked them. The room was very
quiet. "That's better. Remember this, it's a whole lot easier
for us if you are dead and we do like to make our lives easier." There were chuckles from several as the guns were
taken off ready and slipped back into their leather.

"Calhoun, you, Henry, Peters, and Fitzgerald take first
shift. Hoover, Reynolds, and Sanchez, you take second.
Antonelli, Purdy, and I will roam about inside and outside
and shoot anything that moves. Questions?" Morrison

stuffed some logs in the fire, pulled a flask from his coat pocket and took a long swig of hot whiskey. "Nectar of the gods," he said and passed it to Slim Calhoun.

CHAPTER 26

IT WAS AFTER MIDNIGHT AND BUCK ANTONELLI SAID HE WAS going to step out the door for some fresh air and Purdy O'Neil said he'd join him. "It's a cold one tonight, Buck. Do you think that woman is putting together a group to attack us? Don't think that would be a smart idea myself."

Buck laughed softly as they stepped onto the veranda style front porch. The night sky was showing a few clouds rolling in but with stars bright enough to light up the snow on the high peaks of the Sierra Nevada. "If Chastain is behind it, she surely is putting together something stupid. I don't think it would be an attack, though."

They stepped off the porch, watched heavy clouds move across the moon, and walked around the large farmhouse, looking for trouble. "Storm for sure tomorrow," Purdy said. "Driving coach all these years in this country, I can smell a good winter storm. Wind' ll pick up and then she'll hit, you watch."

Buck Antonelli looked closely at Purdy and then up at the clouds. "Yup," he drawled out. "Those boys just come in tell you anything about your partner?"

"He's stormin' around the lodge but the doc says he's healing slow. When this is all over, I'll never complain about the dull rides across these mountains. Too much excitement for me. Have you talked with Fitzgerald? I don't think he's feeling as good as he's telling Bull. His face is giving him hell."

"I'll have a talk with him," Antonelli said.

The night seemed to take forever to end and the men were tired from expecting something that didn't happen. It was just at sunrise that Mary-Ellen Adams walked up onto the front porch and pulled the door open to look down the double barrels of Morrison's ten gauge.

"Where you been, woman?" He snarled it out, reached out and jerked her into the house. She screamed in fright and Bull pushed her across the crowded room to the fireplace. "Where?"

"I went to see my kids. That hurts. Let go." He had a tight grip on her arm, and he eased up a little but still stood close. "I ain't seen them for two days."

"You bring anyone back with you?"

"No. That hurts," she whimpered.

"What are you doing to my wife?" Charley Adams yelled out from his bed. "You let her go."

"She ain't hurt, Adams. You want her, you got her," he said and pushed her away toward Adams's bed. "Tell him you ain't hurt and get in the kitchen. I better not find out you brought trouble with you." Morrison stalked off to the kitchen to find coffee.

Mary-Ellen Adams whispered, "I brought trouble, Charley. Here," she said, and slowly brought half a dozen knives out of one of her coat pockets. They were skinning knives as sharp as any razor. She fumbled around the other pocket and eased two small revolvers out. "Judge Chastain said he wants one of the pistols. You keep the other and Get the knives to Mason and Saunders.

"The judge wants everything to happen when I'm serving breakfast. Get those knives to the men, Charley. I have to get in the kitchen. The judge will give the word on when to attack."

Charley Adams was amazed at what his wife was doing. He knew she was mean spirited, knew she could hurt someone, but never thought she would do all this. "It will be bad for us if his plan don't work," he said.

"It'll be right fine for us if it does," she smiled. "Have a small little plot of ground right on the bay near Santa Cruz. He'll give you a full-time job on the railroad he's building up into the redwoods, and I'll have a full-time job keeping his house. Charley, it's our dream. Now, get those knives out to those men."

He watched her walk off to the kitchen and eased the knives into his pockets. *I've heard of that redwood country, the Monterey Bay. My God, she's right, it is our dream come true. My leg hurts so bad, I hope I can make that ride across those mountains.*

He sat up and stretched, and using his one good leg, got his bed moved close enough to the fire to drop the knives onto Mason's bed. Mason was glaring at Adams when he turned back after reaching the fireplace. Mason gave a little signal with his fingers, asking, where's my gun?

Charley shook his head and moved his bed closer to Judge Chastain's. He slipped the revolver under the covers. "Glad you're feeling better, son," the judge said. He had one foot manacled to the end of his cot but both hands were free. "You help get me out of this and you and your wife will have a fine life.

Because of the broken leg, Adams only had one wrist in

a set of handcuffs and chained to the bed. It was cumbersome, but the move about was done quietly and quickly.

"Always remember that what we do this morning is morally right. Those men killed my wife, did obscene things with her, and it is our responsibility to see to it that they pay the ultimate price. The marshals should have killed Emerson and Mackenzie on sight and didn't. You'll have no shame nor guilt in what we are doing," he blustered.

Charley Adam's heart was thumping as he made his way back to where he started. People were moving about now, some couldn't get out of bed, others moved slowly from their injuries, and those in on Mary-Ellen's plans were seen to get as close as they could to Loren Mason's bed for a quick chat.

"I don't like what I'm seeing," Slim Calhoun said to Bull Morrison. They were standing near the door to the kitchen, sipping hot coffee. "Five men who've never said two words to Charley Adams stopped at his bed then went to Loren Mason for a chat. I swear I saw something passed to one of them from Mason."

"Mrs. Adams is getting ready to serve breakfast. You get all the boys but one in here. Leave one in the barn. I'll hold up breakfast. Leave Purdy in the barn with two revolvers and a shotgun.

"We'll spread ourselves around this room. Make sure everyone understands that if shooting breaks out to be careful that we don't be shooting each other." He was chuckling lightly as he headed into the kitchen. *Damn I hope that judge starts something. I'm gonna knock heads from now until noon if he does. Yeah, you old codger, you just go ahead and start a fight with me.*

.   .   .

"WHAT DO you mean hold up breakfast? It's already cooked. Those wounded men need their food. You can't do this." Mary-Ellen Adams had trays set out with bowls full of last night's lamb stew and knew Judge Chastain was just waiting for her to start serving them. Men with knives, two men with guns, were waiting for him to give the word to attack the federal marshals. To kill the men who ravaged and brutally killed his wife.

"Those men are hungry, Marshal. You wouldn't let them eat last night. They need their hot food."

"Put the tray down until I tell you otherwise, woman." Morrison walked around the large kitchen table inspecting each tray that was there, looking for hidden weapons. He heard Calhoun bring in the crew from the barn, heard the men move around the ward area and intercepted Doctor Trask as he came downstairs and into the kitchen.

"Hold up, there, Doc. Let's have a quick little talk." Trask joined Bull near the stove and Bull told him to stay in the kitchen until he was told otherwise. "Gonna be trouble, I'm afraid. That judge is stupid," he almost growled. Bull walked to the kitchen door, got the high sign from Slim and motioned Mary-Ellen to start bringing the trays out to the men.

Slim stood about five feet behind Judge Chastain's bed and had Buck Antonelli close by. Gerald Hoover, after being told about Calhoun's worries about Loren Mason, stood behind Mason's bed. Fitzgerald and Reynolds were near the front door, Josh Henry stood near the kitchen door, and Ramon Sanchez and John Peters were spread out from the fireplace.

A wise man would have seen the futility of attempting an escape, but Chastain had only two thoughts in his head. Kill Gus Emerson and Hawknose Mackenzie and escape.

Three men in the barn would kill whoever was guarding them and saddle horses for their escape, while the men with guns and knives would kill the marshals in the main house. In his mind, it was a good plan.

Those involved would be given land and jobs in Santa Cruz when they made their way there. These charges against him would disappear when that foul Marshal Bull Morrison was dead, and he would return to his empire, where what he said and did was the law.

He saw Mary-Ellen move near Harry Saunders and gave him a nod. He screamed bloody loud and kicked the tray from her hands. Chastain pulled the revolver from under the blankets and took dead aim for Bull Morrison, pulling the trigger just as Calhoun smashed his rifle across the back of the judge's head.

Morrison winced as the bullet tore through his heavy woolen shirt and nicked at his arm. His revolver was out, and two slugs tore through Chastain as he fell from the bed. The men with knives attacked immediately and the blasting of weapon's fire echoed through the old farmhouse. Some were wounded, many were dead, and the uprising was quelled.

Mason jumped from his bed, flailing an eight-inch knife at Gerald Hoover who shot him dead from three feet away. The entire fight was over in less than a minute, the room hung heavy with burnt gun powder, and the cries of the wounded mixed with the sound of the marshals forcing people onto the bloody floor.

"Check Emerson and Mackenzie," Calhoun shouted at Josh Henry, and knelt down to see if Chastain was dead or alive. "How you doin', Bull?"

"Just a nick. He dead?"

"Yup. Where's that woman?" Calhoun was back on his

feet, running toward where Mason's bed was. Mrs. Adams was on the floor, on her back, a bullet hole conspicuous in the middle of her chest. "Damn stupid people. Where are you, Charley Adams?" He hollered it out twice before someone said he was dead.

"Those children are orphans because of stupid people," Calhoun muttered.

"Anyone else hurt?" Morrison watched Doctor Trask slowly move through the fouled mess of his once nice home. "Be careful, Doctor. More than one person in this room has been seriously injured by someone who was thought to be dead. Let my men check them first, please. We need you."

Calhoun nodded at Morrison and started running for the barn. "Purdy might need help, Bull." The two pounded across the farmyard, now covered in fresh snow, and into the barn, Purdy stood with his legs spread, a smoking revolver in one hand and the shotgun in the other.

"Easy, O'Neil, it's us," Calhoun said, stopping when the coach driver whirled on him. "Looks like you've got things under control."

"Damn fools tried to attack me. Shotgun's empty now and so's the revolver, and I think I got 'em all," he said, slowly dropping to the dirt floor. Calhoun jumped to his side and saw a deep knife wound in his side. "Get the doc," he howled at Morrison. "Purdy's been knifed bad."

"It don't hurt too bad, Slim. I'm just tired, is all." It was loss of blood not long hours that made him feel tired. It was not a good sign and Calhoun knew he needed to keep Purdy's spirits up. He started ripping the coach driver's shirt and used it to stem the bleeding.

"Well, Mr. O'Neil, you just rest some, then." Calhoun found a saddle blanket and covered the stage driver, making a little pillow from some straw. "Doc'll have you on your feet shortly. I gotta check on the mess you made out there," he said.

"Don't let me die, Slim. They're waitin' on me to get my stage back on the road."

"You ain't gonna die, Purdy. You're too mean to die. Just look at this mess you made out here. Bodies everywhere." Calhoun found one man alive but not able to be a threat and moved him near Purdy. "Doc's on his way, boys."

CHAPTER 27

"It's over, Bull." Gerald Hoover had all the prisoners that were being held under federal laws packed in the two wagons for the long trip back to Placerville, the nearest location with a federal court. A few had been transferred to the jail in Mormon Station, now overseen by Acting Sheriff Martin.

"Me and Calhoun, Fitz and Antonelli will finish up around here. The town's justice court will be quick, I'm sure. Doctor Trask says Purdy O'Neil is gonna make it, but it will be a long healing period. You might want to tell the folks at Strawberry that he'll be fine."

"There will be hearings on Chastain's actions and death, and I'm sure you and your boys will be called on the carpet. I got a wire from Churchill. He understands the situation and says it needs to be in the record."

"Maybe future appointments will be made with a touch more thought to the appointee's ability," Morrison chuckled. "I'm looking forward to those hearings. I love to growl at those people. I'll let you and Peters know when we're wrapped up here so you can give us a nice quiet assignment somewhere peaceful."

"Only peaceful men get peaceful missions, Bull," Hoover laughed. He nudged his horse and rode off to join his deputies and escort the prison wagons over the mountains.

"Glad it's them riding off in this blizzard, Slim. Let's go see if Mr. Jenson has that saloon open."

"The justice of the peace said he's holding court first thing tomorrow morning. Charges against some of those involved were reduced from taking part in a riot to being rowdy in public. The people that created the most trouble were killed."

"Except for two," Bull said. "Gus Emerson and Hawknose Mackenzie are still alive. Don't seem right, neither. Too many people found themselves on the wrong side of the law, too many died because of that, and none of it would have happened if Emerson and Mackenzie hadn't abducted that damn judge's wife.

"They were good highwaymen, good stage robbers. Should have left the kidnapping to professionals." Morrison was letting himself get riled, Calhoun noted, and thought he just might enjoy this little repast at the saloon.

"Somebody's head is gonna get knocked around, sure as I'm walking alongside this man," he muttered, every so quietly.

Cliff Martin was walking down the street from the jail, talking with Josh Henry as Morrison and Calhoun rode into town. "Morning, Marshal," Martin said. "Saw the wagons ride out. County commissioners named me acting sheriff until the spring elections."

"You got something on your mind besides telling me that," Bull said. "I'm not in a friendly mood, but if you'll join me and Slim at the saloon, I'll listen. For a moment or two."

Spike Jenson growled some when the group came in and Slim was amazed that Bull only smiled and asked for a glass of whiskey instead of demanding one. "Let's take a table back there," Bull said, motioning the group to the table that Sheriff Rogers usually occupied. "Don't you agree, Sheriff?"

"Fine with me, Marshal, but I won't be sitting in Rogers' chair, or coming back here when you gents are gone. Which brings me to what I want to talk to you about. Are you taking Josh Henry with you? I could sure use him here."

"Yes, you could," Morrison snapped. "Gonna take you some time to put together a decent sheriff's office here, but you ain't getting Henry. Buck Antonelli filed claim on the boy and he's about to become a deputy U.S. Marshal. Case closed." Bull sat back, took half the glass of whiskey down, and glared at those around the table. Nobody glared back, which frustrated the man.

"I do want you to know that I think I'm a better man after riding with you these past few weeks. A better lawman. Marshal Calhoun, I've never met anyone like you, certainly never anyone like Marshal Morrison, and in a way, I envy Josh Henry right now. I'm going to make my rounds now, but I needed to say that." Cliff Martin stood up, bowed slightly, and strode from the saloon.

"Took the wind right out of your sails, old man," Calhoun laughed. "Turned all your anger and frustration into a bowl of cherry jam."

"Shut up, Calhoun. Not another word," Morrison growled. He poured himself another glass of whiskey, looked at Josh Henry, glared at Slim Calhoun, and burst out laughing. "He did at that, knocked me flat on my fat old butt."

A LOOK AT NAME'S CORCORAN, TERRENCE CORCORAN (TERRENCE CORCORAN BOOK I)

Terrence Corcoran carried a badge in Virginia City, Nevada until one day, in a drunken stupor, he shot the sheriff. Now he's returning to the Comstock looking to get his badge back and stumbles into a conspiracy that might put the sheriff, district attorney, and others in jail for a long time. A lovely working girl is brutally murdered, a Hungarian duke wants a Wells Fargo gold shipment, and the sheriff rehires him after first kicking him in a most tender spot. Corcoran was born on the ship bringing his family to this country, ran away to the frontier at an early age and brings his ideas of the old country and knowledge learned of the west to whatever mess he finds himself in. He's carried a badge, found himself in jail, and stands four-square for right, honor, and truth. You gotta love the guy.

AVAILABLE NOW

ABOUT THE AUTHOR

Reno, Nevada novelist, Johnny Gunn, is retired from a long career in journalism. He has worked in print, broadcast, and Internet, including a stint as publisher and editor of the Virginia City Legend. These days, Gunn spends most of his time writing novel length fiction, concentrating on the western genre. Or, you can find him down by the Truckee River with a fly rod in hand.

Gunn and his wife, Patty, live on a small hobby farm about twenty miles north of Reno, sharing space with a couple of horses, some meat rabbits, a flock of chickens, and one crazy goat.

www.ingramcontent.com/pod-product-compliance
Lightning Source LLC
Chambersburg PA
CBHW052044240626
47153CB00006B/2205